Follow the Yellow School Bus

Follow the Yellow School Bus

to Lincoln Elementary

Ilse E. Arndt

Follow the Yellow School Bus

to Lincoln Elementary

This book is a work of fiction. Any references to real people or real locales are used fictitiously. Names, characters, places, and incidents are the product of the author's imagination and any resemblance to actual events, or locales, or persons, living or dead, is entirely coincidental.

©2011 by Ilse E. Arndt
All rights reserved

International Standard Book Number (ISBN): 1-4505-4856-3

Designed and formatted by Susan Bond

Printed in the United States of America

No part of this publication may be reproduced, stored in a retrieval system, or transmitted, in any form or by any means - electronic, mechanical, photocopying, recording, or otherwise - without prior written permission. A reviewer may quote brief passages in a review to be printed in a magazine or newspaper without permission in writing from the author.

Available from Amazon.com and other retailers

TO: Sharon Peerman,
who helped find my mistakes.

Also by Ilse E. Arndt

City of Looms and Spindles

Southern California

One School Year

		Supply	
	Library		

	Pantry	Kitchen
Multi-Purpose Room		

Staff Room	Women	
	Office	Principal Office
	Health Office	

20	19	18	17	16	Storage
				B	G

Ramp 4

15	14	13	12	11	Custodial
				B	G

Ramp 3

10	9	8	7	6	Men
				B	G

Ramp 2

5	4	3	2	1	Custodial
				B	G

Ramp 1

P
L
A
Y
G
R
O
U
N
D

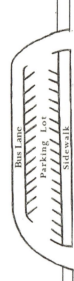

Bus Lane
Parking Lot
Sidewalk

Sidewalk   Street

LINCOLN ELEMENTARY SCHOOL STAFF

Principal: Elizabeth Leski

Grade	Teacher's Name	Aide's Name	Room #
Kindergarten	Carolyn Tyler	Shirley West	1 Am
Kindergarten	Ida Pierce	Gail Wiley	2 Am
Kindergarten	Janice Sexton	Marilyn Rogan	2 Pm
1st	Barbara Selby	Debbie Cranwell	3
1st	Jeanne Curtis	Rosa Torres	4
1st Bilingual	Patricia Campos	Janine Neal	5
2nd	Janet Reeves	Denise Garcia	6
2nd	Susan Woodward	Cathy Brooks	7
2nd/3rd	Karen Ramsey	Ellen James	8
3rd	Shela Dennis	Maria Guerrero	9
3rd/4th	Louise Wong	Carolyn Muldoon	10
4th	Deborah Bradfield	Cynthia Romero	11
4th	Linda Chamberlain	Sara Liebowitz	12
5th	Norma Glas	Louise Adams	13
5th	Fred Martinez	Joyce Smith	14
6th	Mary Ann Duncan	Sandy Ferrer	15
6th	Ray Ogilvie	Patricia Lopez	16
Learning Handicapped	Diana Neblett	Linda Cohan	17
Special Ed. Resource	Rebecca Coulter	Marion Lukens	18
Title I Resource	Margaret Dorner		19
English Second Language	Jose Ortega		20

School Secretary	Annie Kallas
Psychologist	Brigitte Vordstrom
Clerk	Loren Ash
Nurse	Anita Ronco
Librarian	Eloise Mann
Head Custodian	Joe Sullivan
Custodian	Clyde Terrell

SEPTEMBER

It was 90 degrees at seven o'clock in the morning when Annie Kallas stepped into her car to go to work this last day before school started. The temperature had reached 104 the previous day with 12% humidity. The weather report on her car radio said it was expected to be at least 108 today. As she drove, Annie noticed that her arm holding the steering wheel looked dry and flakey. She brushed it with her free hand and tiny bits of skin flew into the air.

"Oh yuck! I forgot to put lotion on. I'll be lucky if my skin doesn't crack open. Between these bags under my eyes and my skin turning to dust, I'll soon be too ugly to be seen in public."

She parked in her usual spot and breathed in deeply the clean, fresh air. The smog from Los Angeles wouldn't drift in until later in the day. Annie unlocked the office door and turned the lights and machines on as she walked to her desk. "Morning, Loren," she said as the clerk arrived.

"Morning, Annie. How're you?"

"Morning, Elizabeth," Annie said to the principal as she came in behind Loren.

"Annie, we've got a lot to do. Please come in and let's work on the mail I didn't finish yesterday."

"Coming." Annie pulled out her steno notebook, grabbed the horn-rimmed half glasses she used for reading, and followed Elizabeth into the principal's office.

The teachers were arriving for work carrying portable fans since the classrooms weren't air-conditioned. The building that housed the office and staffroom was newer and had air-conditioning so it sometimes functioned as a haven from the heat for the staff.

"Hi, Loren. Where's Annie?" asked Susan Woodward, a second grade teacher, her arms full of yards of rolled up different colored butcher paper.

"She's in with the principal."

"You don't happen to know how much we have in our classroom budget this year, do you?"

"Golly, no. I don't even know what a classroom budget is," answered Loren with a nervous giggle.

"We have to get all those supplies from Joe today and I don't want to go over my budget and have the principal give me a lecture. I'll catch Annie later. On second thought, ask her to call me in my room, will you? I'll be there putting up bulletin boards." Susan struggled with the butcher paper as she went out the front door.

When Annie came out of the principal's office with her arms full of papers, periodicals, and catalogues which she deposited noisily on her desk, Loren said, "Annie, Susan Woodward wants you to call her in her room and tell her what the classroom budget amount is."

"Okay. You listen to what I tell her so you'll know the answer next time somebody asks you." Annie punched the buttons on the intercom and called.

"Susan."

"Yes?"

"Pick up the intercom, please."

"Yes, Annie?"

"Loren said you wanted to know about the budget. You have $150 again this year for all your classroom supplies from the supply room or anything you want to buy from a vendor."

"You know that's not enough."

"Sure, everyone knows that but if there is no money, there is no money, so it's $150 until further notice. Didn't Elizabeth speak to that at the faculty meeting yesterday? It was on the agenda."

"She might have," Susan answered. "She talked about everything. I couldn't remember it all."

Annie laughed. It had been a full agenda - three pages long. "Well, that's the way it is - same as last year."

"Okay, thanks."

Annie looked up from her desk a few minutes later and watched Loren as she helped a father enroll his two sons. She was friendly and helpful and had the appropriate answers to his questions at her fingertips. He, on the other hand, was clearly overwhelmed by Loren's blonde, green-eyed beauty. He couldn't take his eyes from her. Annie smiled as she watched his expression. He was as awed as if he had been introduced to a movie star but she appeared to be totally oblivious of his feelings.

Loren had been the clerk at the school only since the previous April and, in Annie's opinion, was slightly lacking in both initiative and judgment but she was young and inexperienced so Annie hoped she would grow into the job as the days went by. This, her first beginning of school experience, would either make her or break her. Annie wasn't sure which it would be.

Janice Sexton, a kindergarten teacher, asked "Annie, when are we going to get our class lists? I have to have all those name tags made up for Monday and I'm running out of time."

"I'm going to start on the final draft of them right away. I can give you the first draft now if you want. But, you know, we always wait until the very last minute to finalize the class lists so we can include those children we're enrolling now."

"Please give me whatever you've got so I can get going. I can't believe I have so much left to do." She got a catch in her voice which caused Annie to look at her.

"Hey, Janice, it'll be okay. You'll get it all done in time." Annie squeezed her hand.

Janice took a deep breath and said, "You think so, Annie? I can't remember being this frantic last year but I suppose I was."

Annie laughed. "You don't remember? You were in a state of shock, I guess. It was worse last year so be consoled. Things are improving even though it may not feel that way right now. After all, this is your second year.

You know what you're doing now." Annie made her a copy of her class list with the names of her students on it. "Here you are - go make tags for all your little darlings."

Joe Sullivan, the head custodian, came banging into the office with a case of tissues and a case of copy paper on his dolly. "Wow! It's got to be over a hundred already and it's only ten o'clock."

"I hope our air conditioner holds up."

"It's working all right, isn't it?" asked Joe, creating deep creases in his forehead as he frowned.

"Yes, it's okay now, but like the rest of us, it's getting old. Joe you remember last year when it got so hot how the thing sputtered and carried on and when there are no windows that open, the air conditioner going out is a catastrophe."

"I know, Annie, but let's not borrow trouble. I got my hands full enough right now. I'm trying to get all these teachers' orders filled today, but I'll tell you... It seems like they're ordering for the whole year. I got one teacher's order that's five pages long. Can you beat that? How many pencils and crayons and paper can one teacher use?"

Annie laughed. She knew one of Joe's favorite pastimes was complaining about teachers' orders. He hated the part of his job that required him to distribute supplies to the teachers. It could be kept under control after school started but on this day Annie knew he was overworked. She looked at him and smiled. She was very fond of him and treated him like a younger brother. He knew women considered him sexy with his black wavy hair, sky-blue eyes, and beautiful smile, so he kept his body slim and flexible by working out in a gym at least four nights a week. Annie had dated him a few times when he was first hired but soon realized he only wanted to play around and include her in his string of conquests, so they agreed to stop dating and only be friends.

The teachers came in and out of the staffroom throughout the day to get colored butcher paper for the background of their bulletin boards, to run copies for student math or spelling work, to get a coke, or just to rest in the coolness of the air-conditioning. It was 105 degrees at twelve o'clock.

Annie concentrated on getting the students' names, addresses, and all other pertinent information into the computer in order to compile the class lists for the teachers. There were about five hundred fifty students divided into eighteen classrooms with new students enrolling every hour. It was a massive data entry job.

"Annie, were you the one who arranged this heat wave to make sure I could tell I wasn't in Canada any longer?"

Annie turned from her computer and smiled as she looked at Ray Ogilvie and held out both her hands to grasp his. "Don't I wish I had that kind of power. I'd sure turn the heat off again if I did. How are you doing, Ray? Getting back into the swing of things?"

"Yes, slowly," he answered as he held her hands. "I'd almost forgotten how much there is to do in the days before school starts. How have you been, Annie? I haven't had a chance to talk to you before this. Everything okay with you?"

"Everything's fine with me, but what about you? Did your change of scene help?"

"That and time. I've pretty much gotten over the shock. Of course, I still miss Helen - I probably always will - but life continues, doesn't it?"

"Yes, it does that. Well, we're glad to have you back, Ray. The school wasn't the same without you. We all missed you."

"You, too, Annie?"

"Sure, me too. I missed you a lot. I missed the philosophizing we used to do and the talks we had. It's always been nice having you around, Ray."

Ray flushed with pleasure. "I've always enjoyed our talks, too, Annie." He dropped her hands and patted her shoulder. "Well, I know you're busy and I still have lots to do. I'll see you later."

She watched him as he walked into the staffroom. He certainly was nice to look at and even the gray that had crept into his hair since his tragedy made him more attractive. He was thinner, too. Poor man, he must have really suffered when his wife died so suddenly in the car accident. It was too bad because he was such a great guy.

By three-thirty when it was time for the teachers to go home, the temperature had reached 108 degrees. They were cranky and sweaty from the hard work of trying to get the classrooms in order. Annie could hear snatches of their conversations.

"...it's inhuman to expect us to work in those rooms."

"...I sure hope it's not this hot on Monday."

"...it'll ruin the first day if it's this hot on Monday."

"...it's not fair that the rooms aren't air-conditioned. How can we work like this?"

Even the temperature inside the office was climbing as the old air-conditioner labored to try to combat the heat. Annie took a sheet of paper and used it as a fan. "It's 88 in here, Loren," she said, glancing at the thermometer on the wall. "I sure hope this thing can keep going. We'll be in big trouble if it konks out."

Annie could feel the beads of perspiration on her upper lip as she worked at her computer. The class lists had to be finished and hung up outside the office before they could go home so parents could come over the week-end to see what classrooms their children would be in when school started Monday.

At exactly four o'clock Loren went to the front door of the office and locked it. "That's it, no more new enrollments now until Monday. How're you coming on the lists?"

"They're about finished. You can start running copies if you will. I need three copies of each sheet."

"Okay."

"How are you coming with those lists, Annie? I see we're getting a group congregating at the front door waiting for them to go up," Elizabeth asked.

"I only have the learning handicapped class left. Loren is running the copies. We'll be ready to post in a few minutes. We promised to have them posted by five o'clock so we're on schedule."

At four-thirty, Loren, who was the tallest, taped the class lists up onto the front door and window. The waiting children were either happy or dejected according to whether or not they were assigned the teacher they wanted or their best friend was in the same room with them.

With that task done, they packed up to go home.

"Loren, remember to get a good night's sleep Sunday night. Tell little Patrick not to wake mommy up during the night 'cause Monday will be the worst day of mommy's life," Annie said as she waited for Loren to get ready to leave.

"Is it really that bad, Annie?"

"It sure is. I'm perfectly serious about it. The first day of school is the worst day of the year. Take my word for it and be prepared."

"Okay, I'll see to it that Patrick and I are both asleep by eight o'clock and wake up fully rested and eager to go on Monday morning."

* * * * * * *

"I'm next. I've been waiting at least a half hour. This is really disgusting. Why don't you people get extra help if you can't handle it alone?"

Annie looked up at the speaker who was a woman with a baby in her arms and a five year old by the hand. "One of the reasons we don't get additional help is that there is no money, and the second reason is that no one expects everyone will wait until the first day of school to register their children. We've been open for registration for the last three weeks."

Annie caught herself. She had broken article number one of the school's creed: never get sharp with a parent. She needed to control herself or she'd only make things worse.

She checked over the woman's enrollment papers and said, "I'm sorry, ma'am, your daughter's shots aren't up to date."

"What do you mean, not up to date? She's had every shot known to man. What more do you people want?"

"Yes, ma'am, but she's missing the last two booster shots." Annie reached for the health department form, wrote the child's name on it, and checked off the shots needed. "As soon as you get the last two shots and bring in the proof, she can start school. Here's the form. It has the health department phone number on it if you want to call them."

"Do you mean to tell me that after I've waited all this time I can't leave my child here? It's outrageous!"

"I'm sorry, but those are the rules and we have to abide by them. It is for your daughter's benefit, you know."

"Well, I didn't want my child to go to this school anyway. I'll put her in a private school." She grabbed the girl by the arm and pulled so suddenly the child stumbled as she was dragged out the door.

Annie smiled at the remaining people and asked, "Who's next?"

The next person to approach the counter with completed papers in hand was a young Asian man with a five year old boy. The enrollment paper said the boy was born in Viet Nam. The man spoke very broken English. "I want my niece in school," he said, making an effort to sort the proper English word in his mind.

"Your niece? Isn't that a boy?" Annie asked while taking another look at the child's boy's haircut and boy's pants.

"Yes, him boy."

"Okay, you mean your nephew. I would like to see the birth certificate or passport and the shot record, please." Annie spoke slowly and distinctly but tried very hard not to raise her voice. She didn't want to be one of those Americans who expect foreigners to understand English if only it is spoken loudly enough.

"I have passport here and here shot record."

After reading the papers, Annie said, "Here are the passport and the shot record back, Mr. Nguyen. Is that how your name is pronounced?"

"Yes, that right, that right," he nodded at her and smiled. Annie smiled back at him.

"Does the boy speak any English at all?"

"No, lady, no English."

She looked through the kindergarten class lists for a Vietnamese looking name in hopes she could find the child a friend but there was none. She decided to place him in the morning kindergarten class with the most experienced teacher which would make it room two, Ida Pierce. Mrs. Pierce had been a teacher for twenty years and would be able to figure out how to teach this little boy.

"Sir, I am placing him in room two in the morning kindergarten class with Mrs. Pierce as the teacher. Is that all right?" Annie asked.

"That good, lady," he said as he nodded his head.

"Since you live on Peach Street, Twan will be a walker. Will someone pick him up today?"

"Yes, lady, I be here."

"Let's go to the classroom." Annie led Mr. Nguyen and his nephew out of the front door and set a rapid pace over to room two. She opened the classroom door, ushered them inside and waited for Mrs. Pierce to interrupt what she was doing and come over to them. "Mrs. Pierce, I'd like you to meet Mr. Nguyen and his nephew, Twan."

"How do you do, Mr. Nguyen. I'm happy to meet you. And how are you, Twan? Welcome to our class." She smiled at him.

"Twan does not understand or speak English. He's only been in the country for six weeks, Mrs. Pierce," Annie said.

"That's fine. We'll manage. Will you pick him up today, Mr. Nguyen? At twelve o'clock."

"I be here. Thank you, teacher," he said with a heavy accent. He bowed to her. He added some words to the boy in Vietnamese. The boy nodded. He seemed to have tears in his eyes but gave no sign of unease. He took the teacher's proffered hand and went with her. Mr. Nguyen and Annie slipped out of the room unnoticed.

As they walked back to the office, Annie said, "Twan will be put into the English as a Second Language program. He will go to a special teacher three times a week and that teacher will help him with his English. Is that all right with you, Mr. Nguyen?"

"That good. Thank you, thank you, lady."

"Good-bye now, don't forget twelve o'clock."

"Good-bye. I remember," he waved as he walked off.

As Annie went back into the office, she noticed it didn't seem to be as hot as it had been at this time of day the last four days. Maybe they were going to be lucky and the heat wave had broken. She registered another four or five children as she wondered what there was in human nature that prompted so many people to leave things for the last minute.

The bell rang for first recess and shortly thereafter Annie heard some of the primary teachers, grades one through three, in the staffroom. "Loren, I'm going to take a minute to see how the teachers are doing. Call me if any of these parents finish writing."

"Okay, go ahead. I'll handle it here."

The teachers and aides in the staffroom were loud, exuberant, and happy. They were standing around or sitting at the tables in groups of two or three all talking at once. A few people had brought in chips, dips, and cookies. It seemed to Annie that teachers were always hungry and she had often wondered why it was so.

She walked up to Janet Reeves, a new second grade teacher, twenty-three years old and just out of college. She had been nervous on Friday about what this first day of school was going to bring.

"Janet, how's our new teacher doing?" Annie asked.

"Okay, I guess. I kept control this morning. They didn't run all over me. That's what I've been having nightmares about. I guess the worst is over."

"Don't believe her, Annie. She was great this morning," said Denise, Janet's aide. "She had the right combination of discipline and freedom and the children love her."

"You can stop giving us any more new students. I think we've all got enough," teased Barbara, a first grade teacher, from the other side of the room.

"Yeah sure, wouldn't that be nice? I don't want any more coming into the office, either. Barbara, you've only got twenty-seven. You know you're going to get some more."

"Annie," Loren called from the doorway. "We're ready for you."

She went back into the office and assigned a few more classrooms and bus stops.

Annie approached one of the PTA volunteers, Mrs. Stanford, and asked, "Do you have time to deliver all these new students to their rooms now?"

"Sure, be glad to. What do I do?"

"Here's the teacher's copy of the enrollment form. I've marked the room number on each form and put the forms in order by room number. Just make sure you get the right child into the right room."

"I understand," answered Mrs. Stanford, who seemed proud she could be of some genuine help. "Come on, children, let's get started. You come along with me and I'll get you to your rooms." They went with her with somber faces and looks of fearful anticipation.

"You know, this phone has rung at least one thousand times so far this morning. I never want to answer a phone again as long as I live," Loren said.

The phone rang. Annie laughed. "Too bad, I'm afraid you'll have to anyway."

Two more parents came in with their completed papers. Annie assigned rooms and bus stops. Mrs. Stanford wasn't back yet, so she said, "Come on, kids, I'll take you to your rooms. Let's see, we have a room four and a room seven." She took the first grader's hand. She was a little girl all dressed up for her first day of school. Her thick dark hair was parted in the middle and braided into two braids which hung down her back and were tied with yellow checked ribbons. These matched the yellow checked dress she wore. Her yellow socks and black patent leather "Mary Jane" shoes completed the outfit. She seemed full of confidence as she held Annie's hand.

"You sure look pretty today, Cheryl," Annie said.

"I know. My mommy bought me all these new clothes so I could look real pretty today." She looked up at Annie and they both smiled.

"We'll deliver Cheryl first in room four and then Billy in room seven, okay?"

"Okay," they agreed, nodding their heads.

"Cheryl, here we are - room four. See the four up there on the top of the door? Your teacher's name is Mrs. Curtis. Can you say that?" Annie asked, knowing she could.

"Mrs. Curtis," she repeated.

"That's good. Billy, you wait outside - stay there. I'll be right back. Come on, Cheryl." They went inside the room and waited by the door for the teacher to come over to them. "Excuse me, Mrs. Curtis. I've brought you a new student, Cheryl Adams." Annie handed her the enrollment sheet.

"Hello, Cheryl. Don't you look pretty! We're glad to have you with us. My name is Mrs. Curtis." She took Cheryl's hand and led her over to an empty desk. Annie left.

"I'm ready for you now, Billy. Your teacher's name is Mrs. Woodward. Let's hear you say it - Mrs. Woodward." But Billy had decided he wouldn't say anything. He was a stocky second grader with blond hair, blue eyes, lots of freckles and an infectious grin. Right now, though, he wasn't smiling. "Here we are. See the seven on the top of the door?" Annie opened the door and found she had to pull Billy inside. Mrs. Woodward came over to them. "Excuse me, Mrs. Woodward. This is Billy Mitchell. He just moved here from San Francisco."

"Hello, Billy. We're glad to have you with us. We need another boy." She led him over to a seat.

Annie hurried back to the office. When she got there, she found Loren in the health office trying to soothe a little girl who was vomiting into the toilet while two women were standing at the counter waiting to be helped.

"Sorry to keep you waiting, ladies. What can I do for you?"

"We want to pay for our children's lunches for a month. How much is it?"

"It's $2.30 a day, so $46 covers a school month of 20 days. If the child is absent, the money is carried forward. We don't send out notices if the money's run out. That's up to you to keep track of. We do accept checks if it's more convenient for you." When they were finished, she put the checks in her desk drawer until she had a chance to make up lunch cards for the children.

"Annie, I'm starving. Any chance I could go to lunch early?" Loren asked.

"Sure. What have you got in the health office, anything serious?"

"Not really. The little girl who was vomiting has a temperature of 102. I phoned her mom and she's on the way. The other girl just didn't feel well - no temp - so I let her rest but I think she's ready to go back now." She turned to the child, "Your bell just rang. Are you ready to go back to class?" The child nodded. "Okay, run along then."

"Everything's under control, Annie, so can I leave now? I'm going to eat and then go to the bank."

"Go ahead, Loren."

Annie leaned on the counter to get a moment's rest when another parent came in. "Hello, may I help you?" she asked.

"Yes, I have two children I want to get registered."

As Annie explained the registration forms to the woman, a small boy struggled to get the heavy front door open enough to get himself inside. He pulled the knob with one hand while holding a paper in the other but could only move the door a few inches. He then transferred the paper to his mouth and held it between his teeth while he used both hands to open the door enough to slip inside and gave the door a final, triumphant push with his butt.

Annie wondered if she should help him as she watched him struggle, when she noticed a snake about two feet long slither past the boy into the office and under the front table. Without thinking she said to the parent, "Oh, look, a snake came in and is lying under the table."

The woman became rigid, screeched, grabbed the papers and ran. "I'll be back," she called as she went out the door. She almost knocked the boy over in her haste.

Annie peered over the counter to see if she could still see the snake. It was curled up next to the wall under the table. "Yes, young man, what can I do for you?" she asked the boy who seemed oblivious to the commotion his entry had caused.

"My teacher told me to give this to the secretary. Are you the secretary?" He was about seven years old.

"Yes, I am." He handed her the attendance sheet. "Thank you very much for bringing it to me. You can go back to your room now." She tried to hurry him along so she could do something about the snake before someone else came in. She held the front door open for him while she took another quick glance at the snake. It appeared to be perfectly content where it was. After the boy left, she went to the intercom and rang for Joe.

"What do you need?" he asked.

"Joe, there's a snake loose in the office. I need you to come and get him out."

"Are you kidding me?"

"No, of course not. A little garter snake came in and it's under the front table. I'd just as soon not handle it if I don't have to.

"Well, I guess you're going to have to. I hate snakes and no one can pay me enough to come into that office until the thing is caught and out of there."

It took Annie a moment to digest what he said. "Do you mean to tell me you're going to leave me here with a snake wandering around the office and not help me?"

"Sorry, but I do not handle snakes," he said and hung up.

Annie banged the phone down so hard it almost broke. How dared he? He was supposed to be her friend! But right now she had to figure out what to do about the snake before Loren got back and fainted dead away and created another problem. She took a quick look at the snake.

It had moved over into the corner, was curled up and seemed to be asleep.

As she stared at it, she wondered what she should do. Perhaps if she could find a box nearby, she could get the thing into it quickly without having to touch it too much. She hurried into the staffroom, found a suitable box, and hurried back into the office. She hadn't been away more than two minutes but the snake was gone... gone! She stood and stared at the empty corner. She couldn't believe it! The snake was gone!

She searched every inch of the office, the principal's office, and the health office all the time hoping Loren wouldn't come back until it was found; Annie knew Loren would go hysterical but the snake seemed to have disappeared. She wondered for a fleeting moment if Joe had changed his mind and sneaked in and gotten the snake. But it couldn't be because she would have heard the front door open. The truth of the matter was they had a snake loose in the office. She shuddered. She didn't mind them as long as she knew where they were but now she wouldn't know if it would come slithering across her desk, be sitting on her chair when she wanted to sit down, or come crawling up her leg while she was typing.

Annie called Joe back, explained the situation to him, but all he said was, "I do not handle snakes," and hung up. She vowed she would never speak to him again.

When the principal returned, she told her about the snake. Elizabeth laughed - Annie admired her spirit - and told her not to tell anyone about it or they might have a staff riot on their hands.

Well, they never told anyone and they never saw the snake again but Annie had a rough couple of days wondering when or where it would slither toward her. She never did figure out how it managed to get out of the office without anyone seeing it.

Annie gathered up her lunch things and went wearily into the staffroom. Ray and the other upper grade teachers were there talking and laughing and comparing notes. He smiled at Annie and she smiled warmly back at him. After fixing her coffee, she sat in the vacant seat next to the new sixth grade teacher, Mary Ann Duncan, and directly across from Ray.

Mary Ann was a little older than the usual first year teacher. She had told Annie she was thirty-three with three children of her own. Her husband had fallen in love with his secretary and gotten a divorce. She was determined she wasn't going to struggle along on alimony and child support - which half the time didn't arrive - for the rest of her life so went back to college and got her teaching credential. She would have her hands full being a first year teacher and the single mother of three.

"How's it going, Mary Ann? Everything all right?" Annie asked.

"Everything is much better than I expected. Sandy is invaluable. I hadn't realized what a difference an aide makes."

"Oh, sure, they're great. That's the reason we budget for them each year. Did your kids behave pretty well?"

"I couldn't ask for anything better. If it continues on like this, I'll have a great year."

Annie laughed. "This is the first day of school, remember. You may be having a honeymoon. And how's your day going, Ray?"

"Great. I spent the first half hour this morning explaining to my students that my classroom is not run as a democracy. It is run as a dictatorship and I am the dictator. Once they understood that fact of life, everything went along just fine."

Annie laughed along with him.

The bell rang and the teachers left the staffroom to get their students from the playground and take them back to class. Annie went into the office where only two parents were filling out forms. She guessed they were over the worst of the first day enrollment crunch. She pulled out some of the new registrations and started working on them.

As the long day drew to a close, Annie asked, "Well, Loren, now do you believe me that the first day is a monster?"

"Annie, I'll tell you the truth. I never want to answer another phone as long as I live. This phone must have rung four thousand times today."

"Yes, I know. Let's go home. We've earned our pay for today."

Annie was getting into her car when Joe called to her, "Annie, wait a minute."

"I don't want to talk to you ever again, Joe."

"Please let me explain."

"What could you say that would make it all right? You didn't help me when I needed help and that says it all. We were supposed to be friends and friends are supposed to help each other when they need it. You let me down."

"I know, Annie, but there's a good reason. Will you listen a minute?"

Annie looked at his concerned face and said, "All right, go ahead."

"Annie, you know I was in the Marines."

"Yes."

"Well, one night I was sleeping out in the field when something woke me just as it was getting light. I was immediately alert thinking it was the enemy, but it turned out to be a snake had gotten inside my shirt while I was sleeping. I panicked and almost went crazy. Ever since then I can't be anywhere near a snake. I'm sorry, Annie, but I can't help it."

"Oh, Joe, I'm sorry, too. Of course, I didn't know." She hugged him and said, "Okay, you're forgiven. I can understand it and from now on I'll handle my own snakes."

* * * * * * *

"It's amazing! The only papers parents return immediately when we need them are the free/reduced lunch applications. We sent them home yesterday and just look at the amount we have back already. I must have a hundred of them in my box. You're going to have to do this next year, Loren. I'm only doing it this time because this is your first beginning of school experience."

"I appreciate it, Annie. I'm sure I couldn't handle it on top of all these registrations and stuff." Loren giggled.

"You know, Loren, this school has one of the highest free/reduced lunch counts in the school district. We have about 55% of the students on free lunch and about 20% on reduced. That makes 75% of the school. Let's see, 75% of an enrollment of about 550 equals 412. That's 412 applications we have to process. Parents seem to think we can get that all done in about 45 minutes. They'll start calling up in about an hour to see if they've been approved."

"Annie, I have a lady on the phone who wants to talk about free lunches."

"Okay, I got it." She picked up her extension and said, "This is Mrs. Kallas, the school secretary, speaking. May I help you?"

"This is Mrs. Young. You know, Charlton and Amy's mother. You sent our free lunch form back because it needs a social security number on it."

"Yes, that's right."

"Well, my husband says he don't want us to put our social security number on it. He says it's none of your business."

"Mrs. Young, the government says if you want the free lunch for your children, you must list your social security number on the application. If you don't want to do it, of course, you don't have to but then you don't get the free lunch either. It's up to you."

"My husband says we won't take it then."

"Well, that's all right. It's entirely up to you."

"Bye," Mrs. Young said pleasantly as she hung up the phone.

"Honestly, those people... I know they're on welfare and would qualify for free lunches. They've put it on their application for the last two years and now they've suddenly decided they don't want to give it out."

As Annie answered another call: "Yes, Mrs. Armstrong, I remember your application. ...No, I'm sorry, there's nothing I can do about it. I'm sorry, Mrs. Armstrong, but four people in the family with an income of $85,000 a year doesn't qualify you for free lunches."

* * * * * * *

Ray reached across the table and took her hand. "I can't tell you how happy I am that you agreed to come to dinner with me, Annie. I've been lonesome for someone I can talk to and be comfortable with."

"I know it must have been hard for you to come back to the house where you and Helen were so happy for, how many years, 20, 25?"

"Exactly 25 years." He released Annie's hand. "We were married when I was 22. It was a happy marriage even though we weren't lucky enough to have kids." He appeared deep in thought and shook his head. "The house is empty without her. I feel like I'm rattling around in a big barn by myself."

"Ray, you need to be with people as much as possible."

"Sure, that's what everyone says. Everyone I know has been trying to fix me up with blind dates and dinner parties and barbecues and all that stuff. I feel like I've met more single women in the last six weeks than I did in all the years before I married. It's been awful, Annie."

She looked at his woebegone expression and laughed. "Some men would figure that was heaven. You're in a unique position, Ray. You're a mid-life, single man. You're an eligible, single man. Do you know how many mid-life, single women there are out there looking for someone just like you?"

"I don't want to know. I discovered I hate to date. I feel like a used car that's for sale. People come around and kick your tires, check your speedometer, turn on your motor to see if you can start, and then drive you around the block to see if you can still perform. I get so self-conscious at this obvious examination that I can hardly speak much less do anything else."

While Annie laughed at this description, he added, "That's why it's so nice to be with you. I don't have the feeling that I'm being examined. I'm comfortable with you. We're friends - we speak the same language - I admire you and I think you admire me and that's it. I don't feel I have to prove anything to you or perform for you and it's very comfortable."

"Yes, I know. I feel the same way. I finally gave up dating because I couldn't stand the examination either. I decided I'd rather stay home by myself than go through the trauma of dating. I was so self-conscious, I seldom had a good time with anyone."

Reaching for her hand again, he said, "Well, Annie, do you think you could have a good time with me? I'm learning how to cook. Maybe sometime you could come over and let me try a new recipe out on you. How about it? Could we keep each other company?

Putting her hand over his, she said, "Yes, Ray, I would love to sample your new recipes and think we could keep each other company very nicely."

OCTOBER

"She wants you to check her head, Annie. Aaaannie!!! The girl wants you to check her head. She says you do it much more thoroughly than anyone else!" Loren's voice got loud and vehement in an attempt to get Annie's attention.

Annie looked up slowly from the attendance report she was balancing and tried to concentrate on what Loren was saying. "What are you talking about? Am I getting a reputation for being a good head louse finder? Wow, of all the things I'd like to be renowned for, I can assure you that's not one of them."

She walked up to the counter and faced the girl who was waiting there. She must have been a sixth grader because she looked like a ninth grader. She was a neat and clean blonde with beautiful long, shiny, wavy hair half way down her back. She was as tall as Annie. She had make-up on but had done a good job of it with light blue eye shadow accenting her bright blue eyes, a little blusher, and faint pink lipstick. The girl was a beauty.

"You want me to check your hair. Have you ever had it before?"

"Yes, Mrs. Kallas. You found them the last time I had it last year. You do a good job, so I want you to check for them. Sometimes the nurse gets in a hurry and isn't really careful. I know you'll be thorough."

Annie stared at her. She talked, thought, and acted like an adult. She was perfectly poised and knew what she wanted. If she wanted Annie, Annie guessed she could have her. Maybe it was a little flattering to be the best head louse finder on campus. She smiled at the thought.

"What's your name?"

"Sandy."

"All right, Sandy. Come on into the health office. Would you sit there, please?"

She sat down where Annie pointed and folded her hands in her lap.

Annie stood in front of her and was about to part the hair above her forehead when she saw it. Without even touching Sandy's hair, Annie could see a louse walking on top of the hair spray she had on. She was stunned. She usually saw only the white eggs - the nits - that had been laid. She seldom ever saw the lice themselves because they liked to hide under the hair, right next to the skin and they scurried out of sight when someone went poking around disturbing their warmth and darkness. If this child had one on top of her hair, Annie shuddered at the thought of how many were hidden underneath the hair spray. "Well, Sandy, you have them all right. Is anyone home?"

"Yes, my mom's home."

"Please call her and tell her to come and get you. Then you can get your stuff out of your room. I'll call your teacher and tell her." Annie called the classroom. "Mrs. Duncan, please pick up the intercom."

"Yes, hi," she answered.

"This is Annie. Sandy has a very bad case of pediculosis and will be going home. I'm sending her to the room for her things."

"Good heavens, what's that?"

"Oh, I forgot you're new. It's head lice."

"Oh, my heavens, Annie, are they catching?"

"Sure, they're catching. If people put their heads close together or share combs or brushes, these little bugs just love running around from head to head."

"My head itches just thinking about it."

"Hey, relax. Come down later and I'll check your head for you."

"Oh, I'd be so grateful if you would do that. This is terrible, terrible."

Annie laughed at her reaction. Mary Annie Duncan was having a hard enough time this first year without having to worry about catching head lice. By the end of the school year, she'd be hardened and would take this type of thing in stride.

She went back to her desk and picked up the attendance report again.

"Look," whispered Loren.

Annie growled in irritation. Sandy had returned from the classroom and brought four friends with her.

"What's this, Sandy?"

"Mrs. Kallas, these friends of mine were at a slumber party at my house on Saturday night and they would like you to check their heads, too. Will you, please?"

How could she resist this child with her good manners and polite way of speaking? She sighed and said, "All right, girls, into the health office." They went in and took seats. "Who's going to be first?"

"I'll be first," offered a little brown-haired girl.

Annie stood before her, parted the hair over her forehead with her fingers and looked for the white eggs. Nothing there, so she moved to the right ear, nothing there, so on to the middle of the back of her head. One of the louse's favorite spots was the indentation where the neck joins the back of the head. Nothing there, so on to the left ear. Nothing. "You're okay. Who's next?" Annie washed her hands.

"I'll be next," offered an African-American girl. Annie hesitated for a moment wondering if she should tell her she didn't have it. African-Americans seldom, if ever, got it. She then thought, no, she needed to be treated the same as the others. Annie looked through her hair - forehead first, then right ear, back of head, then around to the left ear. "You're okay. Who's next?" She washed her hands.

"Me." Annie went through the same routine but found nothing. She washed her hands. The fourth girl, unfortunately, had a few nits on the back of the head. Annie told her to phone her mother and told Loren to call the teacher. Annie completed the paper work on two cases of pediculosis for the nurse.

With another sigh, she went back to her desk. She had spent an hour and a half chasing bugs on heads instead of on her paperwork. She finally balanced her attendance report through the second grade when she was distracted by a loud, piercing voice.

"It's this filthy school, that's what it is. I'm going to report you to the health department. We never had anything like this in the family before. I want to see the principal. I'm going to have you all arrested."

Loren, who was supposed to handle all counter work, stood in front of the woman, apparently hypnotized, unable to utter a word. Annie walked beside Loren and said in a very quiet and firm tone of voice which the school psychologist had once told her would help to soothe all troubled parents, "Excuse me, ma'am, I'm the school secretary, Mrs. Kallas. May I have your name, please?"

"I'm Mrs. Pelham, Sandy's mother," she continued screeching. "Sandy called me and told me you said you found lice in her hair. Lice! Are you crazy? We don't even know what lice look like in our family. We're clean people and I consider it an insult to me and mine when you say we have lice."

So much for the psychologist's theory. Wishing wholeheartedly the principal would return from her meeting, Annie asked the mother to follow her into the health office. "I'm sorry, but the principal isn't on campus just now. If you'll come in here, I'll show you what I found in Sandy's hair."

Sandy was sitting on the cot in the health office while Annie pointed out to Mrs. Pelham the lice in Sandy's hair.

She started screeching again, "It's this school. We never had them before in our family."

Annie looked at Sandy, remembering what she had said about having had them the previous year. If mother was telling the truth, how was Sandy knowledgeable enough to suspect she had them? Sandy met Annie's eyes and smiled slightly and they both knew mother was lying.

"Mrs. Pelham, anyone can get head lice. Sandy is obviously a very clean girl but she could get them from using someone else's comb or leaning her head against her girlfriend's head. The nurse will check all the students in Sandy's classroom. That's our normal routine. When one student in the room has pediculosis, we check everyone in the room.

"Here's some information on what kind of shampoo to use and what else to do to make sure you kill them all in your couch and carpeting and all over the house." Annie handed her a pamphlet. "The shampoo will kill them but our school district policy requires the hair also be free of all eggs before the student can return. Sandy will have to be cleared through the office before she can return to school. I know it's a nuisance but these things happen. It's no reflection on you or Sandy."

Mrs. Pelham snatched the pamphlet and grabbed Sandy and pulled her toward the front door. "As soon as I get home I'm going to phone the health department and report this school as being filthy, full of bugs, and a danger to the students."

"Yes, ma'am." Annie watched her leave and wondered how that mother could have raised such a well-mannered daughter.

She returned to her attendance report and was able to work on it until the teachers started coming out to lunch.

"Oh, there you are, Annie. I've been looking for you. Can you check my head now? It itches something terrible."

It was Mary Ann Duncan, Sandy's teacher. Annie laughed and said, "That's only the power of suggestion, Mary Ann. Don't you know the white man's head louse won't crawl on the black man's head? Even our lice are prejudiced."

"What it really is, is that lice will crawl on the heads of peasants but not on the heads of royalty," Mary Ann answered.

Mary Ann Duncan was an absolute prize in Annie's opinion. She was the school's second African-American teacher. The first one was cool and reserved and stayed to herself but on her very first day on the job, Mary Ann fired off jokes and all kinds of remarks about blacks and whites and their relationships. She shocked a lot of people at first, but she was like a breath of fresh air swirling throughout the school. She forced things out into the open that many people had never discussed in public before.

"Anyway, please check my head - just to make sure this louse isn't color blind."

"Sure, come on into the health office with me." They found Loren had a multitude of students in there with bumps and scratches from lunch recess.

"Let's go into the principal's office. Elizabeth's on the playground." Annie had Mary Ann sit by the window so the sun would shine on her head and give her good light. She went through her hair thoroughly but as she expected - nothing.

"Thanks, Annie. Is it really true that blacks don't get head lice?"

"That's what I read. There is a variation of louse blacks can get but it's fairly rare. You're not immune but your chances are slim," Annie assured her.

"Just like with everything else in this cold, cruel world, our chances of getting what you people get are slim."

Annie laughed, gave her a friendly slap on the arm, and pushed her toward the staffroom. "Go on and eat knowing that you have a clear head."

"Oooooohhh, Annie," she groaned at the pun.

Annie could hear the children's noise as they lined up in front of the cafeteria. "Wow, it must be lunch time already."

"Annie, what am I supposed to do with this child?" Barbara Selby, a first grade teacher, left a little boy at the counter and came to Annie's desk to whisper to her, "He's got a big hole right in the front of his pants and no underwear on."

"And, so," Annie finished for her, "when he sits down, his 'thingee' shows and disrupts everyone?"

"How'd you know?"

"I've been around a long time. See if he's got a phone

and call mom to come and repair him. If there's no phone, see if any of the clothes under the sink in the health office will fit him."

"Annie, I'm on my lunch hour and I only get a half hour. Could anyone here do that for me?"

"Sure, Loren will do it. You go eat."

"Thanks, Annie." The teacher went to the boy and told him they would take care of him. "His name's Jimmy Cates," she called as she went into the staffroom.

"Loren, call the boy's mother and ask her to bring some pants for him."

"There is no phone, Annie," she said after looking at his record in the computer.

"Well, Loren, think it through. You know what the problem is. How are you going to solve it?"

"I don't know. Shall I take him home?"

Annie was aghast at the question. "Geez, Loren, don't you remember I told you clerical and other Classified employees NEVER take students home? It's a matter of liability. If you get in a car crash on the way to the kid's house, you want to be responsible and have his mom sue you? We let the nurse or the principal, the Certificated employees who get paid for that kind of stuff, do it. You don't remember that I already explained all of this to you?"

"Yes, I guess so. I just forgot."

"Is there a grandmother or aunt or somebody listed as an emergency contact person? If not, dig a pair of pants out of the health office box of clothes and make him put them on. Then send him to lunch. It's time for me to go to lunch, too. The principal should be back any minute but if you need me, I'll be here in the staffroom."

Annie gathered up her lunch sack and coffee cup and went into the staffroom. It was like going into bedlam. When teachers got tired, they got quiet and the staffroom was like a morgue. Judging by the level of the noise, everyone was feeling good today. This was first lunch so these were all primary teachers. Five instructional aides were also eating lunch at the table. Everybody was talking. She filled her coffee cup and found a seat. As she ate her sandwich, she listened in on the conversations going on at the same time around the table.

Barbara Selby was talking to Jeanne Curtis, also a first grade teacher. "I brought him into the office and they're trying to find his mother now to come with some underwear or change his pants or do something. Jeanne, I can't believe how aware of their bodies first graders are and how sexually aware they are.

"We were sitting in a circle on the floor. I was reading to them when all of a sudden this little girl, Karen, started whimpering. She wouldn't stop so I asked her what was wrong. As soon as I did that, she burst out crying, ran up to me like someone was chasing her and pointed hysterically at Jimmy and his torn pants crotch with his penis very noticeable through the hole. I'll tell you - that really killed the reading lesson.

"The whole class, of course, had to get in on the act. I guess they all, except Jimmy, have been well briefed that one does not show one's private parts. The boys teased him, the girls got dramatic and acted like they were going to be molested - even though they don't know what molested is.

Jimmy must be used to the draft in his pants 'cause he couldn't figure out why everyone was so excited. It was incredible! It seemed as if in one minute we went from a well organized, well run, happy reading lesson to a hysterical, chaotic, disorganized mob. I was literally saved by the lunch bell. Annie, are you going to be able to solve my problem with Jimmy?"

"Loren is working on it now. I can assure you Jimmy will return to class with his private parts private or he will not return at all." Everyone laughed.

Susan Woodward, a second grade teacher, was involved in a three way conversation with the other second grade teacher, Janet Reeves, and second/third combination class teacher, Karen Ramsey. Annie heard Susan saying, "That boy and his mother are going to drive me batty. He wets his pants in class every day! He's seven years old and wets his pants every day! His mother came in this morning at seven-thirty at my request and we had a nice conference. It consisted of mother telling me not to worry so much about Steven doing this because it's a family trait."

"A family trait?" asked Karen. "You mean, it's inherited?"

"Can you believe it? It seems she wet her pants every day all throughout her school career and didn't stop until she got to high school."

Almost everyone at the table was listening to this story. They moaned and groaned at the last statement.

Susan continued, "So now, of course, she thinks I'm crazy because I don't consider this normal behavior for a seven year old."

"Can't somebody insist the boy get a physical check-up?" Janet asked. "If it was my child, I certainly would."

"They went through that last year, Janet. Weren't you his teacher, Barbara?" asked Susan.

"No, I was," said Patricia Campos. "It was the same thing, wet pants every day. I finally took it to the principal, who called the mother in. The mother told her the same thing about how it runs in the family. Elizabeth didn't buy it and insisted mom get a doctor's statement, which she finally did. The doctor said he couldn't find any evidence of any type of bladder or kidney dysfunction."

"Yes, and as long as mom regards it as normal for their family, we don't get anywhere. What do I do now? Any suggestions?" Susan asked.

The room was quiet for a minute.

"How about asking the school psychologist to test him to see if there is anything emotionally wrong with him," said Barbara.

"Try giving him a reward every day he doesn't wet," suggested Janet.

"Why don't you make it uncomfortable for mom every time the kid wets. Call her to come to school and change him every day. That ought to make something happen," said Patricia.

"Those are three good ideas," said Susan. "I think I'll use all three of them."

The bell rang and they had to go back. Annie still had fifteen minutes for lunch and the sudden quiet was deafening. She leaned back and closed her eyes but before she knew it, the bell rang again. It was time for the next lunch, a new batch of teachers, and for Annie to get back to work. She usually waited a minute to see if someone on the next lunch wanted to ask her something.

Norma Glas, a fifth grade teacher, was the first one in. Norma was one of Annie's favorites even though she enjoyed shocking people, but Annie liked her because she thought for herself and didn't follow the crowd. She didn't spend a lot of money on things for show like clothes, cars, or furniture. Instead, she saved up and went traveling every summer. She was still under thirty and she'd been to the Brazilian jungle, the African veld, China, and next summer was going to Russia.

"Hi, Norma, how're you doing," Annie asked.

"Okay, Annie. How do I go to a store to buy something for my class?"

"Where do you want to buy it?"

"At the local market. We're going to fix an Eskimo dinner," she answered.

"Good heavens, what does that consist of?"

"You'll see. We'll fix you a plate. What do I have to do?"

"Come see me later and I'll give you the paperwork.

* * * * * * *

"Lincoln Elementary, Mrs. Kallas speaking," Annie said into the phone.

"Can the children wear their costumes on the school bus?"

"No, ma'am. They have to carry the costume in a bag."

"Well, that's terrible! How am I going to get him fixed up? I have to put all this make-up on him. It takes a half hour to put it on."

"I'm sorry, ma'am," Annie answered, wondering if her hearing was going. "I thought you asked if he could wear a costume on the bus. He can, of course, wear make-up. The bus drivers feel that the costume itself and the mask might present a safety hazard when there are ninety children on the bus. Make-up is not a safety hazard."

"That's good. Thanks very much."

Today was the big day - Halloween. They had been leading up to this day for the last few weeks. The office showed the right spirit with a bulletin board covered with pumpkins and witches to greet anyone coming in. It was put up by Miss Wong's room ten.

At ten o'clock the annual school Halloween parade was to be held. From eight o'clock until ten o'clock there was a stream of parents coming into the office to deliver costumes or masks or forgotten make-up, money, lunches, etc., to their children. Annie and Loren were kept busy calling students from their rooms to meet with the parents.

At about nine-thirty Jackie Montenegro, a thin fourth grade girl with stringy brown hair, came in quietly and asked to use the phone.

"Have you got a phone pass?" Loren asked.

"Yes, here it is."

A few minutes later she stood hesitantly in front of Annie's desk.

"What do you need, Jackie?" Annie asked.

"No one answers," she said sadly in a worried tone of voice. "Can I call again in a few minutes, Mrs. Kallas?"

"Sure. What's wrong, Jackie? Anything we can help you with?" The child was upset about something.

"Mrs. Kallas, did my mother bring my costume into the office and you maybe didn't get a chance to call me?" she asked.

"No, honey, not to me. What about you, Mrs. Ash? Have you seen a costume for Jackie?"

Loren thought a minute. "No, I haven't seen anything, Jackie." The girl looked so disappointed and sad that Loren added, "I'm sorry, Jackie."

"Why don't you just wait in the health office by the

phone and try every few minutes, Jackie? Maybe she just had to go out for a minute?"

"Okay, Mrs. Kallas."

Annie waited for her to go into the health office. She and Loren looked at each other. "I could kill some parents, sometimes. I bet that mother forgot all about it," Annie muttered.

"And her kid's sitting here waiting, embarrassed, and scared to death she's going to be left out."

Annie picked up the intercom and called Jackie's teacher. "Mrs. Chamberlain, please pick up your phone."

"Yes, Annie?"

"Linda, Jackie Montenegro can't reach anyone at home. Do you by chance have an extra costume for her? She's getting pretty upset."

"Well, I'll tell you...," she said slowly in a teasing way. "Since I'm a well-organized teacher who always thinks ahead and is well prepared, I always keep a spare sheet or two for those who want to dress up like ghosts. Tell her to come on back and we'll get her fixed up."

"Thanks, Linda, that's great." She went into the health office where Jackie was sitting on the cot with her hands folded in her lap. She was staring straight ahead trying to control her sobs, with the tears rolling down her cheeks. Annie crouched down in front of her, took her hands, and said, "Jackie, Mrs. Chamberlain has a ghost costume you can wear. She says to tell you to come on back so she can fix you up in it."

"Really?" asked Jackie, looking at Annie as if she was trying to see inside her mind.

"Really." Annie took a tissue and wiped her tears and handed her another tissue. "Here, blow your nose. It's all going to be all right. Your teacher is going to take care of it. Okay? You going to give me a smile?" Annie lifted her chin and looked into her eyes.

Jackie smiled. Annie gave her a hug and a push. "Hurry to your room now. It's almost ten o'clock"

At ten o'clock Annie said to Loren, "Come on, let's lock the office and go watch the parade, too."

"Oh, can we? That would be wonderful. This is the first one I've ever seen. I was hoping you'd let me."

Annie smiled at her. Loren was a pleasure to be near sometimes in her delight and enthusiasm at small things. They locked the office doors and walked to the playground to the west of the school. On the way, they saw the classes lining up outside their rooms. The principal was going to ramp four to start the line of students making a large circle around the perimeter of the playground. When ramp four was on its way, she went to ramp three and got them going and did the same on ramps two and one. Those students who had to wait were jumping up and down in excitement.

In a few minutes, they were all out on the playground, walking around in an orderly fashion. It was fun watching them, so proud and excited, in their various costumes. Jose Ortega, the English as a Second Language teacher, had volunteered to lead the parade. He was dressed in a Mexican costume with sombrero and serape. There were an abundance of monsters of various descriptions, numerous witches and vampires, ghosts in mother's (or teacher's) sheets, little girls dressed as fairies or brides, little boys as cowboys. Everyone laughed at the teacher dressed as a woman just getting up in the morning: curlers in her hair, bathrobe and slippers on. They ooh'd and aah'd at the pretty teacher in a fancy wedding dress.

There was one little girl in authentic Japanese ceremonial clothes. The parade lasted about half an hour and was a great success.

When Loren and Annie got back to the office, they found four parents standing angrily outside the locked door.

"Hello, may we help you?" Annie asked, knowing what was coming.

"I have a costume for my son. Where's the parade?" one mother asked.

"I'm afraid the parade is over. It started at ten o'clock sharp. It is now ten-thirty."

"Well, I got here at about ten-fifteen, but I couldn't get in the office to let anybody know I was here. Why wasn't anyone in the office?"

"Because at ten o'clock we closed up to watch the parade. The children were already lined up and parading. It would have been too late for anyone to deliver a costume at that time. At ten-fifteen your son was out in the field, ma'am." She unlocked the door and everyone went inside the office. Loren went to her desk and let Annie handle the parents. This woman wouldn't let go.

"Your note that came home said the parade started at ten-fifteen."

"No, ma'am. Here's a copy of the letter that went home." Annie reached over on the counter where there was a supply of the letters. "You see, it clearly states ten o'clock." She handed her a copy. "But, you don't have to worry. If your child didn't have a costume, the teacher probably provided something for him. Are any of you the parent of Jackie Montenegro?"

They all murmured, "No."

"Is there anything else I can do for you?" Annie smiled at them wishing they would hurry and let her go back to her paperwork. Three of them turned around, grumbling to each other as they left. The fourth said, "I would like to talk to my daughter and explain why I was late."

"Yes, of course. What is her name and room number?"

A call to the room and the girl was on the way. "She's coming. You might want to meet her outside."

"Loren," Annie said after the mother went out. "You notice there's no sign of Jackie Montenegro's mother."

"Yes, I noticed. Jackie would have been sitting here waiting a long, long time."

* * * * * * *

"You're getting to be a very good cook, Ray. I'm surprised."

"Why are you surprised?"

"I don't know. Maybe because I hate to cook so much it's always a surprise when I find someone else enjoys it."

"Well, I'm surprised at that. I don't understand why someone wouldn't enjoy it."

"Because you can spend hours working on a meal and if it's good it's devoured within fifteen or twenty minutes. If it's not good, it's garbage within five minutes. I find as I get older I don't want to put the energy into being careful when I'm cooking, so more and more of what I cook becomes garbage."

Ray stared at her for a minute and then laughed. "I'll tell you what. Don't cook any more. Just come over here and eat. It's much more fun being able to cook for someone else than just myself."

"You got a deal. You cook and I'll do the dishes."

"Annie, why don't you go into the living room and wait for me. I'll put this food away and be right with you."

"Okay, if you're sure you don't need me to help."

Annie walked slowly from the kitchen, through the dining room, across the entry hall and into the living room. She had been in this house a year ago last Christmas. At the time, Ray and his wife had hosted the staff Christmas party and Annie remembered what a pleasant, comfortable home it was. But now she also remembered that Helen had been an admirer of modern art and Annie shook her head in disbelief at the split heads and staggered eyes that looked down at her from the pictures on the walls. Annie didn't understand modern art and didn't understand anyone who did understand it.

"That piece you're holding was one of Helen's favorites."
"Why?"
"Why?"
"I'm sorry, Ray. It's just hard for me to understand how something that looks like a doughnut can be anyone's favorite piece of sculpture. Where's any beauty in it?"

Ray laughed. "I have to laugh, Annie, because that's about what I said to Helen when she brought it home. She tried to explain it to me but we both finally agreed to allow each other our own tastes in art. This stuff isn't for me but she enjoyed it so here it is. I suppose I should get rid of it but I'm not ready to change the things in the house yet. She's still here in her things and it's a comfort to me right now."

"Yes, of course it is."

Ray turned on the stereo and said, "Come sit with me on the sofa." As she started to sit, he added, "Here, next to me." He put his arm around her shoulders and they leaned back and listened to the music. After a few minutes, he said, "Annie, you must know you mean a lot to me. Being with you has helped me more than you could know since I came back from Canada. I sometimes wonder how I would have managed without you."

She turned her body so their lips were almost touching. "You've made a big difference in my life, too, Ray."

He bent down and kissed her. He looked at her and with one hand guided his fingers over the contours of her face as a blind person might do. "I never realized what a lovely face you have, Annie. Did I ever tell you I think the sexiest thing about a woman is her hair?" He ran his fingers through her hair and then bent down and kissed her hungrily.

Annie felt dizzy as she responded to his kiss. However, just as she felt herself floating into the fire, she found herself being pushed away.

"No, no, I can't do it. I'm not ready. I'm not ready." Ray

stood up and looked down at her as she struggled to right herself on the couch. "I'm sorry, Annie. I can't. I'm not ready. I'm still too close to Helen. I can't do it."

Annie reached up and took his hand. "It's okay, Ray. It's okay. I understand. It's all right." She stood up and put her arms around his neck. "Hey, we're friends. It was nice kissing you and it's nice being your friend. Let's let it go at that. If more happens someday, that's fine; if not, that's fine, too, we can be friends. I'd better go home now," she said as she released him. "Thanks for dinner. Invite me again when you have a new recipe you want to try out on someone." She kissed him lightly on the lips and turned to go.

But he pulled her back." Is it okay? Can we continue on?"

"It's okay and we will continue on."

Suddenly she couldn't wait to get away. She almost ran out of the house and into her car and drove away. After she'd gone a block, she pulled over to the curb and parked. She stared blankly ahead and then put her face in her hands. She'd almost let herself go. She could feel herself drifting away to never-never land when he stopped her. How could she have been so stupid? She should have known he wasn't ready. She should have known better than to be so eager to let herself go.

She sat and thought about what had happened. It was wonderful when he held her. Was she starting to care too much about him? She hoped not. She had gone through it with her former husband and didn't want to do it again. She needed to be careful and not throw her hard-won equilibrium away. No, no, of course, she wouldn't. Ray was nice and she wouldn't mind getting closer to him but she could take it or leave it - just as she'd told him. There, she felt better now she'd gotten it clear in her mind.

* * * * * * *

"Excuse me," a quiet voice said.

Annie looked up from her computer to the counter. A small, thin, young woman stood there. Annie had no idea how long she had been waiting. I'm sorry, I didn't hear you come in. What can I do for you?"

"Today was my daughter's first day at this school. I came to pick her up. Can you tell me what room she's in? Her name is Cynthia Miller. She's in the first grade."

"Yes, of course. Let me see..." Annie looked in the box holding new enrollments. She had an uneasy feeling - she didn't remember seeing this woman before. If the child had been enrolled today, she ought to have some recollection of the mother.

"May I have your name, please?"

"I'm Cynthia's mother."

"No, I need your name, please."

"I'm Lurette Miller. Is there anything wrong?"

The name checked with the mother's name listed on the enrollment sheet. "No, Mrs. Miller, there's nothing wrong. I just don't remember you. Were you in to enroll Cynthia?"

"No, I was at work. I had the babysitter, Mrs. Gadson, bring Cynthia in this morning with the enrollment papers."

"Oh, sure, I remember Mrs. Gadson. I'm sorry if I seem to be giving you a hard time, but we have to be very careful about who picks up a student. It's for the child's protection, you know."

"I understand. It's a good idea and I appreciate it." She nodded and smiled.

"Cynthia is in room three. That's the third room in the first ramp nearest the street. Down that way."

"Thank you," Mrs. Miller said as she hurried out.

Mrs. Miller returned to the office a few minutes later accompanied by Barbara Selby, Cynthia's teacher.

"Annie, Mrs. Miller came to pick up Cynthia but she left with the walkers. Did you tell me this morning to hold her for her mother?"

Annie shook her head as she struggled to remember exactly what she had said when she delivered Cynthia to her room. "I think I only pointed out that on the enrollment sheet it said she was a walker. That's all the babysitter, Mrs. Gadson, told me."

"I asked her if she knew she was a walker and she said 'yes' so I crossed her. Did she expect you to pick her up, Mrs. Miller?" the teacher asked.

"I told her this morning but she probably forgot what with the excitement of the first day and all. I guess I better hurry and see if I can catch up with her."

"Let us know what happens, will you?" asked the teacher.

"All right, I'll call the school when we get home."

Annie and Barbara looked at each other after the mother left.

"I hate this feeling," Barbara said. "This feeling of dread - of catastrophe about to happen. You feel it right in your stomach - like a rock sitting in there. I hate it! It's the biggest drawback to teaching lower grades. Every time there's a lost child, I promise myself I'll switch to sixth grade next year."

"Hey, don't worry. She'll show up."

"Yes, well, let's keep a positive thought. I'll go back and finish cleaning up my room and then come back here and wait to hear something. If I'm still in my room and you hear anything, call me right away."

"Sure, Barbara. Take it easy. It'll be all right, you'll see."

Barbara Selby had just returned to the office and was sitting at the front table correcting arithmetic papers when Mrs. Miller walked in again.

"Hi, Mrs. Miller, did you find her?" Annie asked in a cheerful tone of voice hoping it would create the answer she wanted to hear.

Mrs. Miller started to talk but her voice broke. She bit down on her lower lip and waited a moment to still the trembling. "No, I didn't find her. I walked home in the only logical way to walk home and she wasn't anywhere along the way. I asked some of the children I met but no one had seen her. Mrs. Selby, what do I do now? Should I call the police?"

Barbara put her arm around the mother in an attempt to reassure her and could feel how thin and bony her shoulders were. "Don't worry, Mrs. Miller, we'll find her. Why don't you walk home again, looking as you go but then stay home by the phone," Barbara suggested. "I'll get in the car and go up and down the streets. If you find her, please phone us immediately. If you don't find her, why don't you wait at home and we'll call you there if we hear something. There's not much you can do without a car. And then you'll be home if she comes walking in. Keep the phone free as much as you can, okay?"

"Yes, sure, I understand. I'll go right now."

"You know, Annie," Barbara was deep in thought as she spoke, "Cynthia was walking with Tricia Collins when they left school. I think I'll call Mrs. Collins and make sure Cynthia isn't there."

When Barbara returned from the phone, she said, "Mrs. Collins says Cynthia walked with Tricia but had continued on home after getting to Tricia's house."

"Wait a minute, Barbara," Annie said, "look here." She walked over to the school area map on the wall. "Tricia lives down here on Somerset." She pointed to the map. "If Cynthia walked to Tricia's house and then continued on, she was headed east when she should have been going west to get to her house over here on Blanton."

"Oh, wow! Who knows where she is by now? She doesn't know the way home. I'm going to get in the car and drive east and see what I can find. Annie, did you notice how Mrs. Miller was shaking? She had to clamp her mouth shut to keep her teeth from chattering."

"Yes, I noticed. Poor thing, she's scared to death. Wait a minute, let's take a quick look to see if there's a Mr. Miller." Annie looked at the enrollment sheet. "No, no father listed. No siblings, either. There's just the two of them."

"I'm going. I'll report back."

"Good luck, Barbara."

"Yes, let's hope so."

About fifteen minutes later, the mother came back in. "Have you heard anything yet?" She stood at the counter and looked at Annie with terror in her eyes and her lips pinched together. Annie noticed she seemed much older than when she first came in an hour ago.

"No, not a thing," Annie answered in a calm, kindly tone of voice. "Mrs. Selby is out looking, too, but in a different direction." She explained how Cynthia had walked to Tricia's house.

"So I've been looking in the wrong places?" The mother sighed and sat down.

"Can I get you something, Mrs. Miller? Coke, coffee, or a glass of water?"

"Yes, a coke, please. Maybe it will perk me up again."

"Sure." Annie took change out of her purse and quickly got Mrs. Miller a coke out of the machine in the staffroom.

"Thanks." She sat at the table, looking out of the front window. Annie went back to her desk and there was silence for a few minutes.

Mrs. Miller finished the drink, stood up, and said, "I have to get started looking again. I'll walk around those other streets where you said she went but if I don't find her soon, I'll have to call the police."

"Mrs. Miller, don't you think it would be a good idea for you to wait at home by the phone? Someone with some information may be trying to call you right now. Mrs. Selby is looking for Cynthia in her car. She can cover a lot more territory than you can on foot."

"Yes, maybe you're right. Maybe I should be home in case the phone rings or if Cynthia comes home. But it's so hard to sit there and not do anything. Well, I'll look around once more and then I'll go home." She wasn't trembling any more. She only looked exhausted.

"Try not to worry, Mrs. Miller," Annie said in an effort to soothe her. "I've been in this job for nine years and the lost children always turn up again. Hang in there, I know she'll be found."

"You hear such terrible stories, you know, especially with little girls. If anything happens to her, I'll never forgive myself. Why wasn't I here a few minutes earlier?" Her voice broke and she started crying. Annie grabbed a box of tissues and hurried around the counter. She put her arm around Mrs. Miller and offered her the tissues. Mrs. Miller took two and wiped her eyes. "Thank you. I'm not going to break down." She patted Annie's hand. "I'm all right. I'm small but I'm strong."

"Well, you have a lot of courage and I admire you for it. Why don't you go on home now? Maybe Cynthia is waiting on the steps for you."

"Yes, I will. You'll call me..."

"Yes, of course."

Annie watched the door close behind her and walked slowly back to her desk. Damn it! Why hadn't she asked the babysitter when she enrolled the child whether or not Cynthia was going to be picked up? Usually, if the child was a walker someone picked him up until he got used to his new neighborhood. If anything happened to this little girl, Mrs. Miller wouldn't be the only one not forgiving herself. She picked up a pencil and angrily broke it in half and threw the two halves onto her desk. Damn, damn, damn! She sat at her desk staring at the opposite wall. She was interrupted by Barbara Selby's return.

"Hi, Barbara, any luck?"

"No, nothing. Have you heard anything?"

"Not a thing."

"I went up and down every street within our school boundaries but no sign of Cynthia. Where on earth could she be, Annie?"

"She's playing in some kid's backyard where no one can see her. She'll be all right, you'll see. We haven't lost one yet and we're not going to lose one now."

"In my opinion, this is one of the hardest things in the world." Barbara was close to hysteria as her words followed one another faster and faster. "It's enough to drive someone out of teaching. It makes you feel guilty and responsible even when you're not guilty or responsible. If anything happens to that child, I'll feel it's my fault for not being careful enough. Oh, God, let her be safe!" Barbara dissolved in a flood of tears and ran into the staffroom.

A few minutes later, the babysitter, Mrs. Gadson, came in. This was the woman who had originally enrolled the child. "Hear anything yet?" she asked.

Annie shook her head. "No, nothing."

"Well, I'm going to drive up and down the street all night if I got to. That woman don't have a car, you know. She don't have nothing except that lil' gal. There's just the two of them," she said in a Texas twang. "And maybe that lil' gal is lost 'cause I didn't tell the teacher to hold onto her until her mom got there. Maybe it's my fault."

"You keep looking. But, you'll see, it'll be all right. She'll be found. They always are. We have a dozen children every year who don't go straight home as they're supposed to and everyone gets frantic. Most of the time they stop off at someone's house to play and they don't realize how late it is. It's not until it starts to get dark or they get hungry for dinner that they realize they better get home and they're probably in trouble."

"Yup, I know. It happened to one of mine one time. I'll keep on looking though. Thanks for your help, ma'am. Bye."

Annie watched the door close behind Mrs. Gadson and started pacing back and forth. Maybe if she could get up and do something she'd feel better. Cripes! She didn't care if the principal did say their official responsibility ended at the curb line. This time she did feel responsible. She had not made it clear to the teacher or the child how Cynthia would get home. This wasn't only a case of the child playing on the way home but a case of the child not being instructed properly. She had to take her share of the blame for that. Cynthia was only six years old, it was her first day of school, and it was a new neighborhood. They had gotten careless - and she hoped and prayed mother and child didn't have to pay the price for their carelessness.

Annie tried to concentrate on some paperwork but it was impossible. It was almost four forty-five now - long past the office closing time. She knew Barbara Selby was in the staffroom sitting and waiting for some news. Barbara should have gone home by three-thirty. Everyone had gone home except the night custodian. But Annie knew neither she nor Barbara would leave until Cynthia was found or the case was turned over to the police. And before that happened, Annie would have to find the principal, who had left early that day, and let her know what was going on at her school.

The sudden, loud ring of the phone made her jump. She picked it up while it was still on the first ring.

"Lincoln Elementary. Mrs. Kallas speaking."

"Is this the school?" an old woman's quavering voice asked.

"Yes, ma'am, it's the school. What can I do for you?"

"Are you the principal?"

"No, ma'am. I'm the school secretary. May I help you?"

"Well, I found a little girl," the woman said slowly as if each word was an effort. "She says she's lost. I don't know what to do with a little lost child so I called the police. Did I do the right thing?"

Barbara came into the office to see what the phone call was about. Annie gave her the okay sign with her fingers. Barbara stood there listening to Annie's end of the phone conversation - not saying a word - but with tears running down her cheeks.

"Yes, it's all right that you called the police. But it's good that you called the school, too," Annie said into the phone.

"Well, this little girl says today was her first day at school and I guess she got lost going home. I was outside in my front garden when she came along my sidewalk. She was crying so I asked her what was wrong and she told me she was lost. Her name is Cynthia Miller. Do you know where she belongs?"

"Yes, ma'am. Would you tell me your name, please?"

"Why, I'm Mrs. Holmberg. I live at 4840 W. Haven St., phone 267-6329. Been here for 45 years. One of the old pioneers, I am. What should I do with the girl?"

"Would you please just hold onto her? We'll phone the mother immediately and make arrangements to have Cynthia picked up. If the police should come to your house first, don't let them take Cynthia. Please, have them call me here. Thank you very much, Mrs. Holmberg. We have all been worried sick about Cynthia. Thank you so much for rescuing her. I'll call her mother right away, so she'll be seeing you in a few minutes. Thank you so much."

"Well, that's all right," Mrs. Holmberg said. "I only did what should be done. Good-bye."

"Good-bye," Annie said as she hung up. She then dialed Mrs. Miller who picked it up on the first ring.

"Mrs. Miller?" Annie asked.

"Yes, who is this?"

"This is Mrs. Kallas at Lincoln School. Cynthia is found. She's okay."

"Oh, thank God, thank God." The seconds of silence ticked on as she absorbed the news. "Where is she? How did you find her?"

Annie started to tell her and found her own voice wouldn't behave. It quivered and broke. She pressed her teeth into her lip and fought to keep the tears from falling. She blinked her eyes rapidly and took a deep breath. She was determined she was not going to show any emotion. She was the professional. She had to be in control of herself and the situation always. She took another deep breath and explained to Mrs. Miller about Mrs. Holmberg finding Cynthia. After giving her all the pertinent information, Annie asked if she had a way to get Cynthia.

"I have to walk."

"Oh, no. Mrs. Selby and I'll come and get you and take you there. We'll be there in a few minutes."

As Mrs. Miller got into Barbara's car, she asked, "Do you know where this street is - W. Haven St.? I never heard of it. That's where Cynthia is - 4840 W. Haven St."

"We looked it up on the map," Annie answered. "It's a good ways from the school - about ten or twelve blocks. Cynthia had herself some walk. She'll be ready for bed tonight, I bet."

"There it is - 4840. The lady's name is Mrs. Holmberg." When the car was parked, Mrs. Miller jumped out and ran up to the front door and rang the bell. She saw Cynthia peeking through the front window curtains.

"It's my mommy. It's my mommy," Cynthia called. In another minute, she had the front door open and was squealing, "Mommy!" They ran into each other's arms. Small and thin as she was, the mother had the strength to pick up the six year old and hug her and twirl her around. Cynthia had her arms tight around her mother's neck and her legs around her waist. She kissed her face and neck unmercifully and kept repeating, "Mommy, mommy, I'm so glad you came."

They finally collapsed in a heap on the front lawn. "Honey, are you all right? No one hurt you or anything, did they?"

"No, mommy, no one hurt me. But I got losted and I was scared. I walked and walked and got scareder and scareder." Tears overflowed. She brushed them away and they were replaced by a quick smile and giggle. "Mrs. Holmberg found me and gave me milk and some good chocolate chip cookies and she found you."

Mrs. Miller scrambled to her feet, brushed pieces of grass from her dress and said, "We have to thank Mrs. Holmberg."

She hadn't noticed Mrs. Holmberg standing in the doorway watching the reunion. "No, no, you don't need to thank me. I only thank heaven it turned out all right."

Cynthia ran to her, hugged her so hard around the waist she almost toppled the fragile old woman, and said, "And thanks for those yummy chocolate chip cookies."

After regaining her balance, she said, "Do you want some more to take home?"

"That would be super, Mrs. Holmberg."

"I'll go get some."

When she returned, Mrs. Miller held out her hand and said in a shaky voice, "I can't tell you what you've done for me. If you hadn't taken her in, who knows what might have happened to my daughter. God bless you!"

Mrs. Holmberg took her hand and patting it said, "I understand, young lady. But you don't have to thank me. Some day you pass it on by helping someone yourself. She's a sweet, lovely child. Good luck to both of you. Go on home, now. I know you want to get your daughter home. I'll telephone the police and tell them it's all right now."

Amid joyous thanks and good-byes, they got into the car and took Cynthia and her mother home.

As they parted, Mrs. Miller said, "Thank you so much for helping me. I was so frightened. I can't believe I actually have her here with me. I'm so lucky she's safe. How can I ever thank you both for your help? Thank you, Mrs. Selby," she said as she shook hands with Barbara. "Thank you, Mrs. Kallas," she said as she shook hands with Annie.

"Well, that's all right. We've only done what should be done. Good-bye."

Barbara drove Annie back to the school to pick up her car. They hugged each other silently in the parking lot with tears flowing down both their faces.

"Good-night."

"Good-night. See you tomorrow."

NOVEMBER

That did it! If Ray didn't come and talk to her today, Annie was determined to corner him and find out what he was thinking. He'd been avoiding her ever since the incident at his house when they had almost gotten carried away, but a couple of weeks of confusion was a couple too many. She thought she knew what was wrong. He was embarrassed about what happened and didn't know what to say to her. Well, she knew what to say to him and she was going to say it today.

The phone rang as she opened the office door. "Lincoln School, Mrs. Kallas. May I help you?"

"Is there school today?" a woman's voice asked.

"Yes, there's school. Why did you think there might not be school?"

"Because that's what my kids are sitting right here telling me. They're saying there's never school on the first Monday of November. They're trying to put one over on me and they're going to pay for it!" She banged the phone down.

"Uh-oh, somebody's going to catch it. That's a pretty cute trick if they could have gotten away with it." Annie had to smile as she started her morning opening routine.

The phone from the district office rang.

Judy, whose job it was to call substitutes, asked "I have a list of your substitutes, are you ready?"

"Yes, go ahead." Annie wrote down the names of the teachers who were going to be absent and their substitutes. As she was doing it, Loren came in amidst a commotion at the door.

The buses were starting to pull in and unload the children. Four boys, all about ten years old, entered in the middle of a shouting argument. Behind them was a bus driver. She was simmering. "I've given all of these boys tickets for shoving, getting out of their seats, and arguing with me. Here are the tickets." She slapped them down on the counter. All four loudly proclaimed their innocence and called her a liar.

"You better go," Annie said to her. "I'll take care of it."

"Thanks." She flashed Annie a grateful smile and left.

"I want all of you to sit down at the table and be quiet." Annie said in her most authoritarian voice. "You are not going to leave the office and go to the playground until you have quieted down and have shown me you can be responsible citizens. Now, you're already in trouble on the bus - I know you don't also want to be in trouble in the office."

"But, Mrs. Kallas, it wasn't our fault on the bus, she --"

"No, I don't want to hear a word of it. You'll get a chance to tell your side when the principal calls you in to discuss the ticket. Right now you just be quiet."

"Annie, I think something is wrong with the intercom," Loren said.

"What? I certainly hope not. You take care of those two children who just came in and I'll check the intercom. What's it doing?"

"Nothing, that's what the problem is."

Annie picked up the intercom receiver and heard a dial tone. She punched the buttons for one of the rooms. Nothing happened, just the unbroken dial tone. She tried the all-call which went over the outside horns but still the dial tone. "Darn it, how are we going to function without being able to call the classrooms or they to call us?"

She picked up the regular telephone and dialed the maintenance department. While the phone rang, she looked at the counter. There were six children there, all talking loudly. Two parents were waiting to be helped and

Loren was in the health office slowly, slowly, putting a band-aid on a child.

"Maintenance, Catherine speaking."

"Catherine, this is Annie at Lincoln. Our intercom is totally non-functioning and there is absolutely no way we can run a school without an intercom. Please have someone come out immediately."

"I'll get someone out as soon as I can. We have other things to do, too, you know."

"Sure, I know you do, just like the rest of us. But one cannot have a functioning school when there is no communication between the office and the rest of the campus. We have to be able to talk to the classrooms. I would very much appreciate it if you would get someone out here right away."

"I'll see what I can do," she said and hung up.

"Grrr," Annie muttered. In her opinion, the maintenance department had a certain amount of room left for improvement.

Loren was still fooling with the child and his band-aid. Annie went to the counter which now had eight children standing at it and three parents. "What are all you kids doing in here?" She shouted above the noise in her meanest voice. There was immediate silence - it was wonderful. It lasted three seconds. Then they all started talking at once.

"Quiet," Annie roared. "One at a time. You," she pointed at a small, brown-haired, freckle-faced boy. "Why are you here?"

"I gotta use the phone. I forgot my homework," he sniffed with tears in his eyes.

"Do you know your number?"

"I think so."

"Okay, come on." She brought him through the swinging gate and pushed the button to get a line on the phone for him, handed him the receiver and told him to punch in his number.

She went back to the counter. "What do you need?"

she pointed to a little girl from India with long black braids and a crisp English accent.

"I have lunch money."

"Anybody else with lunch money?" Annie called out. Two others said yes. "Loren, will you get finished in there, please, and come take this lunch money?"

"Yes, I'm coming."

Annie next pointed to a group of three sixth grade boys standing against the wall. "Yes, boys, what is it?"

"Ricky and Danny and Charles are out to get us. They followed us to school and kept saying they'd catch us at recess," the boy named Jason said.

"You three boys go sit in the principal's office. She's at a meeting this morning but I'll get Mrs. Dorner to take care of you in a few minutes."

Loren had taken care of the lunch money students and was giving registration papers to the three parents. When they saw how much paper work there was, two of the parents decided to take it all home and do it. Annie told the four boys who had been in trouble on the bus they could go to the playground and complimented them on their good behavior in the office.

Another woman walked in. "May I help you?" Annie asked.

"I'm Marcia Ooner. I'm a second grade substitute today."

"Come on in. Sign in here. You're for Susan Woodward, room seven. Here's the key and you have after school bus duty at the crosswalk." Annie studied her face and said, "You haven't ever been here before, have you?"

"No, I haven't been at this school before."

"Well, I'm Annie, the school secretary, and this is Loren, the clerk. If you have any problems, send a runner down with a note. Our intercom is broken. Here's a map of the campus. See, here's your room." She pointed out to her how to get from the office to the classroom.

Annie took her into the staffroom to show the substitute her mailbox and noticed all four of the copy machines were cranking out math and spelling papers for the students to work on while the teachers were all talking at once.

She went over to the chalkboard and wrote on it that the intercom was broken and then she shouted, "See what I've written - the intercom is broken!" Everyone groaned.

She went up to Maggie Dorner, the Title I coordinator, who was talking to two other teachers, and told her she needed her when she had a minute. Maggie Dorner was the principal's designee. When the principal had to be away from the campus, someone had to have the authority to make decisions. Maggie had been chosen, mainly because she didn't have a classroom of her own and so had more mobility.

"This day is going to be a disaster without the intercom and without the principal. I can feel it in my bones."

"Oh, Annie, you were in the other room - the intercom is working again."

"What! What happened?" She picked up the intercom and called the library. The call went through. "Just testing, thanks," she said to Eloise, the librarian. "Well, that's a relief. I better call maintenance and cancel the service call."

"This is Annie at Lincoln. Our intercom suddenly decided to work again."

"Okay," said Catherine in a disinterested tone of voice. "I'll cross your name off the list."

"Here I am, what's up?" said Maggie.

"I guess Elizabeth told you she'd be in meetings most of today so that makes you the principal for a while. I have a few problems for you already. First, there are three boys in the principal's office complaining that other boys are out to get them and they're afraid to go on the playground. When you get finished with that, I have four bus tickets. All four boys proclaim their innocence. I've sent them to their rooms until we're ready for them."

"Good. I'll see what's up with this bunch first." She went into the principal's office and closed the door.

The bell rang for school to start. "Thank heavens, now maybe things will quiet down in here," Annie said.

Suddenly, without warning a brrr-boom, brrr-boom

noise like a motorcycle warming up on a cold winter day came out of the intercom. "Judas Priest, what happened? What's going on?" she asked Loren.

"I don't know but what are we going to do?"

Annie dialed the maintenance department again. She was lucky - the head of the department answered the phone. "This is Annie at Lincoln. I want you to hear something. Listen." She put the phone next to the intercom.

"What's that noise? It almost sounds like the fire alarm."

"It's our intercom, Phil. It's been doing all kinds of weird things lately but this takes the cake. Will you come right over and fix it? We sure can't live like this all day. The noise is terrible."

"I'll be right there," he promised. Annie went into the health office, got a blanket off the cot and wrapped the intercom phone in it. The noise was still loud and clear but no longer excruciating.

"Well, obviously, we have no intercom again. Gad, what a pain."

"Annie, how long are we going to have to listen to this noise? I'm not going to be able to stand it."

"You have to. Just tune it out. Don't hear it. It may be like this all day. I don't know if Phil can fix it or not. I have to get some work done. This morning's been so busy I haven't even taken anything out of my desk yet. I have to work on teacher's budgets. I haven't done it for so long they may all be overdrawn and no one would know."

But before she could get started, a young, tall, exceedingly handsome Latino man with a little girl came in with completed registration papers in hand.

"Is she kindergarten?" Annie smiled.

"Yes," he gave her an answering smile. He pulled out the birth certificate and shot record. The child's age and shots were both in order.

"What school has she been attending?" Annie asked.

"She has never been in school. We have just decided the time has come for her to start."

"Oh?" Annie would have liked to ask why he kept his

child out of school until November but since attending kindergarten wasn't required by law, she felt she didn't have the right to ask. "Would you like morning or afternoon kindergarten?"

"Do any of those teachers speak Spanish?"

"No, I'm sorry they don't. Is that important to you?" She was puzzled. His English was perfect.

"Yes, it is. My daughter does not speak English yet. I thought a Spanish speaking teacher might be of help to her," he explained.

"Oh, I thought I saw she was born here. Did she leave the country?" Annie wondered if she had stayed in Mexico with grandmother or something.

"No, she's always been here. But my wife and I speak Spanish at home and all our friends speak Spanish, so she has never learned to speak English," he answered.

Annie was so surprised she stared at him a minute. The child was born here, had never lived outside the country and couldn't speak English.

"Well, Mr. Gutierrez, we do have an English as a Second Language program your daughter could be in. A special teacher is here two and a half days a week to teach non-English speaking children. Your daughter would be called from her classroom to this teacher's room. Is that all right?"

"That will be fine."

"Do you want a morning or afternoon kindergarten?"

"Morning is good," he said. "What are the hours?"

Annie gave him all the information and he said he would start his daughter the next day. "I have to ask Fred about this one," she promised herself.

Maggie opened the principal's door and the three boys she had in there came out looking pleased and happy. She was good as a conciliator and arbitrator.

Annie went into the office. "You ready for the bus tickets yet?"

"Give me a few minutes to write up what I just did for Elizabeth and then I'll start the tickets."

"Sure, let me know when you're ready."

A mother and three children came in and asked Loren for registration papers. "What's that terrible noise?" she asked.

"The intercom is broken."

Phil Saturn, head of maintenance, walked in, "It is making a racket, isn't it? Well, let's see if I can at least turn it off if not fix it," he said.

"We'd sure appreciate anything you could do."

"I called the engineer from the company who installed it to come and see what the problem is. It doesn't sound like anything I know how to fix but I'll take a look anyway." He went out to the room where the mechanism was housed.

Annie went back to her desk and tried to concentrate on the budget. A couple of minutes later the brrr-boom stopped. "Thank heaven, he got that much fixed," she said to Loren.

"It's such a relief. I have a terrible headache from all the noise." She rubbed her beautiful eyes which today looked green, reflecting her green sweater.

"Well, you're not allowed to get sick. Take some aspirin," Annie said as she handed her the staff aspirin bottle.

"As I expected, I don't know what the problem is, Phil said. "But Gus is on his way and he'll be able to do something."

"I sure hope so. It's very hard and could be dangerous when the teachers can't contact the office."

"Yes, I know. We'll do the best we can, Annie."

"Thanks, Phil. I appreciate it."

"Gus will call me when he knows something. I've got to get to another school but he'll be here soon."

"Okay, bye, and thanks for coming out so promptly."

* * * * * * *

After the terrible morning, Annie was properly grateful when the engineer told her at eleven-forty that the intercom was fixed. She immediately got on the all-call and announced to the entire campus that, happily, the intercom was fixed.

Annie caught up with Fred Martinez before he left the staffroom at his lunch time. Fred was a fifth grade teacher, one of two regular staff members who were Latino. The other was Patricia Campos, first grade bilingual teacher.

"Fred, have you got a minute to explain something to me?"

"Sure, Ann, I've got about four minutes," he said glancing at the clock on the wall.

"I'd like your interpretation of something that happened this morning."

"I'll give it a try. Go ahead."

"A young Latino man came in to register his daughter for kindergarten. He wore a business suit and was very well spoken. His English was perfect. The girl was born here, has not left the country and can't speak a word of English. I couldn't believe it. He didn't seem to think it was unusual. He wanted to know if we had a Spanish speaking teacher to help her. What do you make of that, Fred? I think it's incredible."

"Well, it's not incredible. That's the way it is in some circles. A lot has to do with where you live. If everyone a child comes in contact with speaks Spanish, the child only learns Spanish. Grandparents, parents, cousins, friends - everyone speaks Spanish."

"But what about going to the store - shopping and stuff?"

"Father is probably the only one who drives, so when they go to the store, father does the talking. The small corner store within walking distance for mom probably has employees who speak Spanish. Father had to learn English in order to work and drive, but the rest of the family has no push to learn," he explained.

"But don't they realize what they are doing to their daughter? How far behind she will be?"

"I don't think they fully understand that," he answered. "They feel it's most important she not lose the culture and customs of her people. In order to do it, they feel she must speak her language at home. They feel she's got plenty of time to learn English. There's the bell -- I have to go."

"Bye, thanks," Annie called as he hurried out of the door. She shook her head. "Suppose the girl wants to become a lawyer or something? Would she ever be able to catch up those five years again?" she wondered.

The big event of the afternoon was that it rained. It didn't rain much but since the last recorded rain had occurred almost seven months before in April, even a little rain was an experience.

Some of the students were so young that with their short memories they couldn't remember ever seeing rain before. When the bell rang, half the student body wanted to phone home to get someone to pick them up at school. They didn't understand how they could be expected to walk home their regular way when it was drizzling and many of the parents didn't expect it. The parking lot was full of mothers in their cars picking up their children.

* * * * * * *

Even the school architects in Southern California didn't make provisions for rain when they designed the schools. They built overhangs over the walkways leading from the rooms to the cafeteria or the library but no provision was made for the wind driving the rain under the overhang and the few times a year when it did rain hard, the children invariably got soaked as they had to walk around the campus.

There was no inside gymnasium so when it rained the students had to stay in their classrooms during recess. By the close of a rainy day, teachers were exhausted trying to control the students who were filled with energy which had no outlet during the day.

All the school staff hated a rainy day. It upset all schedules, created double the work for the custodians as they had to clean up all the mud being tracked indoors, made more work in the office as Annie and Loren had to make

arrangements for dry clothes for wet kids, and exasperated the principal as she had to help keep everyone else's temper under control.

But this was only a little rain and Annie went to the door and sniffed in the sweet freshness of it and said, "Smell that, Loren, doesn't it smell great? You can even smell some of the orange blossoms in the air."

"Oh, Annie, close the door quick - you might let some of the wet in and we'll all catch pneumonia."

"Honestly, Loren," she said in disgust as she closed the door. "Have you ever been anywhere where there's real weather?"

"No, I haven't and I'm not planning on it. I like it to be eighty degrees and sunny and that's where I want to be."

* * * * * * *

As soon as the bell rang for the close of school, Annie went to Ray's classroom to speak to him. She sat on one of the student desks and waited until he dismissed the pupil he was talking to. "Hi, Ray," she said as he approached her.

"Hi, Annie, I'm glad to see you."

"Well, you haven't come to see me, so I figured I'd come to see you. How've you been?"

"Okay, I guess." He hesitated. "Truth of the matter is I feel like a fool, Annie."

"Why?"

"Because of the way I treated you. I'm embarrassed about it."

"There's no need to be embarrassed. I told you I understood. It was perfectly natural. Hey, let's forget it. We agreed to be friends, didn't we? So let's act like friends. I've got a tearing desire for Chinese food and there's a good movie I want to see at the Westgate. Will you keep me company?"

"When?"

"Now. Today. After I get off work."

As Ray hesitated, Annie wondered if she had read him wrong. "You don't have to if you don't want to, Ray."

"No, no, it's not that. But I promised Mary Anne Duncan I'd give her some tips on disciplining and lesson plans this afternoon. I'm not sure exactly when we'll be finished."

"Oh, okay. Well, we can make it some other time. Just let me know when you're in the mood for Chinese."

"No hard feelings, Annie?"

"No, of course not. No hard feelings."

Annie left his classroom feeling she'd been slapped in the face and some confusion as to whether she was justified in feeling that way. After all, they were both sixth grade teachers and Mary Anne was a new teacher and could probably use some tips on teaching techniques from an old hand like Ray. But again, he could have limited their meeting to a couple of hours and still had time to go to dinner with her if he'd wanted to or even offered to make plans to go out another day but he didn't say anything at all about seeing her again. There was no getting around it. She'd been put down. So, that would be her last effort to continue her friendship with Ray. The ball was in his court now. She had to work hard to control the hurt and embarrassment she was feeling.

* * * * * * *

"Who takes lost and found?" Sara Liebowitz, the aide in room twelve, asked.

"If it's a coat, leave it there on the counter," answered Loren.

"If it's money, I get it but I don't want to be bothered with anything less than fifty dollars," Annie said.

"How'd you know? That's exactly what I have for you," Sara laughed as she opened up a fifty dollar bill and held it up in front of her.

"I was only kidding, honest. Where on earth did you get it?"

"A boy gave it to me out on the playground. Says Cameron Ritchey gave it to him."

"I wonder if Cameron has any more to give to me?"

Sara laughed. "Yeah, me too. Anyway, the kids are saying Cameron got it out of his mother's wallet. Here it is. I leave it up to you to play detective."

"Thanks for bringing it in, Sara."

"Elizabeth," Annie stopped the principal as she went into her office. "Here's a fifty dollar bill that needs to find its owner. The kids say Cameron Ritchey took it out of his mother's wallet."

"Well, we'll give Mrs. Ritchey a call and see if she knows anything about this." Five minutes later she came out of her office to tell them, "Mrs. Ritchey says fifty dollars is missing out of the money she had saved for the rent. She'll be here in a few minutes to claim it and wants Cameron to have a talk with both of us together. Get him down here, will you?"

Mrs. Ritchey arrived in ten minutes. Cameron was nervously waiting at the front table. "I'm Mrs. Ritchey," she said as she stood at the counter.

Elizabeth came out of her office. "Come in, Mrs. Ritchey. I'm Mrs. Leski, the principal."

"What am I going to do with that boy?" was all Annie heard before the door closed. Soon after, Elizabeth called Cameron into the office and Annie could hear the mother yelling at the boy and then Elizabeth's quiet voice speaking to him. A few minutes later, the door opened.

"Thanks, Mrs. Leski. Thanks for your help. Call me again if he gets in any more trouble. No child of mine is going to act like this." She grabbed Cameron's arm, "Come on, you're going home. You're on restriction for the next ten years."

"Aw, mom," pleaded Cameron.

"Quiet," she yelled at him as they went out the door.

* * * * * * *

"Annie, can you help me here?"

The aide from room four, Rosa Torres, was standing at the counter with a boy from her room. "Sure, Rosa, what's up?" she said as she walked to the counter.

"This is Robert Abados. He doesn't feel well. We think he needs to go home. He's the one with leukemia, remember?" she whispered.

"Oh, that's right. I've heard about him." Annie looked over at the boy who stood there quietly. She smiled at him. "Don't feel so good, Robert?"

"No, I wanna go home," he said on the verge of crying.

"Go and sit down in the health office. We'll get your mother for you. Loren, see if you can find someone at home." She turned back to the aide. "Is it getting worse? He's never been in here before. I know we have a health alert on him but I don't think I've seen him since he was registered."

"His mother told the teacher he's dying," answered Rosa. "They've found a brain tumor now."

"Oh, how awful!"

"Yes, it's really bad. I feel so sorry for the poor mother. It's unbelievable the things that happen to some people. Did you know her husband was killed in a motorcycle crash about three years ago? And now her only child is dying. And she's only twenty-five years old. It's just terrible."

"Geez, that is terrible. It makes you wonder sometimes, doesn't it?"

"It sure does. Anyway, he loves school and she wants to keep him in school as long as possible. You notice he's bald. That's from the treatments."

"I noticed. Chemotherapy does that, doesn't it?" Annie asked.

"Yes. You know, the other children are really good with him. They're only first graders but the teacher explained to them about Robert being sick and his hair falling out and all and they never tease him about his bald head."

"Robert's mother is on her way," Loren called to them.

"Do you have everything out of his room? A coat and books and stuff?" Annie asked Rosa.

""He's got his coat on and some papers to do at home if he feels like it," she answered. "I've got to get back. The teacher will wonder what happened to me. Bye, Robert, hope you feel better," she said as she looked into the health office. "Your mom's on the way."

"That's good," he answered.

"Bye, Rosa," Annie said as she left.

A few minutes later, a young, wan looking woman came in. "I'm Mrs. Abados. You have my son?"

"Yes, ma'am, he's right here. Please sign the register to show you've taken him out." Robert heard his mother's voice and came out of the health office.

"Don't you feel well, Robbi mio?"

"No, mama. I wanna go home."

She finished signing. She took him by the hand and led him out the front door. "Thank you very much," she said as they went out.

* * * * * * *

"Annie, you won't be able to guess what I heard today."

"Oh, what did you hear?"

Loren was obviously excited as she imparted her news. "Ray Ogilvie and Mary Anne Duncan have a thing going. Can you imagine? A white man and a African-American woman getting interested in each other! And right here on this campus." She was deep in thought for a minute. "What do you think of that?"

Annie hid the shock and hurt she was feeling and answered, "What do I think of what?"

"Of a African-American woman and a white man dating? Maybe even having an affair? Do you think that's terrible?"

"No, of course not. What difference does it make if they're African-American or white? If they care about each other and will be good to each other, what difference does it make? Besides, you're just listening to gossip."

"Well, maybe it's just gossip but everybody's talking about it. An aide told me they were seen having dinner together in some restaurant one night so they're at least friendly."

"That's good, Loren. Everybody on the school staff

should be friendly with each other and I don't want to listen to any more gossip, okay?"

Annie turned away to give herself an opportunity to absorb the news. She was surprised at the hurt she felt at the thought that Ray was interested in someone else and then was angry at herself for feeling hurt. He didn't owe her anything. She had no right to expect anything at all from him so she had no right to be hurt at anything he did.

When Annie passed Joe later on as he walked to the office with some supplies she asked, "What are you doing tonight, Joe?"

"Nothing much. You got any ideas?"

"I don't feel like staying home tonight. How about going for a ride in your convertible? Out toward Palm Springs? It's going to be a beautiful night."

Joe looked pleased at the invitation. "Sounds good to me. What say we pick up some picnic fixings from the deli and have a picnic in the desert under the moon? Doesn't that sound romantic?"

"Sounds great. Pick me up at...say, six o'clock?"

"I'll be there with bells on." Joe continued on with his duties whistling as he went.

Annie felt slightly guilty as she watched him walk away so happily. She suspected she was using Joe to soothe her bruised ego. It was always comforting to be with him because she was certain that in his own way he was very fond of her.

"This is unbelievably beautiful, isn't it, Joe?" Annie asked as they drove along the freeway toward the desert. The moon was just rising as they drove east away from the Los Angeles basin with its haze and reflected lights. The sky got darker and darker and it seemed that one by one the stars came out and flickered down on them like friendly little fireflies.

"I'm going to turn off the freeway up ahead, Annie, and take one of these side roads and we'll really be able to look at the stars. We can find a place to park and have our deli dinner. Sound all right to you?"

"Sounds great! I'm so glad you got this convertible, Joe. There's nothing like driving on a warm night with the air smelling all sweet blowing through your hair. It makes me feel all new and clean inside. Know what I mean?"

"Yeah, I do. It sure helps to get rid of the cobwebs, too. I used to take a ride like this whenever I'd get so mad at my wife I'd be afraid I was going to hit her. That was in my old convertible before Rhoda and I got divorced. That old car got me out of many a tight spot and by the time I got back from the ride I'd be calmed down and able to see things more clearly. That's one of the things I like about you, Annie, that you like to take rides like this, too."

"It's one of the things I like about you, too, Joe."

They were climbing along the side of the San Jacinto mountains and were traveling on a gravel winding road not meant for heavy traffic. "Look over there, Annie, you can see miles and miles of nothing but Joshua trees and way over there on the other side the lights of Palm Springs."

"I see them. Let's stop along here somewhere and eat, Joe. I'm getting weak from hunger and this is a beautiful view for us to look at."

"Okay. Soon as I find a wide spot in the road."

As they ate their sandwiches and potato salad, they tried to identify all the stars they could. "There's Venus going down in the west. See it, Joe?"

"Yeah, and there's Jupiter over there rising in the east."

"And there's the Big Dipper."

"And there's the... No, I guess not. I don't know what that is."

Annie sat quietly for a few minutes after she finished eating, breathed deeply and enjoyed the peace and quiet of the environment. "It's so lovely here. It smells so good, do you notice, Joe? You can even get a whiff of the pine trees in the mountains up there. And it's so beautifully quiet and deserted. Joe, thanks for taking me out here tonight. I guess I needed this. There's something about the desert that's calming. Even though we know it's crawling with all kinds of creepy-crawlers, some of whom can kill you, it's still peaceful. Especially if you look at the stars instead of the ground. Joe, do you think there's life out there somewhere on those stars?"

"Well, if you want to get technical, most of those twinkling lights you're looking at are suns, not planets, so they wouldn't have life on them but maybe they have planets going around them with life on them. I like to think about it and try to imagine all the different kinds of beings who maybe evolved on different planets. You know, like some that have four arms and are eight feet tall because they have light gravity on their planet and can jump ten feet at a time. Things like that are fun to imagine - for me, anyway."

She laughed and said, "Why, Joe, I had no idea you were a science-fiction fan."

"Yeah, I read it all the time." He pulled her toward him and bent to kiss her. "But I like this better."

"Now, now, Joe! You remember we agreed no hanky-panky, just good friends."

He groaned and in mock horror said, "I must've been crazy to agree to that. Couldn't we forget that agreement for one night?"

She laughed. "No, I don't think so. Come on, we better go back. There's too much temptation in this car."

As he pulled up in front of her apartment house, Annie said, "Thank you for a wonderful evening, Joe. It was magical."

"We could have made it more magical, Annie."

"It was fine the way it was. Good night, sleep tight."

* * * * * * *

"You know, Loren, I can't believe it. It feels like school just started and here it is almost Thanksgiving. Look what the messenger brought from the district office." Annie held up a half sheet of blue paper she had taken out of the box. "These are the notices to parents about the canned food drive for needy families for Thanksgiving. Will you see to it these notices go home tomorrow?"

"Sure."

"I'll get Joe to get a big box to put in the cafeteria for the cans when the children start bringing them from home."

"Annie, did you read that each school has to submit the name of a needy family for a Thanksgiving basket. How are we going to do that?"

"I don't know. I'll give a notice to Elizabeth. It's the principal's job to figure it out."

When Elizabeth came into the office, Annie showed her the notice. "We'll let each teacher pick a family name and when we have them all, we'll let the nurse decide which family to recommend to the district office. Annie, will you make sure that item gets on the next faculty meeting agenda?"

* * * * * * *

"Hi, Annie. How're you doing?"

"Well, hi, Ray. I'm just fine. How're you?"

"Good. Very good but I suddenly realized I haven't had a chance to talk to you for quite a long time and I realized I miss you. Weren't we supposed to go out for Chinese awhile back?"

Annie laughed. "Ray, that was a couple of weeks ago."

"Was it? Time gets away from me. Well, how about it? Can we do it soon?"

"Sure, whenever you're free."

"How about this Friday? Can you make it then?"

"Friday would be fine. Pick me up about six?"

* * * * * * *

"What do you feel like eating, Annie? Italian, Mexican, Chinese, American?" Ray asked as he picked her up that evening.

"I feel like plain old spaghetti. How about you?"

"Italian's fine with me. Why don't we go to the place on Cason Avenue?"

Annie studied him as he turned the car around and headed in the direction of the restaurant. She couldn't sense any feelings of unease in him. She did in herself, though, and wondered why. She felt awkward and, remembering the gossip about Mary Anne, wondered where she fit into his scenario. She decided she'd find out tonight or not go out with him anymore. It wasn't much fun on a date when one felt awkward and insecure.

But Ray solved the problem of how to approach the subject for her. As they ate their salads, he said, "You know, Annie, I've been feeling kind of awkward on campus lately."

"Oh, why?"

"I don't know if you've heard it or not but my aide told me there's some gossip going around about Mary Anne Duncan and me. I thought my aide was kidding me but I guess it's true. Mary Anne wanted to treat me to dinner one night to thank me for the time I spent giving her some pointers on discipline and organizing her work and someone saw us in the restaurant and jumped to all kinds of untrue conclusions. I can't believe people can be so interested in another person's life that they have to do that kind of gossiping."

Annie chewed on some lettuce as she sighed a giant internal sigh of relief as he spoke. So there wasn't anything to the gossip. She should have known. Ray was really something of an innocent even if he was forty-seven. He'd been happily married for so long that he didn't realize what a catch he was in the world as it was now. In many ways, he was still in the protected world of his marriage where the thought of playing around with other women probably never entered his head.

Annie felt a sudden warm, protective feeling toward him. He was like a babe in the woods in the new world of single people he had been thrown into. She could foresee some of the pitfalls he could unknowingly stumble into without some guidance. Should she attempt to guide him? She didn't relish the role of mother to him. That wasn't the role she was interested in.

"As I mentioned to you before, Ray, you're a very eligible man and I think as such you have to expect that people, especially women, will be curious as to what's happening in your love life. Because of that you and I need to be a little circumspect about our friendship. I have absolutely no desire to be gossiped about."

"I can't imagine who would dare to gossip about you. The staff has too much respect and is too scared of you to gossip about you."

"I don't think that staff is scared of anything. They'd probably love it if, after all these years, they could find something about me to gossip about. But I think it's up to us to be a little discreet so the problem won't arise."

"Sure, I can be discreet but I won't hide. If somebody sees us together, they'll see us together. There's nothing we can do about that, Annie."

"I guess not. What do you want to do now, Ray? Feel like taking a walk?"

"Yes, let's do that."

Annie threw her sweater over her shoulders as they left the restaurant. It was the end of November but it was pleasantly warm as they strolled around the block. "Look at that moon, Ray. It's like a floodlight sitting up there lighting our path for us. Isn't it beautiful out? I just love this weather with a nip in the air and the smell of orange blossoms everywhere."

"Are you a confirmed southern Californian, Annie? Didn't you come from another state?"

"Yes, New York. And no, I'm not a confirmed southern Californian. Actually, I hate the heat. I like the winter here, such as it is, when it does manage to get a little chilly and I enjoy the fresh crispness of that. It seems like every year the heat feels worse to me. I left New York to get away from the cold - but now I'd like to get away from the heat. People are never satisfied, are they?"

"Maybe. I'm from Minnesota and came here to get warm but I'm still enjoying being warm."

"Have you still got family there?"

"A couple of cousins, that's all. I go back every few years but no ties of any consequence. How about you?"

"No, my parents died a few years ago so I have nobody left. I only have my two daughters and their families. Speaking of families, Ray, do you have plans for Thanksgiving?"

"Well, Mary Anne Duncan invited me over and so did some other friends but I can't say I'm really interested."

"We always have Thanksgiving at my oldest daughter's house. You're certainly welcome there if you'd like to come along." Annie was aware that this would be his first Thanksgiving without his wife and must be a painful one for him. "They're just home folks, Ray, nobody special but warm and loving people. This daughter, her name's Alicia, is married to a man who is a sculptor in wood. He makes the most beautiful statues of animals you've ever seen."

"He sounds interesting. Do they have kids?"

"Yes, my only grandchild. Two year old Justin."

"What about the other daughter?"

"Ilene hasn't, as they say, found either herself or a husband yet. She's always been crazy about horses and works on a ranch. She's not small enough to be a jockey, so she's thinking about being a large animal vet. She dropped out of college for a year to try to make up her mind. That girl could easily drive me crazy if I let her."

Ray laughed. "They sound interesting. Would they mind if I came along to dinner?"

"They wouldn't mind at all. Mike, my son-in-law's, parents might be there, too, so it'll be a nice party. Want to make it for sure or do you want to think about it some more?"

"Let's make it for sure. I'll phone you in a couple of days and you can tell me what I should do or bring, okay?"

"Great."

As he dropped her off at her door, she asked, "Want to come up for some coffee?"

He hesitated a minute, "No, Annie, I don't think I should. Some other time, okay?"

"Sure. Thanks for a nice evening. 'Night."

* * * * * * *

"Annie, is the principal around?"

"Here she comes now."

"Elizabeth, I've found the family that in my opinion should be given the Thanksgiving basket," Anita Ronco, the school nurse said.

"Oh, good! I'm glad to hear the decision is made. Who is it?"

The Mirandas. Eight children and mother. You have the two youngest children at this school. The others are spread through the junior high and high schools. The father was killed in a single car accident last year - no insurance. Mrs. Miranda refused to go on welfare and they're struggling along on her motel maid's pay plus what the older children can bring in with after school jobs. They're all working hard and deserve a hand up if we can give it to them."

"Sounds great, Anita. Go ahead and make the arrangements."

The school cafeteria prepared and served its Thanksgiving dinner of chunks of turkey with gravy over mashed potatoes, string beans, rolls, salad, and pumpkin cake with whipped cream for dessert. This meal was the students' and staff's favorite and almost everyone ate it. The lunch count stood at four hundred and sixty - the highest of the year.

After the heavy lunch, everyone needed a nap. They all struggled through the afternoon and were glad when it was time to go home.

* * * * * * *

"I always feel amazement at how beautiful the beach is at this time of year. Everything's so clear and crisp with the sun shining hot on us -- it's really God's gift." Ray squeezed her hand to share his joy. "Do you agree, Annie?"

"Oh, absolutely. This is the perfect way to spend the day after Thanksgiving. I love the beach. I love the wind and the smell and the clean freshness of it and the different birds and the little crabs scurrying around in the sand. It's marvelous. It's one of my favorite places to be especially at this time of year when it's not crowded. I'm so glad you suggested it yesterday. Take a deep breath, Ray. Isn't it great? C'mon, let's go up on the pier and see if anybody's catching anything."

They walked through the sand to the wooden pier which jutted out into the ocean. Lining the railings were people: sometimes one alone, or husband and wife, or father and son, or two old fishing buddies with their tackle boxes and pails. Ray and Annie peered into the pails as they strolled along and complimented the fishermen if the pail was full or sympathized with them if the pail was empty. Everyone was friendly and seemed glad to share fishing information with them. They walked the length of the pier on one side and as they got nearer to the end, they noticed how much stronger the wind blew the further out from land they were. It whipped around their heads until Annie took her scarf from around her neck and tied it around her head to keep her hair from getting uncontrollably knotted.

By the time they finished their walk around the pier, Annie remarked, "I'm getting hungry. How about you, Ray? Ready for lunch?"

"My stomach's growling - trying to tell me something."

They headed back to where they'd left their blanket and picnic basket. As they walked Ray said, "You don't know how grateful I am to you for helping to make this Thanksgiving vacation a pleasant one for me. I have to admit I was worried about what to do with myself while school was out. It reminds me again what a boon work is. When you're working, you don't have time to feel sorry for yourself as you can do when you're off work. I don't know if you know it or not, Annie, what a nasty feeling it is to feel sorry for oneself. It seems to stymie all growth in any direction. I know I'm doing it and I hate it but I don't seem to be able to stop."

"You will, Ray, you will. Gradually, it'll pass. It was a terrible tragedy and because it was so unexpected makes it much harder. If Helen had been sick for a long time and you'd had the opportunity to get used to the idea of losing her, it would be a different story. But, it must be a terrible, terrible shock when one moment the person you love is there and the next moment they're gone. Gone forever. It seems to me that it would take a long time to get over the shock of such a thing. You'll recover at the pace your body and your mind can handle. You can't criticize yourself because you're not recovering any faster. It's not really a choice you can make.

"But right now let's feed that body of yours so it, at least, can heal all the faster," Annie said as they reached their blanket. She opened the picnic basket and pulled out the tablecloth which she spread over the blanket. She handed Ray the bottle of wine to open while she put the plates of fried chicken, potato salad, lettuce and tomato salad, pickles and olives, and bread in the center of the tablecloth. "There we are. If the wine's ready to pour, we're in business."

Ray filled their glasses and toasted, "To friends like you, Annie, and the goodness they bring to others' lives."

After they ate their fill, they laid down side by side on the blanket and let the sun warm them. "Are you warm enough, Annie?"

"I'm fine. This is a warm jacket. If we get cold, there's the extra blanket." As Annie lay there beside him, she wondered how long it would take for him to heal. She knew he would heal in his own good time as she had told him but she was beginning to admit to herself that he was getting important to her and her desire for him was growing every time she was with him. She was finding it more and more difficult to keep from caressing him.

The wine and the food and the sun combined to make her drowsy and when she awoke, she found herself cuddled in the crook of Ray's arm. She opened her eyes without moving and realized her face was against his chest and his face was resting in her hair. His breathing was quiet and steady and she knew he was asleep. She tried to feel by the heat of the sun how much time had passed. The wind had picked up and she felt chilled and knew they should be moving but being this close to Ray felt so intimate and comfortable, she hated to wake him. But just then he stirred and the next minute was awake. He was embarrassed when he found himself with his arm around her. He sat up quickly and said, "I don't know how that happened, Annie. Hope it didn't disturb you. You must have felt so good while I was sleeping that I wanted to get closer. I'm sorry."

He looked so contrite Annie laughed. "Don't be silly. It was nice cuddling. I enjoyed every minute even though I was asleep. But I think we need to go now. The fog bank's coming in - look over there. It's going to get really cold soon."

As he dropped her off at her house, Ray said, "It was a wonderful day, Annie. Maybe someday soon we can do that cuddling for real."

DECEMBER

When the staff members congregated in the staffroom the first day back from Thanksgiving vacation, the noise level reached a roar as they laughed and talked and shared the interesting events of the four day week-end.

Annie watched them a minute with a pleased smile on her face. She felt as if these people were her family who enjoyed being together and were interested in each other. She was proud of them for the way they got along, and, of course, Lincoln reaped the benefits of their camaraderie because they made suggestions to each other, helped each other, and planned grade level projects together. Annie had heard rumors that in some of the other schools the teachers divided into cliques which sometimes didn't even speak to each other but, thank heaven, that hadn't happened at Lincoln.

Loren was giggling as she came into the office from the staffroom and Annie could feel her staring at her. As she looked at her, Loren quickly looked away. "All right, come on, tell me what it is. You know you'll never be able to keep it to yourself." As Loren hesitated, she added, "For heaven's sake, Loren, what is it? You look like the cat that swallowed the bird and is scared someone will find out about it."

Loren giggled as she gathered her courage and finally said in a rush, "Everybody is talking about Ray Ogilvie going over your house for Thanksgiving dinner."

"Judas Priest! What is there to talk about? He needed a place to go, so I invited him to go along to my daughter's house for our family dinner. That's all. There's nothing to gossip about."

"Okay, Annie, okay. Don't get mad. You sure would make a nice couple, though," she said with a giggle as she ducked into the health office.

Annie fumed at the thought of the staff discussing her

private life and started getting angry at Ray but stopped herself as she realized that someone had probably asked him what he did at Thanksgiving and he'd innocently answered that he had spent the day with her at her daughter's house. He wouldn't lie about it and probably had no choice but to answer truthfully. She only hoped he didn't mention the trip to the beach the next day. But Loren didn't mention it so Annie assumed he had remembered to be as discreet as possible.

As the day progressed, she noticed that twice when she entered the staffroom a conversation between a small group suddenly stopped and the people involved looked embarrassed. She sensed they were discussing her and relishing the thought of a possible romance blossoming on campus but it infuriated her.

Even Joe had to get into the act when he saw her later. "Annie, are you aware that everyone on campus is talking about Ray spending Thanksgiving with you?"

"Joe, for heaven's sake, I told you I had invited him. There was nothing to it. I only wanted to make sure he wouldn't be sitting home alone." In an effort to change the subject, she added, "Did you have a good time in Montana?"

"Sure. As good a time as you can have visiting your sister. But it was good to see her and her kids and, you know, I really like being on the ranch with the ridin' and ropin' and stuff. It's good to keep my hand in." After a pause, he added, "So, I assume you had a good time with good ole Ray."

Annie ignored his sarcastic tone, "We had a very nice time. He seemed to enjoy the family and they liked him, I think, so it went very well. My son-in-law's parents were there, too, so it was a little bit of a crowd."

"Glad to hear it. Gotta get to work. See you later."

* * * * * * *

Thoughts needed to be directed to the future. If Thanksgiving was over, it meant Christmas was coming. Orders needed to be sent to the purchasing department at the district business office for the materials necessary for Christmas: sequins, glitter, beads, paint, and anything else to be used to make presents for parents. The big Christmas show for parents had to be organized, costumed, directed, and practiced. The next three weeks would be busy ones for everyone.

* * * * * * *

It was eight-fifteen and the office was in it's usual uproar and confusion before the bell rang for class to begin. In the midst of it, a fifth grade girl came in with a friend on either side - as if for moral support. Since Loren was busy with a bus driver, Annie asked the girls if she could help them.

One of the friends spoke. "Mrs. Kallas, she's handcuffed."

"What?" Annie asked.

The other friend said, "She's handcuffed!"

"Can't she speak?"

"Go ahead," the friends prodded the girl in the middle.

"Mrs. Kallas, I'm handcuffed," she said.

"To what?"

"To myself. See?" She held up her hands which were handcuffed together.

Annie shook her head in exasperation. "Have you got the key to that thing?"

"No."

When the girls first came in, their attitude was this was exciting and interesting. Since Annie showed she found it irritating - not exciting - the picture suddenly changed.

"I've got to get to class, Dawn. The bell's gonna ring in a minute. I'll see you later," said one friend.

"Yeah, me too," said the other.

"Okay, Dawn, where did you get these handcuffs? Are they play ones?

"No, Mrs. Kallas. They're my father's. They're not play ones. They're real ones."

"Has your father got the key?"

"No, I don't think so. He never had the handcuffs closed."

"Wow, what did you do a dumb thing like that for? What did you close them for if you didn't have the key? How're we going to get you loose?"

"I don't know. We just thought it would be fun to be handcuffed like a real criminal. Will I have to be like this forever?"

"No, I don't guess so. One way or another we'll get them off of you. Go and wait in the principal's office. I'll call the custodian. Maybe he has some kind of tool that will work." She went to the intercom, punched the numbers for the all-call. "Mr. Sullivan, please come to the office. Mr. Sullivan. Dawn, what's your last name and what room are you in?"

"Rappaport and I'm in room fourteen."

"I'll tell your teacher you're here, so he won't mark you absent." She punched the buttons for room fourteen. "Mr. Martinez, please pick up the phone."

"Martinez here."

"Fred, I have Dawn Rappaport here in the office. She's got a pair of locked handcuffs on. She'll be here until we can figure out how to get them off."

Fred laughed. "What did she do that for? Who's got the key?"

"No one, as far as I know. The custodian's coming to see what he can do. We may have to call the father. I'll keep you posted."

"What can I do for you ladies?"

"Joe, I have a young lady in here who thought it might be great fun to be handcuffed like a criminal, so she put her dad's real handcuffs on and never gave a thought as to how she was going to get them off again. She doesn't think her dad has a key." Annie led him into the principal's office while she talked. "I thought you might have some kind of tool to open them."

"That was smart, wasn't it?" he said to the girl as he examined the handcuffs. "These look like regular police handcuffs to me. Is your father a cop?"

"No."

"Where'd he get these from?"

"I don't know." She got tears in her eyes.

"Dawn, don't cry. We'll figure it out. Is your mom or dad home?" Annie asked.

"Yes, I think my dad's home."

Ann beckoned Joe out of the office. "I don't want her all upset and crying."

"Well, Annie, I sure don't have any kind of tool to open police handcuffs. You'll probably have to call the cops to get her loose. How'd her dad get the cuffs in the first place?"

"Don't know. I'll call him now and see what he can do. Thanks, Joe."

"Sure. Let me know what happens."

Elizabeth walked in from the playground and Annie told her the story. She agreed Annie should phone Mr. Rappaport.

"Mr. Rappaport, this is Mrs. Kallas, the school secretary at Lincoln Elementary," she said into the phone. "We have Dawn in the office with a pair of locked handcuffs on she says are yours. Do you have a key?"

"Did that gal get into my handcuffs?"

"Yes, sir. That's what she says. Do you have a key to them?"

"No, never did get the key."

"Do you have any way to open them?"

"Well, never had to open them before. I can bring my toolbox down and give it a try," he said with a hearty laugh.

Since Annie failed to see anything funny about spending her morning trying to get handcuffs off a little girl, she asked spitefully, "These look like police handcuffs. Are you a policeman?"

He laughed again. "No, no, no. I ain't no policeman. So, Dawn got into my cuffs, eh? She's a little devil, she is."

"Mr. Rappaport, could you come down here and see what you can do with these cuffs?"

"Sure, I'll be right there. Wanna see Dawn all cuffed up."

"He'll be right here. He thinks it's funny," Annie told the principal.

"Call the police and ask them to send a car out. They can get the cuffs open and they may be interested in asking Mr. Rappaport where they came from."

"Okay." Annie dialed the police number.

A female voice asked, "Is this an emergency?"

"No," she answered.

"One moment, please," the voice said.

"May I help you?" a pleasant sounding gentleman came on the phone.

"This is Mrs. Kallas, the school secretary at Lincoln Elementary School. We have a child locked in handcuffs. We can't get her loose. Wonder if you could help. We think they're police handcuffs."

"How'd she get into police handcuffs? Her father an officer?" he asked.

"No, I don't know where he got them from. He's on his way down here. Thought you might want to talk to him."

"Yes, ma'am. We'll have a car out there in a few minutes."

"Thank you."

She fixed herself a cup of coffee and took it back to her desk. She had taken two sips when the front door opened and a tall, gaunt man walked in carrying a tool box. He had long, sandy colored hair and a long sandy colored beard. He wore faded, dirty army fatigues with an army cap on his head.

"I'm Mr. Rappaport. Where's my gal?" he roared merrily.

Annie walked up to the counter to greet him. As she got closer, she noticed he wore a Nazi insignia pinned onto his right breast pocket and a pin shaped like a marijuana leaf pinned to his left breast pocket. Annie could feel the anger rising inside her. How dared he come into a school wearing that junk!

"Come this way, please, Mr. Rappaport." She led him into the principal's office and introduced him to Mrs. Leski. She saw that Elizabeth noticed the pins but she greeted him pleasantly. Annie closed the door to the office as she left. "Shooooot," she said disgustedly as she sat down at her desk.

She pulled out the word processing she needed to do and took another couple of sips of coffee. The police arrived. "Come in, officers. This way, please." She led them into Elizabeth's office and closed the door behind them.

Five minutes later the police left, Dawn was free and went back to her room, and Mrs. Leski was pleasantly saying good-bye to Mr. Rappaport who was still laughing heartily and left with the cuffs in his hand.

After they were gone, Annie went in to see Elizabeth. "What happened? Where'd he get the cuffs?"

"He says he found them. There's nothing the police can do. They have no proof that he's done anything wrong. Having handcuffs in one's possession is not a crime. Anyway, they got Dawn loose and I don't think she'll try it again."

"Elizabeth, I've been dealing with the public for a long time and I realize it means all of the public and I know it's a big part of my job. This is the first time I can remember really feeling resentment at having to deal with somebody but I feel I shouldn't have to accommodate someone who is wearing a Nazi emblem and a marijuana leaf. Of the two, the Nazi sign is the most offensive. That's like wearing a Klu Klux Klan sign. I resent it and I resent not being able to tell him to take it off before he comes onto school grounds."

"Yes, I understand how you feel, Annie. But, of course, we can't do that. He has his constitutional rights - just like the rest of us. Remember the first amendment? ... Freedom of speech and expression. He's got the right to express himself with those emblems even if we don't like them." Elizabeth patted Annie's shoulder and said, "It takes all kinds to make this republic and I sometimes think Lincoln Elementary has to live with them all."

"Sure feels like it sometimes, doesn't it?"

* * * * * * *

"Annie, could I talk to you a minute - privately?" It was Ellen, the aide in room eight, speaking.

"Sure, Ellen, we can go into the principal's office. She's out on the playground." She got up hurriedly, wondering what on earth Ellen could want to talk to her about. Ellen was not one of her favorite people. She was, in Annie's opinion, a prissy old lady although she was only about fifty. She closed the door behind them in the principal's office and asked, "What can I do for you, Ellen?"

"Annie, I don't know quite how to say this..."

"Just say it, Ellen. Come on, just tell me," Annie coaxed impatiently.

"Well, have you heard any rumors about Joe?" she asked, gathering her courage.

Annie could feel herself bristling. "No, I haven't heard anything. What about Joe?"

"Well, the rumor is he's fooling around with the aide in room thirteen. It's a disgrace, Annie. That's a disgrace! I don't want to be a gossip, Annie, but it's a disgrace."

Annie struggled to hide the shock this information gave her. Could this be true? Why would Joe do such a thing? "For heaven's sake, Ellen, Joe's single. He can do whatever he wants." She could feel her anger swelling.

"But, Annie, the aide is not single."

"I'll look into it," Annie said. She opened the office door and signaled Ellen to precede her out. She watched the aide leave the office and then said to Loren, "I'm going out to find Joe. I want to discuss something with him. I'll be back in a little while. Call me on the all-call if you need me."

"Okay."

As Annie walked slowly to the supply room where Joe spent a lot of his time, she struggled to decide what to say to him. Should she repeat what Ellen had said? Should she warn him that everyone would be talking about him and the aide? Annie had no illusions Ellen would stop at discussing it with her. By the end of the day everyone on campus would have heard the story. It was what Annie had always feared might happen to her concerning either her friendship with Joe and now with Ray. She and Joe had both been careful but also lucky in that everyone expected the secretary and the head custodian of a school to be friendly because their jobs as the principal's right and left hands required it.

But Joe was a grown man and knew what he wanted to do. She decided against telling him what Ellen had said but, instead, see him just to be friendly and find out if he seemed happy. She found him checking the inventory of various papers the teachers used. "Hi, Joe, thought I might find you here."

"Hi, Annie. How're you doing? What brings you to my end of the campus?"

"Just a friendly visit but I also had a complaint about your night custodian I need to share with you. What's he up to these days?"

"For crissake, what's he done now?"

"Well, Elizabeth got the following note from a teacher. I'll read it to you. 'Please find out what Clyde has done with my rat. He dumped the rat's water out a couple of weeks ago, so the rat went all week-end without water. Now the rat is missing. I want my rat back.' It's signed Norma. That's room thirteen."

"Yeah, I know." Joe sighed and sat down heavily on a stack of boxes. "Clyde hates rats."

"I can't say I blame him."

"He doesn't think he should have to clean a room with a rat in it," Joe continued, "even if the rat is in a cage. He probably took it out and killed it. I'll talk to him when he comes in today. Shit! This job gets to me sometimes. Between these supplies, the night man, and these teachers, I wonder if it's worth it. I could live on my Marine retirement. I don't have to do this."

"You'd die of boredom without a job and this one is interesting, you must admit."

"Yeah, it's interesting all right. At six o'clock in the morning, I'm sweeping up used rubbers and empty beer cans out of the parking lot, 'cause the idiots who live in this neighborhood figure the school parking lot is a lover's lane. Then I go around with the can of paint to cover up the gang names and messages that little bastard has spray painted on the outside walls again in the middle of the night. One of these days I'll catch him and then watch out. He's playing games with me now but I'll catch him."

"You still think it's Tricky Dicky?" Annie referred to a former student who had caused endless trouble when he attended school there.

"It's Richard, all right, and one of these days I'll catch him and be able to prove it."

She laughed. "Now, Joe, you know you'll never give up this job with all these interesting challenges."

"That's what you think."

Annie searched his face and saw only the usual discontent with his job. His attitude toward her seemed normal and she felt it was the right decision not to discuss Ellen's information with him. "Well, I need to get back to the office. See what you can find out about the rat, okay?"

* * * * * * *

The front door burst open and a woman came staggering in. "Help me - help me, please," she sobbed.

"Ye gads!" Annie ran to the woman and led her into the health office. She recognized her as one of the parents. She was so small and thin she seemed like a brittle leaf about to crumble.

Loren still sat at her desk, gaping at them with her mouth open.

"Loren, get moving and get some ice," Annie ordered sharply. "Mrs. Wallace, what on earth has happened to you?" Annie sat her down on the cot, took her hands away from her face and looked for damage. She had a bump and a small cut on her forehead, a cut lip, her nose was bleeding, and her left eye was rapidly swelling. There was a lot of blood flowing, but Annie couldn't see any sign of serious damage. Loren finally got back with the ice. "Mrs. Wallace, pinch your nose like this to get it to stop bleeding and hold this ice cube on your mouth," she directed. She wrapped some more ice in a paper towel and put it onto the cut on her forehead and one on her eye.

"Loren, you can go back to your desk. I'll take care of Mrs. Wallace."

"Okay," Loren giggled nervously, relieved she wouldn't have to be involved and make decisions.

After a few minutes, Annie said, "Mrs. Wallace, please come over here to the sink and let's see if we can get some of the blood washed away." They moved together to the sink. With her free hand, Annie wet a paper towel and wiped away the blood which was smeared all over her face. Mrs. Wallace stopped pinching her nose and they waited to see if it had stopped bleeding.

"Does your nose feel all right? You don't think it's broken, do you?"

"No, it feels all right," she answered as she gingerly felt it.

"It seems to have stopped bleeding." Annie cleaned all round the nose as gently as she could. "Why don't you hold the piece of ice in your mouth and wash your hands off here?" she suggested. Her upper lip was split, her lower lip wasn't cut but was badly bruised and swollen. Annie removed the ice she had been holding onto her forehead and found the cut had stopped bleeding but the ice needed to stay on awhile to get the bump down.

"Loren, please get us a couple of new pieces of ice," Annie called to her.

"Okay."

"Does anything else hurt you, Mrs. Wallace? We've taken care of the bleeding but is there anything else? Are your teeth loose, ribs broken, or anything like that?"

"No, he only hit me in the face. No, nothing else is

hurt. Only my face." She started whimpering, was shaking violently, and then finally broke into sobs. Annie held her and let her cry in her arms, fighting back the tears herself. "Could the 'he' be her husband?" she wondered.

Annie remembered when they enrolled. The reason she remembered was because the children were so polite. They had just moved here from down south - Alabama or somewhere around there. They all had beautiful southern accents and the children had been taught to say "Ma'am" or "Sir" when an adult spoke to them. It was so unusual in this environment that the children made an impression on the whole staff. The parents were in their mid-twenties. There were three elementary age children and two pre-schoolers. They had left their home and extended family to come to California to find and participate in the "good life."

When Annie got their application for free lunches for the children a few months later, she knew things weren't working out the way they had hoped. They stated on the application their income came from Aid to Dependent Children. Annie guessed coming from a farm in Alabama did not qualify the husband for many jobs in cosmopolitan southern California.

Mrs. Wallace finally stopped sobbing and said, "Miz Kallas, I'm so sorry. I got your blouse all wet an' bloody. Look there. It's a blood stain."

"That's okay. Don't you worry about it. I'll get it out in a few minutes. Do you feel better now?" She had stopped shaking and managed a small smile from her swollen mouth.

"Yes, ma'am, thanks to you."

"Let's go into the principal's office and talk. We need to leave the health office for the students. Recess is starting." Annie moved her into the principal's office and then called on the loud speaker, "Mrs. Leski, please come to the office. Mrs. Leski, to the office, please."

Elizabeth came to the front door a couple of minutes later. "What's up?" Annie briefed her on what she knew and they went into her office. "Hello, Mrs. Wallace.

Mrs. Kallas tells me you've had a little trouble." As she talked, she examined Mrs. Wallace's face. "Really just superficial wounds. They'll be much better in a couple of days," she reassured her. "Mrs. Wallace, do you want to tell us what happened?" Elizabeth asked her while holding one of her hands.

"Yes, ma'am, I guess so. I got to do something. Well, my husband's been drinking a lot lately an' he got mad 'cause the vacuum cleaner made so much noise he couldn't hear the ball game on TV. Mrs. Leski, I got to vacuum sometime. He jumped up and grabbed me and hit me while he was yelling that I would do anything to keep him from having a little fun out of life. I got to vacuum sometime and he's always watching TV. I tried to get away but he just kept slapping me. Then he threw me down and I hit my head on the edge of the TV. I kind of blacked out. When I woke up, he was gone. That's when I ran down here. All the blood scared me and I didn't know where else to go. I live just down the street and I knowd y'all would help me." She wiped tears away with her hands. Annie got a box of tissues from Elizabeth's counter and offered them to her.

"Miz Leski, what am I gonna do? I'm scared of him. When he drinks, he don't know what he's doing. He never used to be like this. Back home he was always sweet and gentle. Out here he's so different. Back home he used to always be working. When it was too dark to work outside, he'd come in and work in the house. He'd always be fixing something, or making something for us, or even helping me with the kids. He's the only man I ever knowd who'd help with the kids. Out here he can't find work and won't do nothing round the house. He won't help with the kids and won't help me. And now he don't even want me to vacuum. We can't live like pigs, Miz Leski." She started sobbing again. "What am I gonna do? I'm scared, I'm scared."

"Mrs. Wallace, would you like to go to a shelter home for a few days? We can call someone who can make the arrangements," Elizabeth asked her.

"What about my kids? I can't leave my kids. The little ones are playing over my neighbor's house right now. I gotta go get them. My neighbor will be wondering where I am."

"Your children can go with you to the shelter home. If you want me to, I'll go with you to pick up your children and bring them back here. What do you think, Mrs. Wallace? Do you want a day or two in a shelter home to think things over?"

"Yes, ma'am, I guess so. All I really know is I'd be scared to be home with him tonight."

Elizabeth turned to Annie and said, "Call and get Deanna James of Social Services on the line for me."

Annie soon had Mrs. James on the phone. Within a few minutes, Elizabeth had made all the arrangements for the Wallace family to go to a home for battered women. Mrs. James would meet Mrs. Wallace at the school in a half hour. Mrs. Wallace and the principal would go to the neighbor's house to pick up the two pre-school children while Annie rounded up the three children who were in school and have them wait in the office.

Mrs. Leski and Mrs. Wallace left. Annie called room six. "Mrs. Reeves, please pick up the phone."

"Yes, what is it?"

"Please send Mary Jane Wallace to the office with enough work for a few days and her coat and whatever else she might have but don't tell her anything. I'll explain to you later. Okay?"

"Sure, will do."

Annie followed the same procedure for the twins Jimmy in room four, and Tommy in room three.

"Why are we here, Miz Kallas?" asked Mary Jane, a pale, blonde, seven year old in a worried voice.

"Mary Jane, it's okay. You don't have to be worried," Annie reassured her. "You're just going to visit someone with your mother for a few days. You'll have a good time and then you'll be back again. Your mom will be here to pick you up in a few minutes."

"Oh. All right." She accepted the explanation and they all sat and read the books on the front table while waiting patiently for their mother to arrive.

About fifteen minutes later, Mrs. Leski, Mrs. Wallace, and the two pre-school children came in the door. While Mrs. Wallace greeted her older children, Elizabeth asked if there was any sign of Deanna James.

"No, not yet. Wait, maybe this is she."

"Yes, it is." Elizabeth walked up to the young woman who had just entered. "Hello, Deanna, good to see you again," Elizabeth said as they shook hands.

"You're looking great, Elizabeth. Being a principal agrees with you, it seems."

"It has its ups and downs. Keeps one on one's toes."

"Mrs. Wallace, this is Mrs. James. She will see to it that you get settled and are made comfortable."

"I don't know if I'm doing the right thing," said Mrs. Wallace, her face crumbling into tears again.

Deanna answered, "It'll be all right, Mrs. Wallace. We're just arranging it so you can have a couple of days to think things over. It will give your husband a chance to think things over, too, and then you can decide what to do."

"Okay, I guess so. Bye, Miz Leski. Thanks for helping me."

"Good-bye, Mrs. Wallace. I'm glad we could be of help."

After they left, Annie followed Elizabeth into her office. "It's so sad. Why does he have to be such a bastard and hit his wife? I'd like to hit him with a two by four."

"Sure, I understand how you feel but, remember, there are two sides to every story."

"There's no excuse for a man hitting his wife. She loves him, she's a good wife and does the best she can with the children. What more does he expect? Especially when they're living on welfare and there's never enough money."

"No, I'm not saying there's an excuse. I'm just suggesting there is a likely explanation," Elizabeth said.

"Oh, what's that?"

"Do you remember when they first enrolled, they said they had left the family farm down south to get the 'good life' here?"

"Yes, I remember."

"Well, I think they left an environment where they and their parents were known and respected, where they knew everyone and everyone knew everything everyone else did. They might have been poor farmers but they came from a stable society where the limits were recognized and mostly obeyed. Marrying at seventeen and having five children by the age of twenty-five was commendable and showed their fertility besides providing more hands to do the work.

"They left that life for Southern California which has an unstable society in which everyone makes his own rules and limits are set only by the individual or the police. They don't know anyone and no one cares what they do. Early marriage here is considered stupidity and five children without enough money is considered sheer lunacy. With the few marketable skills he has, of course, he's been unable to find a job. To sum it up, everything that made him admirable and respected where he grew up is scorned here. I would guess the man has lost his self-respect. He considers himself worthless because this society considers him worthless."

"Well, if that's true, why don't they just move back home?" Annie asked.

"Probably because they would be returning in defeat for all to see. And perhaps, there still is hope for a decent job here somewhere."

"That's really sad, Elizabeth."

"Yes, it's very sad, Annie. And what's even sadder is it's likely to get worse. A person who considers himself worthless is very likely to become worthless."

They stared at one another for a few seconds while Annie shook her head.

* * * * * * *

Mrs. Wallace brought the children back to school the following Monday. "Hello, Miz Kallas," she called with a happy smile on her bruised face. "Do I have to do anything to get the kids back into school?"

Annie walked up to the counter where she stood. "No, you don't have to do anything. They can just go to class. What's happening? Are you back home?"

"Oh, Miz Kallas, I'm so happy. My husband was so sorry and begged and pleaded for me to come back home. I stayed at the shelter home for three days. There were all those other wives who had been hit by their husbands and we talked a lot and had a counselor talk to us and I learned a lot. I made a lot of friends. When I called Tom, my husband, on the second day he just cried and cried on the phone. He was so sorry he acted so crazy. Now I'm back home and we're all happy to be together again."

She bubbled over with joy. Annie wondered how women could so easily forget their bruises to be with the man who represents 'home' to them? She was so loving and so trusting. Annie wished her well while at the same time shuddered for her future. "I'm glad everything worked out, Mrs. Wallace, and we're glad to have the children back in school."

* * * * * * *

"Loren, have you noticed all the flies in here?" Annie asked.

"Sure have," she answered.

There was one fly buzzing around Annie's head and another buzzing around the computer keys. She waved at them with her hand but they refused to stay away. "Loren, please get the flyswatter and kill these flies. We must have a hundred of them in here. I've got to get this report finished before the mail leaves."

"I'm sorry, I don't kill flies," Loren said without looking up from her desk.

Annie turned and asked, "What? What did you say?"

"I do not kill flies," Loren repeated in a determined tone of voice.

"For heaven's sake, why not? Are they an endangered species?"

"No, they're not but I won't kill them"

"Why? And what do you do at home? Won't you kill them there either?"

"No, I don't kill them at home either. I just don't like to kill them and I won't!"

With growing irritation, Annie asked her, "How do you get rid of them?"

"I wave them away."

"You realize, of course, when you wave them away, they come over to me."

Loren didn't answer.

Annie picked up the flyswatter and swatted the two who had been bothering her. One fell between her computer keys and by the time she got the body out, it was squished and in pieces. She was losing all patience. She went into the principal's office and killed a few in there. She got about five or six on the front office window. She went into the staffroom and killed about twenty. It was a massacre. She got all the bodies up and thrown away. It was with a feeling of great satisfaction that she returned to her desk. "Murder must be good for my coordination," she thought as she finished the report with a minimum of effort.

The atmosphere in the office was strained between Annie and Loren for the next hour.

* * * * * * *

Norma Glas was sitting on a chair in front of the file cabinet which held the cums, short for cumulative records, for each student. These were the folders which traveled from school to school with the student and held all of his educational history. "What are you doing there, Norma? It's almost time for us to close the office."

Norma answered in disgust, "I'm going through my cums to see what information I can glean from previous teachers' notes or report cards. The principal sure picked a bad week to require us to submit a list of possible retentions."

Annie laughed heartily at the outrageousness of the statement. She knew Norma's work habits well enough to know anytime she was required to do paper work for the office, she would leave it for the last minute. "Sure, Norma," she answered as she tousled her curly hair playfully, "and you haven't known since October you would have to do this?"

Norma laughed with her in acknowledgement. "I'd like to retain half of my class. Think I can get away with it?"

Annie smiled, knowing she didn't mean it. "No." Getting serious, she continued, "But you do have to be careful that any kid you recommend for retention hasn't been retained more than once before. We found a boy at the beginning of the year who we had retained in the sixth grade last June. In October somebody suddenly noticed the boy was fourteen years old. The principal looked it up and found he had been retained twice before. In the first and third grades, I think. Elizabeth had to make arrangements and then take him over to the junior high. It was kind of embarrassing for her. It was really the teacher's fault who recommended retention, although it's hard to blame her either. All she could see was the boy wasn't ready to do seventh grade work. He was small and immature and the extra year here would have done him good."

"Yes, I feel that way about some of my students. If I could just buy a couple more years for them to mature, what wonders some teacher could perform."

"It's a shame in a way. But two retentions per child is the limit and after all, it wouldn't work to have fifteen year olds in the same grade with eleven year olds.

"Well, all I know is I should be working on the Christmas presents for parents project instead of on retentions," Norma complained.

"It's your own fault for leaving it for the last minute and you know it. What's your class making for parents, anyway?"

"Sand sculptures - and it's a lot of work."

"I bet it is. Show me one when you're finished, will you?"
"Sure."

* * * * * * *

Any person knowledgeable about schools could walk onto a school campus blindfolded the week before Christmas and feel it was the week before Christmas. One didn't need to see the construction paper Santas, snowflakes, and Christmas trees which were on all bulletin boards, windows, doors, and hanging from ceilings.

Every day of the last school week before Christmas some staff member brought food for the employees to eat. There were Christmas cookies, breads, and candies and any employee with a foreign background was encouraged to bring in their national Christmas food. As a result, of course, almost all staff members were gaining weight.

There was an excitement in the air which was gradually reaching near hysteria proportions as the last day of school before Christmas vacation arrived. Almost all of the Christmas presents for parents were finished. There were tree ornaments made from clothespins, wishing wells made from ice cream sticks, shadow boxes, sand paintings, student's handprints in plaster, and whatever else the teacher could imagine and the student could make. On the last day, parent volunteers were there to help while room mothers frantically tried to coordinate who was going to bring what for the parties that afternoon.

The PTA owned a Santa Claus suit and arranged for one of the fathers (who even looked like Santa) to dress up that morning and pass out candy canes.

"Annie, where can Mr. Fielding change into his costume?" asked the PTA president, Mrs. Brown.

"He can go into the men's restroom. It's at the end of ramp two. I can give him a key."

"That sounds fine," Mr. Fielding grinned. He was obviously looking forward to the role he was to play this morning. He returned a few minutes later.

"You look great, Mr. Fielding." Loren giggled as she

walked up to him and admired him from all angles in his red suit and hat, black belt and shoes, and white beard and hair. Mr. Fielding had his own rotund figure to fill out the suit.

He smiled gleefully. "Let's get going. Where are my candy canes?"

Mrs. Brown came out of the principal's office. "I have them all in here." She gave Mr. Fielding the bag full of candy and they set off happily together toward ramp one. Mrs. Brown had a string of Christmas bells which she rang as they walked.

Annie had forewarned Loren not to plan on getting any work done this last day but Annie had to complete the attendance report for the current month before she could leave which dampened her party spirit a little. It was always a totally chaotic day. Loren was kept busy dealing with parents coming and going in the office. There were Christmas parties in every room starting right after lunch and the parents started bringing the food and drink from about ten o'clock on. They called students to help the parents get the food to their rooms. Loren tried to find room in the staff refrigerator for all the drinks. This was the one day of the year the cafeteria workers let them use some of their freezer space for all of the ice cream the parents brought.

Santa returned an hour later saying, "This is the most fun I've had in years. The little kids are so surprised and happy to see me," he laughed. "They can't quite figure out how Santa got to their school a few days before Christmas but they get so excited they forget. This is great! Can I do this every year?" They laughed with him at his happiness and Annie was reminded again of the joy children bring everyone. Mr. Fielding stood there flushed and happy with a big smile on his face.

"I need some more candy canes. I've finished ramps one and two. I need this bag filled up again."

"Sure, come on in here." Annie led him into Mrs. Leski's office. "What happened to Mrs. Brown?"

"I left her in the last classroom ringing bells. She's pretty good with those bells. She can play some Christmas carols with them and the kids were singing along with her. They love Jingle Bells. It was really beautiful. I hated to leave but I thought I'd better try to stay on schedule."

"It's probably a good idea. If you get too far off, we'll run into lunch hours."

"Yes, that's what I figured. Okay, that ought to be enough candy. I'll come back if I need more. Thanks, Mrs. Kallas."

"Well, it's my pleasure, Santa."

Santa had no sooner left when there was a commotion at the door. Five students came in, laughing and noisy.

"What are you doing in here?" Loren asked.

"We have Christmas cards for Mrs. Leski. Can we give them to her?"

"She's not here. She's out in the classrooms. Can I just leave them on her desk for you?"

"Sure, will you?"

"Glad to," Loren smiled at them.

"Merry Christmas, Merry Christmas!" they called, laughing as they left.

"What can I do for you?" asked Loren of the next two students who came in.

"This is for Mrs. Kallas to see."

"What is it?" Annie asked as she left her desk and walked to the counter.

"It's a sand sculpture. Miss Glas said you wanted to see one."

"I sure did. It's beautiful! Is it a model of the castle you're going to own some day?" she teased.

"No, Mrs. Kallas, it's King Arthur's castle. You know, in England?"

"Yes, I know. You did a marvelous job. You must be very talented to be able to do it."

"It's not so hard. Anyone could do it," he protested modestly. Both the boys grinned, pleased at the praise.

"Thank you for sharing. I appreciate Miss Glas thinking of me. You be careful carrying it back. We don't want anything to happen to it. Thanks, boys, and Merry Christmas."

As they came to lunch, the teachers dropped off cards or little presents for Annie and Loren in appreciation of their help during the year. Some of the teachers gave each of them the same present their students made for the parents such as a little clothespin soldier painted red and blue with gold trim on his uniform to hang on the tree or a candy cane made out of little red and green beads.

By three o'clock when the students left, everyone was happy but exhausted. The kids were full of sugar on the inside and full of little presents and ornaments and cards on the outside. It was the first day of Christmas for them.

After waving good-bye to their students, the teachers gathered in the staffroom to recover and gather enough strength to straighten up their classrooms and go home. Everyone was tired but happy. They were laden down with cards and little gifts from their students and other staff members and full of nervous energy and were chattering excitedly. Even Joe and Clyde, who had to clean up all the mess, sat and talked for a few minutes and shared the Christmas spirit.

Annie looked fondly around at each of them and thought how lucky they were to have such a great staff and how grateful she was to each and every one of them for enriching her life.

After everyone had gone, Annie and Joe sat alone in the staffroom and talked quietly. "I suppose you and Ray are going to have a merry old Christmas together."

"No, Joe, we're not. He's spending Christmas with his brother in Canada. I won't see him again until school starts. What are you going to do?"

"Just sit around the house, I guess."

Annie laughed. "C'mon, Joe, don't act like a spoiled kid. You've probably had all kinds of invitations to parties during Christmas."

"Well, first of all, remember I have to work during these two weeks that you guys are off. And, second, I didn't get the invitation I wanted so that kind of puts a damper on my Christmas spirit."

Annie wondered if the invitation he wanted was from the aide in room thirteen. "You might have to work but you still get four days off to have a good time. You want to spend Christmas day with us?"

She was surprised to see him flush as he reached for her hand. "Who's us?" he asked.

"My daughters and family. Santa can find you at Alicia's house too, you know, and we cook a mean Christmas dinner. C'mon, Joe, have you had a better offer than that?"

"No," he looked with such fervor into her eyes as he continued to nuzzle her fingers that she was surprised at his intensity.

"So...will you come?"

"Yes."

"Okay, Joe, I'll phone you in a couple of days and we'll make arrangements. Right now, I have to get home. I'm really bushed. This has been a heck of a week."

"Yeah, tell me about it. Okay, kid, I'll be waiting to hear from you."

* * * * * * *

"That sure was a great meal. My hat's off to the cook - or cooks," Joe said as he rubbed his stomach with satisfaction.

"It was mostly my daughter, Alicia. I only helped a little. Alicia is the good cook in the family," Annie smiled proudly at her daughter.

"Well, congratulations, Alicia. You did yourself proud. What do you want me to do now for k.p. duty? Remember I'm the product of twenty years in the Marines. I know all about cleaning up a kitchen."

"Okay, I'll take you up on that offer. Mother and I'll put

the leftover food away while you scrape the plates and put them in the dishwasher. How about that, Joe?"

"Sounds good to me."

* * * * * * *

"Bye, everybody. Joe and I decided to go dancing and work off some of these extra calories we just ingested."

"I had a great day. Thanks to all of you. Hope I'll see you again sometime," Joe added.

"I figured we could go to the Blue Heaven. They have a nice trio playing there. Okay with you, Annie?"

"Sure."

Joe stopped and said a few words to the bartender as they walked to an empty table. "He's a nice guy, Glenn is. You ever been in here before?"

"No."

"Well, it's a good place. Got little groups playing music for a couple weeks at a time. Then they get someone else so you can listen to different kinds of music and it never gets boring. C'mon, this is a good one. Let's dance."

They danced slowly to the plaintive melody. "You're a good dancer, Joe."

"I was just thinking the same thing about you." He held her close a minute and said, "It's too bad we couldn't make a go of it but now it's too late anyway." He waited a minute and added, "There's something I have to tell you tonight. I promised myself I would tell you tonight. I have to get it off my chest."

Annie wondered what this could be about. Joe sounded like he wanted to confess to a crime. Gad, she hoped not.

They sat down opposite one another at the small, round table. Joe took a large swallow of his drink and then holding her hands in his, said, "Annie, I'm in love."

Annie felt a shock at his blunt statement. She looked at him in amazement and then knew. "It's the aide at the school, isn't it?"

He was shocked at her question and took another gulp of his drink. "How did you know?"

"I heard the gossip," she answered and proceeded to tell him about the conversation with Ellen.

He groaned. "Oh, geez, you mean everyone on campus knows?"

"I don't know about that, Joe. Some people may be talking about their suspicions but that kind of gossip takes place every once in a while and then dies out again for lack of fuel. I don't think you have anything to worry about at this point. How did this all happen, Joe? She's married - you know that."

"Yeah, I know. We started talking at the gym when she started to work out a couple of months ago. We see each other there and afterward every Tuesday and Thursday nights. I don't know how it happened."

"What about her husband?" she asked in an effort to make him face reality.

Joe shook his head. "I don't know. I never met the guy. Louise says he's not a good husband but she won't say anything more than that. I don't want to know the details anyway. He's not making her happy so that's all I care about. The rest is his problem."

"Joe, you're on dangerous ground and I don't want you to get hurt."

"No. I won't get hurt. I can take care of myself."

"I meant emotionally."

"Yeah, well, I can't do anything about that. I love her and there's nothing I can do about it."

He looked so downcast Annie could feel tears well in her eyes. She took his hands in hers and said, "Joe, you and I will always be good friends."

"I'll always love you in a way but this gal is different. Man, I haven't felt this way about a woman in twenty years, I bet."

Annie looked at him fondly. "Well, I certainly wish you lots of luck. I hope you find happiness with her. And...I appreciate you telling me about it."

"Let's have one last dance and then we can leave. I want to hold you again for comfort."

As they danced, Annie thought about what a dear person he was. She said a small, silent prayer that he wouldn't get hurt with his new romance.

JANUARY

It was January - the middle of winter. The middle of winter for Lincoln Elementary meant bright, crisp, clear days with no smog and the temperature in the sixties to mid-seventies with a sparkling sun looking down on them. If the farmers were lucky, there would be some rain.

The farmers were lucky on the first day school was open after Christmas vacation. Actually, they had been lucky for the previous three days as well. The greening of Southern California was taking place. Finally, heavy, drenching rain was falling. The foresters and farmers were jubilant as farmland and foothills turned green.

The first day it rained everyone enjoyed it as dusty cars, trees, bushes, and houses all got a good rinsing. The tall, skinny palm trees were dancing in time with the wind and looked gay and happy to be clean again. It had been nine months since the last substantial rain.

The only ones who were unhappy were the mothers of small children. During the first hour of daylight rain and wind they could look out of the window with their children and admire the interesting forces nature was inflicting on them. But after the nature lesson, they had the problem of how to channel those energies that only knew how to run and jump and play out of doors. By the third day of rain, mothers and children alike were hoping and praying their sun - the life they knew - would return to them. But it was not to be. Mothers were finally rescued not by the sun but by the school bus.

Lincoln's staff members were highly indignant there could be rain on the first day back. It was the topic of conversation in the staffroom to the exclusion of all others. They looked out of the windows to see if there was any break in the solid layer of gray clouds overhead. The rain had stopped for the moment but would it start again? Would Elizabeth call the dreaded "Rainy Day Schedule?"

In the middle of all the turmoil and dismay, Jeanne Curtis said loudly, "I have some good news to tell you - I'm pregnant."

"Congratulations, when's it going to be?" they crowded around her.

"I was lucky it worked out exactly the way I planned it. The baby is due July second, so I'll have the summer off and be able to come back to work on time in September. Isn't it marvelous? We're so happy!"

Their congratulations were cut short by the announcement on the loud-speaker, "Rainy Day Schedule - open your classrooms, please, Rainy Day Schedule." They moaned and groaned - the students were not permitted on the playground.

* * * * * * *

Ray lingered in the staffroom after the bell rang in hopes he could have a moment alone with Annie. They stood in the doorway as the door closed behind the last teacher and both said hurriedly, "I missed you," and then laughed together.

"Did you have a good time?" Annie asked.

"Yes. No. I missed you but, of course, it was nice seeing the family again. They all commented on how much better I looked since they had last seen me in August. I almost told them about you but thought that maybe it was too soon. I have to go but can we have dinner together tonight? I really did miss you."

"Sure, Ray, I missed you, too. Are you going to cook?"

"Yes, I'll cook. Come over about six. Okay?"

* * * * * * *

"I have the mother of another first grader working on registration papers," Loren said.

"Geez, aren't there any other kids in the world except first graders?" Annie went into the principal's office. "Elizabeth, I have another first grader out here to be registered. Where do you want me to put him? Everyone is full."

"What have they got?"

Annie showed Elizabeth the class lists. "Selby has thirty-two, Curtis has thirty-two, and Campos has thirty-three. I gave Campos that thirty-third student on Monday when you were at the district office. I didn't know what else to do with him."

"Well, of course, we can go over for twenty days," Elizabeth answered. "We'll have to watch it and hope somebody in the first grade moves soon. Give this child to Selby and the next one coming in to Curtis. And, Annie, better start praying. If it doesn't slow down, I may have to hire another teacher and open another classroom."

"Gad, I hope not! Think of all the paper work." She went back to her desk. "Did you hear that, Loren?"

"Yes, what was it about opening up another classroom?"

"All the first grade classes are full. The teachers' contract with the school district sets a limit to how many pupils can be in a class. The only leeway the district has is that a class enrollment can go over the limit for twenty days. After that, the teacher involved can file a grievance against the district."

The mother was standing at the counter looking over the completed registration papers. Annie took her class lists and walked up to her. "Hi, how are you?" she said to the mother and then smiled at the little boy standing at her side. "Are you going to be coming to our school? We're glad to have you here."

"Does a new kid have to start right away?" he asked in a small, frightened voice.

"Yes, of course," his mother told him. "You have to get into school. You've missed enough."

With that news he turned fiercely to her, put both arms around her upper leg and molded himself to her. "I don't wanna go! I don't wanna go!" he cried.

"Oh-oh, one of those," Annie thought to herself. She

let the mother cope with him while she looked through the registration papers. His shots were up to date, he was coming from a school in Las Vegas, the mother had put zero income on the application for free lunch. "Mrs. Hardasty, I'm not allowed to accept an application for free lunch showing zero income. The state doesn't accept that people have nothing to live on. If you have moved in with another family, you must declare their income," she said as kindly as she could.

"I've applied for welfare. I can show you the proof of that."

"No, I don't need to see it. I can allow your son free lunch for ten days until you can get the paperwork straightened out. As soon as you hear something, please come in and file a revised form. All right?"

"Yes, of course I will. Thanks."

The boy was now laying on the floor with his arms tightly clasped around his mother's ankles. He was whimpering and shaking nervously like a fox cornered by a pack of dogs.

"I notice he's seven years old and in the first grade. Has he been retained?"

"Yes, he has. He went to school in Pennsylvania when he lived with his father and then came back to Nevada to live with me. In Nevada they wanted him to repeat the first grade. So, this is his second year in the first grade."

"We'll mark that on the registration so the teacher will know. The teacher's name is Mrs. Selby, room three. You live near the school so your child is a walker. The school hours are eight-thirty to two o'clock. Will you pick him up today and until he gets used to it?"

"Yes, I'll be here."

"I'll call the teacher and tell her we're coming. Okay, Randy, come on, we're about ready to go." She walked to the other side of the counter where he was lying on the floor holding onto his mother.

He started screaming. "I don't wanna go! I won't go! I won't go!"

The boy was panicking.

While she reached down to pry him loose from her ankles, the mother coaxed, "C'mon, Randy, you didn't behave like this in the school in Las Vegas. What are these people going to think? C'mon, son, get up. You're making me ashamed of you."

He let go of her ankles, rolled a couple of feet and laid on his back flailing his arms and legs and screamed hysterically. They couldn't get near him for fear of being hit by the arms or legs.

Elizabeth came out of her office to see what the commotion was about. "Mrs. Leski, would you please see if you can convince Randy he will enjoy this school?" Annie asked.

Elizabeth, as usual, took command of the situation. She walked behind his head, reached under his armpits and holding him with his feet dragging, pulled him backwards into her office. He had stopped screaming while she made her maneuver because he was so astonished but once in the office he started again.

Mrs. Hardasty and Annie stood spellbound, "Mrs. Leski can handle anything. She'll handle him and make him glad he came," Annie reassured the mother. "There's nothing more you can do. He'll behave better without you around." Mrs. Hardasty was almost crying herself. "It'll be all right," Annie comforted. "In an hour, he will have forgotten all about it. It'll be okay. You go on home. We'll take care of your son."

"Okay," she said, still uncertain. "I'll be back to get him after school."

"Why don't you come to the office about ten minutes early and I'll take you to the room before the teacher excuses the children. Then you can meet the teacher and talk to her a minute if you want."

"Thanks, I'll do that. Bye."

After the mother left, Annie looked through the window of the door to the principal's office to see what was going on. Randy was whimpering in a heap on the floor. Elizabeth sat at her desk doing her paperwork. When he got ready to talk, she would talk to him. Annie went back to her desk.

About ten minutes later, she suddenly remembered Randy and looked through the principal's door. Randy and Elizabeth were sitting at the table together. Randy was telling Elizabeth something. It wouldn't be long now.

A few minutes later, Elizabeth and Randy came out of the office. "What room did you assign Randy to? He's ready to go to class now."

"Room three."

"I'll take him down and see that he's comfortable." They went out the door hand in hand.

* * * * * * *

"Come on in, Annie. It's good to have you here again," Ray said with a pleased smile on his face as he helped her off with her coat.

"It's good to be here, too. It's pouring outside, did you notice? All the cars are slipping and sliding 'cause we southern Californians have forgotten how to drive in the rain. It would be funny if it weren't so dangerous. What's for dinner? I'm starved."

"Pork chops, mashed potatoes, string beans, salad, and sourdough bread. How does that sound? Oh, and chocolate pudding for desert."

"It sounds like you're trying to put some weight on me, that's what it sounds like. Delicious but fattening. Are you?"

"Am I what?"

"Trying to put some weight on me?"

"No, of course not. I think you're perfect the way you are. No, I didn't have time to plan this dinner since I only got home late last night so it's kind of thrown together but it'll taste good and a pound or two won't hurt you. We'll walk it off afterwards."

"We can't, it's raining."

"Okay, okay, we'll do push-ups in the living room. Will that satisfy you?"

"Oh, look what I've gotten myself into now. I haven't done push-ups since high school."

"Serves you right. I'm going to hold you to it, too. But in the meantime, let's enjoy the meal. The chops must be ready."

As they ate, Annie said, "Tell me about your trip, Ray. Did you have a good Christmas?"

"Well, of course, it was the first one without Helen. That's why I felt I had to get out of the house. It would have reminded me too much of all the years of happy Christmases she and I had. Remember last year, Annie, when we had the staff party here? Everybody had a good time. She and I had a lot of fun and a good life together," Ray answered with a deep sigh. "Maybe by next year I'll be able to deal with Christmas here. I'll have to see. Anyway, it was comforting being with my brother and his family. He has such great kids. They all like their Uncle Ray and they're getting old enough now to have fun with and, of course, Christmas is for kids so it's a good time to visit them. There was snow and we got out the sleds and the skis and made snowmen and all the usual stuff. They don't have very much money, so most of the gifts were handmade which I find a desirable and fitting way of celebrating. How about you, Annie? Did you have a good Christmas?"

"It was very nice. Our usual way of celebrating - dinner at Alicia's house. I invited Joe Sullivan to come along because he had nowhere to go and he and I went out dancing afterwards. All in all, it was very nice."

Ray looked at her piercingly when she mentioned Joe and, after a moment's hesitation, asked, "Annie, what exactly is your relationship to Joe these days?"

She looked at him quizzically since his tone of voice seemed tight and strained. "We're old friends. I've told you that before, Ray. This isn't the first time he and I have spent Christmas together."

"Just old friends or more?"

Annie put down her fork and studied him. She was surprised to see that he seemed agitated. "Why are you upset, Ray? You've always known I go out with Joe once in a while but we're really just old friends."

Ray stared at her with an indecipherable expression and then shook his head as though to clear it and answered, "I'm sorry, Annie. Of course, it's none of my business what your relationship is with Joe."

She could feel the tension building between them and not wanting it to happen decided to tell Ray about Joe's new love. "Ray, I'm going to share something in confidence with you so as to help you understand better. Joe has fallen in love with the aide in room thirteen. She's married and Joe is struggling to keep everyone on campus from finding out about it. He admitted it to me while we were out dancing on Christmas."

She could feel the tension in him drain away. "I'm acting like a fool, aren't I?" he asked after a moment's thought.

Annie was tempted to say yes but reminded herself how inexperienced he was in the dating game. "Ray, I want to make sure you understand that I'm very fond of Joe and he of me but we're not 'in love' with each other. We've moved on but we still care and worry about each other. Something like brother and sister. Can you understand?"

After a moment's hesitation, he answered, "Yes, of course. I'm sorry. I'm being stupid. Of course, you're fond of one another. Why shouldn't you be? You've probably been a big help to each other all these years. I'm sorry," he repeated.

"It's okay, Ray, forget it," she said as she picked up her fork again and finished her dinner. "It's good, as usual. You certainly do have a knack with the stove. Bring on the chocolate pudding and then we'll get to those push-ups," she added in an attempt to regain their light-hearted banter.

A half-hour later they were stretched out side by side on the living room floor. "Can't we just stop with this?"

"With this?" Ray hooted. "All we're doing is lying here. That's no exercise. Come on now, turn over and on to the push-ups. Okay, up, one and two, hold it a minute, now down, three and four. Good, now again."

Annie groaned and panted and managed to last through twelve push-ups before she collapsed onto the floor and lay there exhausted. Ray continued on until he counted twenty-one and then laughed as he stopped with the comment, "I better stop or I won't be able to walk tomorrow. I haven't done these in years. You did very well, though, Annie, for a girl," he added with a laugh.

He reached over to where she was lying on her back and leaning his body against hers held her arms at her sides before she could swing at him for his remarks. As she sputtered with indignation, he bent down and kissed her. She responded wholeheartedly to his kiss and pulled her arms free so she could pull him to her. They pressed their bodies against each other in an explosion of sudden desire but, Annie, wanting to make sure this time he was altogether ready for the ultimate step, pulled away and said, "We need to clean up the kitchen and then it'll be time for me to get home. I'm really tired tonight - it's been a hard day."

Ray, realizing what she was doing, kissed her fondly on the cheek and agreed it had, indeed, been a hard day. "Okay, next time we'll both do five more push-ups than we did this time and maybe eventually we'll both get pretty good at it. I'll race you to the kitchen."

* * * * * * *

"Hey, Annie, who's the cute sub? Is he married?" asked Shela Dennis.

"What sub? Who do you mean?" She knew who Shela meant but she wanted to tease her a little. He was cute indeed. He was in his late twenties and looked like one of those blond, handsome surfers in the movies. Everyone who met him at recess or lunch was also impressed with his good manners and charm.

"You know who I mean, Annie. That good-looking guy who substituted in room twelve today." Shela laughed and then pleaded, "Find out for me if he's married or not, please. Get his phone number. Oh, and Annie, find out how old he is."

"How on earth am I supposed to be able to do all of that? For heaven's sake, I can't just go up and ask him, 'How old are you, are you married, what's your phone number? He'll think I'm crazy, Shela."

"Well, when he turns in his key this afternoon, could you just find out if he's married or not? And then if he's not, get his phone number for me?"

She was so sweet in her eagerness and playfulness, Annie couldn't resist her. Shela had had an early unhappy marriage. The staff had gone through it all with her. She'd gotten engaged soon after she started working at Lincoln. She had been engaged for a year and had been so happy - bubbling over with love and joy all the time. The whole staff had enjoyed being around her and shared her happiness.

The young couple married at a big wedding with most of the staff in attendance. Within three months, however, she was looking sad and miserable. She lost weight until she was little more than a skeleton. She seldom talked to anyone and never joked. She didn't share any confidences with anyone on staff but they all guessed something was very, very wrong. She struggled with it for almost two years and then quietly put in a new emergency card with a change of address along with a change in the person to be contacted in the event of emergency - no husband's name on the card. That's how Annie found out it was over. Rumor had it once they were married, he was an old-fashioned husband who believed a wife should be subservient and his rights included physical and verbal abuse. As soon as she had separated from him, she became a changed person. She started talking again, started eating again, and gradually started joking again. They were all glad to have the old Shela back.

"Okay, okay, Shela. I'll see what I can do. Gad! I can't believe the things I do for you people."

Shela gave her a quick hug and went away laughing.

His name was Larry Crandall. He came in shortly after three o'clock and gave Annie the classroom key.

"It worked out all right today, Larry, didn't it?" she asked him.

"I had a great day. You sure have a nice staff at this school. I'd be happy to work here anytime you need a substitute. I'd appreciate it if you would ask for me."

"We'll do what we can, Larry. They usually ignore us when we ask for a specific person but we'll try. Come over here a minute, will you?" She pulled him into a corner and whispered, "I have a couple of people on the faculty who are interested in finding out if you are married or not. Are you?"

It was fun. She watched the startled look in his eyes. The quick thought as he wondered if she was interested in him, then the apprehension as he wondered what he was getting involved in, and then the impish -- why not? "Who is it?"

"I can't tell you,"

He laughed. "Okay. No, I'm not married."

"Would you consider giving me your phone number for publication?"

"Hey, what's going on?"

"The truth of the matter is I moonlight as a marriage broker. I'm trying to work up a commission."

He laughed heartily. He was clever enough to know she was joking. He gave her the phone number and asked, "Can I expect someone will call sometime soon and identify herself?"

"Yes, barring unforeseen circumstances, I expect that will happen."

"Should be interesting," he said with a smile. "Is my time up? May I leave now?"

"You surely may. Thanks, Larry. It's been a pleasure."

Annie called Shela's room and told her what she had found out.

"Hurrah! Did you find out how old he is?"

"No, I didn't. He's old enough for you. The rest you've got to find out for yourself. I've done all I'm going to do."

"Thanks, Annie. You've been a sweetheart."

"Yes, I know."

* * * * * * *

"Loren, I've looked all over but I can't find any large paper clips or large brown envelopes. Do you know where any are?"

"We don't have any. They're both on my list to order from Joe."

"Well, I need them right now. I guess I'll go up and get some. Be back in a minute." Annie took her keys so she could let herself into the supply room. She walked slowly as she savored being out of doors. She often felt the one big drawback to her job was having to be indoors all the time.

She unlocked the door to the supply room and pushed it back all the way so it would stay open. She gasped aloud as she stepped inside the room and saw she had interrupted a passionate embrace between Joe and Louise. They sprang apart as both their faces turned red in an agony of embarrassment.

"Annie, for crissake!" Joe said.

Louise turned her back to Annie so she could readjust her bra and button up her blouse. She felt her hair to see if it was in place and then quickly walked past Annie and was gone.

Annie sat down on a stack of boxes. "Joe, how could you?"

"What do you mean 'how could I?' Where do you get off coming here and checking on me? Stay in your own territory." He stood over her like an angry bear.

"Hey, wait a minute, let's keep the facts straight here." Annie stood up and faced him squarely. "I came here to get some supplies - just as I've done a hundred times before. How was I to know you'd turned the supply room into a love nest? I would have assumed you had more sense."

"Damn." He turned his back to her and walked to the other side of the room and paced back and forth.

Annie sat and watched him. She guessed he was feeling angry at himself for having been caught like a schoolboy. After all, the macho lover should be too adept at trysts to be caught - especially by someone like her whose respect he wanted to keep.

"Joe, come and sit down and talk to me a minute." He sat down on boxes near her. "Joe, what you do is no one's business until you throw it in their faces and make it their business. I've had two people talk to me already about you and Louise carrying on here on campus. If you want to have an affair, go ahead but only a fool does it on the job. What would you have done if it had been Elizabeth who walked in on you? She's got a key, too, you know."

"Yeah, I know. I know all that. The gal's gotten into my blood, though. I can't keep away from her. She's like a doll. She's so little and perfect. And she's so much fun. She's always happy and laughing. It feels good just to be around her. I'm crazy about her, Annie."

"She's married, Joe."

"Yeah, well, I don't know what to do about that. I guess they don't get along."

Annie wondered how Louise could always be so happy and laughing if she didn't get along with her husband. "Joe, maybe you need to cool it on the job and only see her after work. I'm afraid things might get out of hand here on campus and both you and Louise will, at the very least, be put in an embarrassing position with everyone talking about you. What do you think?"

"Sure - you're right. I'll be more careful."

"See you later, Joe." Annie walked out of the supply room, turned away from the office and walked the longest way around. She needed the extra time to calm herself.

When she finally headed back to the office, she knew she had been gone much too long.

"Where's the stuff?" asked Loren.

"The stuff?" Annie stared blankly at her.

"The paper clips and envelopes."

Annie stopped dead in her tracks. "I'm sorry. I got sidetracked. I'll get them later."

* * * * * * *

"What do you need?" Annie asked the little girl, about nine years old, who stood at the counter.

"Can I call home?" she pleaded.

"What for? What's the matter?" Annie asked. Little children always needed to call home for important reasons like they lost their Disneyland pin, or a favorite pencil, or could they go over Mary's house this afternoon. Since there were five hundred and fifty students on campus, if one was permitted to use the phone, all had to be allowed to use it; the rule was made that students must have either a phone pass from their teacher or a very good reason.

"My dog followed me to school. Can I call my mom to come and get him?" she asked as she fought back tears.

"Yes, go ahead."

She knew how to dial her number. Annie could hear it ringing and ringing.

"Nobody answers," she said in a little lost voice.

"Okay, come on. We'll put the dog in the pen. But you have to make sure he doesn't follow you any more. You have to check every morning to make sure he's tied up or in a fenced place. All right?"

"Yes," she answered while wiping tears away with the back of her hand. A small, nondescript mongrel was waiting outside the office door for her. The tail wagged ecstatically when she

appeared. She hugged him. "It's okay, Joshua, I'll put you in a safe place," she reassured him as she picked him up and carried him.

"Joshua?" Annie asked, surprised at the dignified name for the raggedy, colorless animal.

"It's my favorite boy's name, so that's what I named him. Isn't it a pretty name?"

"Oh, ah,...sure. Sure it is. Very pretty."

Annie helped her put him in the pen which was a chicken-wire and plywood concoction Joe had put together to hold the stray dogs. "You hurry to your room now and remember to get Joshua when you go home," she told her when they were finished.

"Okay, Mrs. Kallas," the girl called as she ran off. She went a little way then turned around and waved happily at Annie.

* * * * * * *

The mother and father of three boy students came in to complain to the principal.

"She's in a conference right at the moment. Would you like to wait or could someone else help you? Would you tell me what it's about?" Annie asked.

"No, we have to talk to her," the mother answered in a firm, resolute voice. "She reported us to the Child Protection Service and she had no right to do it. We take good care of our children. We want to complain to her about it."

"Yes, of course. May I have your names, please?"

"We're Mr. and Mrs. Lee," said Mrs. Lee. Mr. Lee wasn't saying anything - just nodded in agreement whenever his wife said anything.

"And the children's names, please?" Annie wanted to make sure she got the right Lee family.

"They're Anson, John, and Alfred," the mother answered.

"Thank you." She went to the card file and pulled the card to give to Elizabeth when she was free. "The principal has another parent in her office, so it may be a few minutes.

Please sit down at the table. May I get the newspaper for you?" She didn't want them to get angrier as they waited.

"No, we don't need it."

Annie went back to her desk. They all waited. She could see Mrs. Lee watching the second hand on the wall clock move. After about ten minutes, but what seemed like an hour, the principal's door opened.

"Thank you very much, Mrs. Leski. I appreciate your help," the parent said as she left the principal's office.

"Good-bye, Mrs. Sanglioux. I'll let you know as soon as I find out anything."

Annie followed Elizabeth back into her office and handed her the Lee children's card. "The parents are waiting. They want to complain about you sending CPS out after them."

"Oh? All right, send them in."

"Mr. and Mrs. Lee, please go in. The principal, Mrs. Leski, will see you now."

They walked briskly and determinedly into her office and closed the door behind them. Everything was quiet for a few minutes but then voices started getting louder and louder. Annie peeked through the window in the door and saw Elizabeth at her desk with Mr. and Mrs. Lee seated facing her. Mrs. Lee was getting loud but Elizabeth was quietly listening.

She can handle it, Annie thought proudly. The lady might be small but most of the time she's seven feet tall in behavior. She sat down at her desk and tried to concentrate but the situation was rapidly deteriorating. Voices got louder and Annie heard Mr. Lee say, "No woman is going to push me around and get me into trouble."

Elizabeth said firmly, "Mr. Lee, if you don't sit down immediately, you will be in even greater trouble. There is a law against creating a disturbance on school grounds."

Annie looked in the door again. She was afraid this might be getting out of hand. Mr. Lee started walking back to his seat but suddenly turned back to Elizabeth, leaned over her with his hands on the arms of her chair and with his face six inches from hers and said something Annie couldn't hear but made Elizabeth turn grim.

"That's enough," Annie said. "Loren, get Joe Sullivan up here immediately. It's an emergency." She went to open the principal's office door - but it wouldn't open. It was locked. She was astounded - how did that happen? She recovered quickly, grabbed her master key to unlock it and slammed the door open.

Mr. Lee stood up immediately and backed away from Elizabeth. It felt as if the pressure which had built up in the room was quickly dissipating through the open door. Annie stood facing them in the doorway ready to do battle. Joe Sullivan came up and stood next to her.

"We'll leave now," said Mrs. Lee.

"Just a minute, Mr. and Mrs. Lee," said Elizabeth as she stood up. "I want to make sure you understand clearly that it is against the law to create a disturbance on school grounds. It is also against the law to threaten a school employee. If either of those events should happen here again, I want you to know I will file charges against you. Do you understand?"

They murmured something and stamped out angrily.

"Wow!" Annie said.

"What's going on?" asked Joe.

"Are you all right, Elizabeth?"

"Yes, I'm all right. But thanks for coming to my rescue."

"What did he say to you? You looked so grim."

"Yes, I'm sure I did. He said, 'I'll get even with you, you bitch'."

Annie gasped. "Elizabeth, you sure you don't want to prefer charges now? That's disgraceful."

"No, I don't think it'll happen again. They don't want any more trouble than they already have. He's a lot of hot air. Let's just settle down and get back to normal."

"One more thing, Elizabeth. How did your door get locked?"

"I don't know. Mr. Lee must have pushed the lock button on the door when he came in."

* * * * * * *

"Annie, got a minute?" Joe asked.
"Sure, Joe, what do you need?"
"Come with me. I want to show you something."
"Where are we going?" she asked as they left the office.
"You remember room thirteen's rat?"
"Yes, did you find him?"
"Yeah, and I want to show you where." Joe led her to ramp four where they went into the small storage room behind the students' bathroom. Joe had some old unused furniture stored there. One of the pieces was an ancient four drawer file cabinet. "Listen." He banged lightly on the cabinet. Annie could hear a rustling noise coming from inside.
"Is he in there?"
"He's in there."
"How on earth did you find him?"
"By accident. I came in here looking for some sixteen inch chairs. I leaned against the file cabinet for a minute and heard the rustling. I knew right away what it was. Whoever put him in there is keeping him alive. There's food and water in there. Want to see him?"
"No. Thanks, but no thanks. Do you think Clyde did it?"
"Who else? Whoever did it has to have a master key to get in this room and into the classroom. It was either you, me, Elizabeth, or Clyde. We're the only ones with the key. My money would be on Clyde. It's his way of protesting having to clean a room with a rat in it."
Annie smiled. "It really is kind of funny. I feel kind of the same way myself."
"It's not funny," Joe said.
"What are you going to do now?"
Joe gave a sigh of exasperation. "I'll have to have another talk with him and tell him again that he doesn't have the right to remove the teacher's property just because he doesn't like it there. The results of my lecture will last about two months and then we'll start the fun and games all over again. I wish the guy would get a job

somewhere else and quit. Well, I've got a box here to put the little critter into. Want to help me?"

"I'll hold the box - not the rat."

"Okay, hold it right there." Joe eased open the file cabinet drawer. The rat was tame so he cooperated when Joe picked him up and put him into the box. Joe closed the cover and locked up the room and they walked rapidly to room thirteen. Annie went along to watch the children's reactions to getting their rat back. When they walked into the room, Joe said, "Excuse me, Miss Glas. I located your rat and brought him back to you."

The students yelled, "Hooray!" They all clustered around Joe and watched eagerly as he took the cover off the box.

Miss Glas picked the rat up and held him for all to see. "There he is. He seems to be perfectly healthy. I'm sure he'll be glad to get back into his cage. We'll go back into the same routine of keeping him clean and fed. Agreed?"

"Agreed," shouted the students.

While the class watched the rat, Joe told Norma how he found it. He told her he would handle Clyde.

"That's fine. You do it. I'm just happy to get the rat back. Thanks, Joe. I really appreciate your efforts."

"Glad to do it."

"See you later, Joe," Annie said as she hurried back to the office.

* * * * * * *

"What on earth is going on?" Annie asked loudly, trying to make her voice heard over the noise of five small voices all complaining at once. "I can't understand you," she yelled, "be quiet. Now, Alisha, you tell me what happened." Annie pointed to a fifth grade girl who she knew was sensible and mature.

"Mrs. Kallas, there's a little first grade girl standing out there by the bus. The bus driver won't let her on the bus because she's got... well, you know..." Alisha hesitated, having trouble getting the words out.

"What? Alisha, she's got what?" Annie prodded her. She had visions of the bus leaving and she would have five students on her hands to figure out how to get home.

"She's got bugs in her hair," said Jimmy. "The driver won't let her on because she's got a paper that says she's got bugs in her hair."

"That's right, Mrs. Kallas. That's why the driver won't let her on," explained Alisha.

"So, now, Mrs. Kallas," added Becky, "the little girl is standing there by the bus crying. It's so sad. And you know, Mrs. Kallas, the driver told everyone on the bus what's wrong with her. It was so embarrassing for her. The driver shouldn't have done it. My teacher says anyone can get head lice - it has nothing to do with being clean," Becky said.

"Your teacher is absolutely right and so are you, Becky," Annie said. She was impressed with the child's astuteness. "Okay, let's go out and see what's going on." She went out the front door with the five students trailing behind her but stopped short at the scene before her. Everyone had gone home. The front of the school was quiet with only the one school bus still parked in the driveway. Everyone was on the bus, including the driver. The door to the bus was closed. Nothing moved.

A little girl was standing alone on the sidewalk facing the closed bus door. She stood quietly with tears running down her cheeks and the incriminating paper in her hand. The tableau was unbelievably vivid. The thought passed through Annie's mind of how many millions of people over the centuries did this picture before her represent? How many children, for how many stupid reasons, had been locked out of some place because someone decreed it and thus wounded some part of their souls?

She walked quickly up to the child, put her arm around her, and said, "We'll take you home, honey, don't cry. It'll be okay."

Annie looked through the glass in the bus door at the driver who reluctantly opened the door. "You kids get on the bus and I want to thank you all for telling me about this," Annie said to the five who had come in the office.

"Bye, Mrs. Kallas," they said.

After they got on, Annie said to the driver, "Come down here please, I want to talk to you."

"I have to get this bus going. We're already ten minutes late."

"If you don't come down right now, I'll write a letter about you and what you've done to this child to your supervisor, with a copy to Personnel and the School Board."

The driver reluctantly got out of her seat and came down the three steps to the ground. The first grader Annie was holding onto stepped behind her to hide as the driver came near.

"Well, what do you want?"

"I want to give you a chance to tell your side of the story," Annie offered.

"There's nothing to tell. The girl's got lice - she doesn't get on the bus. It's as simple as that."

"Oh, really? If it was that simple, why didn't you just bring her into the office instead of getting on your your loudspeaker and broadcasting to everyone on the bus why she couldn't ride? Didn't you think that was a little cruel?"

"No, I wanted everyone to understand if they had lice they couldn't ride on the bus."

"What's your name?"

"I'm Jennifer Radford."

"Well, Jennifer, tell me why you felt you had the right to read the note this child was carrying home to her mother?" Annie asked, struggling to keep her voice calm and controlled.

"She held it out to me so I thought it was for me."

"I see. Well, you have an answer for everything."

"Hey, you know I'm right. Kids with lice don't ride the bus."

"Jennifer, I know kids with lice don't ride the bus. You're right about that. She should not have been put on the bus. What you're wrong about is the way you did it. It was totally unnecessary to shame this child in front of sixty other children on the bus. And it was certainly cruel to leave her standing crying in front of your closed door with no idea of what she had done wrong to deserve not being allowed on the bus or any idea of how she was going to get home."

"That's not my problem."

"Let me tell you what your problem is, Jennifer. Your problem from now on is me. You are an unfeeling, insensitive fool. I certainly hope your judgment while driving is better than when standing still. I'm giving you a warning: if you pull a stunt like this on another of our Lincoln kids, I will write a letter about it and it will be put in your personnel file. Now get this bus out of here. All these parents will be calling to see where their children are."

Annie turned around, took the child's hand and walked back to the office while she tried to control her fury. How could anyone be so idiotic?

"What's your name?" she asked the child as they entered the office.

"Patricia Hernandez."

"Patricia, you sit down there at the table and read a book and we'll figure out some way to get you home. Is your mother home?"

"Yes."

"Do you have a phone?"

"No."

"Well, we'll find someone."

Annie sat down at her desk and said, "Loren."

Loren turned to face her. "Yes, Annie?"

"Loren, how did this child get on the bus with pediculosis?"

"I put her on," Loren answered in her usual sweet, innocent way. "Their phone's been disconnected and there was no other way to get her home. She only has a few nits in her hair. I didn't think it would hurt anything."

"I thought I had explained to you sick children do not go home on the bus - and that includes children with lice. The bus driver was right not to allow the child on the bus. She was wrong in the way she handled it. And you were wrong in the way you handled it. I want you now to handle it correctly. The problem is: you have a child here with head lice. How are you going to get her home? Solve the problem."

Loren blinked back tears at the reprimand and quietly said, "Yes, Annie."

Annie went back to the speech and language specialist's report on a student she had been typing when the five students had come bursting in the door. About ten minutes later, Loren interrupted her, "Annie, I found a neighbor who gave me the number of an aunt of Patricia's who has both a phone and a car. The aunt is on the way now to pick her up." Loren was proud of herself and smiling happily.

"Well, you found a way, didn't you? But you found it about an hour too late and put Patricia through a totally unnecessary heartbreaking experience because of your poor judgment." Loren got tears in her eyes again but Annie was past caring. She was tired of having to tell her the same things over and over again. Maybe shedding some tears would help her to remember what she had been taught.

FEBRUARY

"I'm going to tell on you--"
"You're not going to tell nothin' 'cause I didn't do nothin."
"We want to see the principal."

Annie put on her most icy glare and walked up to the counter. "I'm sure you mean, may we see the principal, please?" She stood in front of them and waited. She looked from one to the other, a little African-American girl and a little white girl, third graders, with tight mouths and sizzling eyes - furious with each other.

The little white girl, Debbie, stared sullenly at Annie a moment and finally said, "May we see the principal, please?"

"That's better. What's the problem?"

"La Tanya stole my valentines. I had thirty-two valentines in a bag - one for everyone in the room - and La Tanya stole them when we were on the bus."

"I did not," La Tanya said. "How can you lie like that?"

"You were sitting next to me and now they're gone. You were the only one who had a chance to take them - and, anyway, everybody knows niggers always steal."

There was a stunned silence as everything stopped short at that last statement. Loren and the mother she was talking to gave gasps of shock and stared at the offending Debbie.

La Tanya was the first to recover and sprang into action. She made a grab for Debbie's long blonde hair and pulled hard. "You can't call me names like that. And you lie!"

Debbie shrieked in pain and retaliated by grabbing hold of one of La Tanya's braids with one hand and slapped her across the face with the other.

Annie was appalled as she realized she suddenly had a full-fledged fight on her hands. "Loren, grab La Tanya and put her in the health office. I'll get Debbie."

They ran to the other side of the counter and pulled

the two girls apart. La Tanya went with Loren and sat down on the cot. She was crying quietly. Loren got an ice pack for her to put on her face. Debbie struggled with Annie as she led her to the principal's office and finally pulled herself free.

"I'll go by myself," she said. She plopped herself down on a chair, crossed her arms on her chest, and stared out of the window.

Annie went to the intercom and called for the principal.

"Yes, what's wrong?" Elizabeth asked when she came in.

Annie explained to her what had happened.

"Since Debbie is already in my office, I'll talk to her first." She went in and closed the door behind her.

"Loren, call both their teachers and tell them briefly what happened. Remind them to mark the girls present on their attendance sheet," Annie instructed her.

She went into the health office to see how La Tanya was doing. She was holding the ice pack to her cheek. "Let me see how it looks, La Tanya. Does it hurt?"

"No, not anymore. Why would she slap me, Mrs. Kallas? I didn't steal her ole valentines."

"Well, La Tanya, you did pull her hair first."

"She called me a name. She had no right to do that."

"No, of course she didn't. You're perfectly right. But you didn't make it better by pulling her hair, either, did you?"

"She had no right," La Tanya repeated.

"Mrs. Leski will give you a chance to tell her how you feel. She's talking to Debbie now. Your face seems to be okay. It's not red or swollen anymore. Do you think it's all right for me to put the ice pack away now?"

"Yes, it's okay."

About ten minutes later, Mrs. Leski opened the door and told Debbie to sit down at the front table. She then called La Tanya into her office and closed the door. Another ten minutes passed and she called Debbie back in. Another ten minutes and Elizabeth opened the door.

"Mrs. Kallas, these girls have phoned their mothers

and explained what happened. La Tanya has been suspended for one day for fighting; Debbie for two days for fighting and being insulting to another student. They both understand now that fighting is not an acceptable way to solve problems and one does not accuse another person of a wrongdoing without some proof. The girls will wait here until their mothers come to get them. They are on their way. I will discuss this with the teachers. La Tanya can wait in the health office. Debbie can stay in my office."

She hurried back onto the campus. The girls were tearful and subdued. La Tanya's mother arrived first.

"I'm Mrs. Moore. I came for La Tanya."

La Tanya walked toward her mother - her head held down with her chin touching her chest, her eyes looking at the floor.

"I never thought a child of mine would be suspended from school."

La Tanya burst out crying. Her mother stood and looked at her and shook her head. "Girl, I've told you and told you to never let a Honkie get to you." Mrs. Moore went out the door with La Tanya following.

Mrs. Wycliffe, Debbie's mother, arrived a few minutes later. "I came to get my daughter. Where is she?"

"Debbie, your mom's here." Annie went into Elizabeth's office and prodded Debbie out. She was obviously very reluctant to face her mother.

Mrs. Wycliffe grabbed Debbie's arm and shook her. "I can't believe you did that. How could you hurt someone's feelings like that? I'm really ashamed of you. Come on, let's get home. You're going to spend the next two days in your room."

Annie and Loren looked at each other after the girls left. "That's a hell of a way to start a day that's supposed to celebrate love."

"I'm sure the rest of the day will be better, Annie," Loren said soothingly in her sweet, naive voice.

And it was. Loren was right. St. Valentine's day was

one of the children's favorite holidays and they were excited and happy. It seemed as if half the school brought valentines to the office and to the principal. Parents came with cupcakes, candy, and Kool-aid for the afternoon parties. When the day ended, everyone was full of sweets and everyone loved everyone else -- at least, as far as they could tell.

* * * * * * *

Ray had invited Annie to dinner at his house and greeted her at the door with a dozen long stemmed roses as a present on St. Valentine's day, the special day for lovers.

"Why, Ray, they're beautiful! What have I done to deserve these?"

"I'll tell you later - after we eat this scrumptious meal I fixed just for the occasion."

"What are we having?" she asked as she tried to hide her surprise at his sudden romantic attitude.

"Well, we're starting with pacific crab puffs as an appetizer, then we'll have asparagus and shrimp vinaigrette salad, the entrée is veal stroganoff and after that a Russian crème for dessert. How does that sound?" Ray asked with a proud smile on his face.

Annie looked at him in amazement. "When have you had time to do all this?"

"I've been working on it all week. It's going to be fabulous because it's been a labor of love. I want this to be a very special meal. Come into the dining room and we'll start on the crab puffs and have a glass of wine while I put the finishing touches on everything."

"I'm stuffed, Ray. That was absolutely the most delicious meal I've ever had. If you ever decide to give up teaching, you could easily be a chef in some fine restaurant."

He laughed in appreciation. "Good, I'm glad you like my cooking, Annie, because I'd like you to start eating a whole lot more of it."

"Sure, anytime. As I told you, I hate to cook but I don't hate to eat and this is the best food I've ever been lucky enough to have someone fix for me."

"Want to take a walk around the block, Annie, so we don't get sleepy from eating? Then we can come back here and dance a little in honor of St. Valentine's day."

As they walked, Ray held her hand and after an extended silence, said, "I have something I want to talk to you about, Annie."

"Oh? Okay, go ahead," she said with a small prickle of fear running through her. Was that great meal a consolation for something? She steeled herself for what was to come.

"Let's go sit on that park bench so I can look at you while I talk to you."

He faced her and took her hands in his. "Annie, I need to tell you how much you've come to mean to me. I find myself waiting from the day I see you until the next day I can see you. Alone, that is, I don't count at school. You've become the bright spot in my life."

Annie listened in silence as she waited for the ax to fall. Was all of this leading up to him telling her he couldn't see her any more because she was beginning to mean too much to him and he didn't want to get serious? Her fear grew.

"You, more than anyone, know how hard it's been for me to get over Helen's death. Every time I enjoyed some other woman's company I felt like I was being a traitor to her. We were married for so long and expected to be married all our lives. We were so close, like two parts of a whole, that I couldn't acknowledge my other part was gone." He paused and stood up and paced up and down in front of her for a minute and then sat down and gathered her hands in his again.

"But it's been a year now and I can feel I'm gradually changing. Nobody can ever replace Helen in my previous life but I'm starting to feel I can and should make another life. Helen would want me to. She wouldn't want me to be sad and alone forever. What do you think, Annie?"

She hesitated. What was he looking for from her?

"Well, I think you're right, Ray. Helen wouldn't want you to mourn forever and she would know you won't ever forget her but she wouldn't want you to be miserable in order to mourn her. Your life has to go on when you're ready. Are you ready now, Ray?" Is that what this is all about, she asked herself.

"I'm getting there, Annie, and I wondered if you would be interested in making the journey with me." He kissed her hands while he looked into her face for an answer.

She wished he'd be a little more specific. Exactly what journey was he talking about? "Do you know where this journey will take us, Ray?"

"To the stars and back, I hope. No, Annie, I don't know exactly where it will take us but if you're willing to take a chance, perhaps the journey itself will be its own reward. What do you say? Will you come with me?"

"I'd like to say yes but I'm not sure of what commitment I would be making."

"Only the commitment to be together as much as possible and see where it leads us." As she hesitated, he added, "You've become so important to me I don't know what I'll do if you said no."

"I won't say no to you, Ray. You're important to me, too. I look forward to seeing you in my life just as you do me. But if we're going to start being more than friends, you have to try to understand me, too, and understand it's become hard for me to trust any man enough to make a commitment to him. It would be something I'll have to learn to do and I imagine it will take a while. I've been out of practice for a long time."

"We can learn together, darling. It can be part of the journey. Just so long as we can struggle with it together. That's the important part. Do you agree? Are you game?"

She leaned over and kissed him lightly on the lips. "I agree. I'm game. When do we set off on this journey?"

"Right now." He jubilantly pulled her to her feet and pressed the length of his body into hers. Then, putting one hand behind her head to hold her still, he kissed her gently and lovingly which turned into fiery passion as she put her arms around him to hold him close.

"We need to go back to the house, now, darling," he said.

* * * * * * *

"I gotta get in m'room," announced a third grader standing at the counter.

"You'll never get it if that's the best way you can ask. It's three-thirty. You should be home." Annie expected to be freed of students by three-thirty. It was always an irritant when they came back after school and needed something. She went back to work.

"Lady, you betta let me in m'room to get m'homework."

Annie looked up again. "Get out of here. You won't get me to do anything for you when you talk to me like that."

The boy looked at her with what he hoped was a fierce look on his face. "You'll do it or I'll shoot. I'm warnin' you - I'll shoot," he said. He waved a toy gun at her.

"You're Jimmy Randall, aren't you?" she asked, walking up to the counter. He was a pale, skinny, blond boy in worn-out old clothes who looked like he needed to eat some fresh vegetables.

"That's me, Jimmy Randall. And I'm gonna be famous. I got this here gun and I'm gonna get famous with it."

"Jimmy, you've been watching too much television. You take your gun and go on back home. If you've forgotten your homework, it's your responsibility. You'll have to settle it with your teacher tomorrow." She walked around the counter, took him firmly by the arm and walked him to the door and gently shoved him outside. "Go on home. I have work to do and I don't want to be bothered with little boys with bad manners." She closed the door behind him, went back to her desk, and immediately forgot about him.

Annie and Loren closed up at four o'clock and went out to their cars. They suddenly heard a noise like a car backfire and then the night custodian, Clyde, give a yell. They looked at each other. "You go on home, Loren. I'll go see what Clyde's into."

"Okay, goodnight. See you tomorrow."

Annie walked over to ramp one to see if she could see the custodian's cart with cleaning supplies outside of a room. Clyde's cart was outside of room three but there was no one in the room. She kept walking toward the end of the building and was going to turn up toward ramp two when suddenly, as she turned the corner to see the playground, Clyde yelled, "watch out" and she heard a shot and something whizzed past her bare arm. She stepped back against the building out of sight.

"Was that a bullet?" she asked. "Is somebody shooting at me?" She was so surprised, she wasn't even frightened. She eased around the corner in hopes she could see what was going on. She took a quick look and then ducked back.

She couldn't believe it. It was Jimmy Randall holding a gun on Clyde. It took a moment to sink in. Was the gun real? For crissake, was the gun he brought in the office real? WAS THE GUN REAL AND LOADED? She could feel her knees getting weak. She slid to the ground with her back against the wall. She took three deep breaths, waited another minute and then stumbled to her feet. She took another look around the corner. Clyde was trying to talk Jimmy into giving him the gun. Good God! Her heart started pounding and she put her hand over her mouth to stifle any sound. Now she was scared! She turned and ran wildly back into the office. She unlocked the door and ran to the phone. She dialed the police.

"Is this an emergency?"

"Yes, yes! This is the school secretary at Lincoln Elementary. We have a student on campus holding a loaded gun on our custodian."

"What is your name, please?"

"Kallas. K-A-L-L-A-S."

"Your first name?"

"Annie. A-N-N-I-E."
"The address of the school?"
"2111 Monterey Drive." She wanted to scream.
"The nearest cross street?"
"Juanita Street." She would have screamed but she knew it would only slow things up even more.
"We'll have a car out there immediately."
"Thank you." She went back outside in front of the school to wait for the police car. She wondered if Clyde was still alive. She didn't know if she would have heard any more shots while she was on the phone. She paced back and forth in front of the school. It seemed like she'd been waiting an hour but it was probably less than two minutes since she'd hung up the phone.

She heard a child screaming. She ran over to ramp one and saw Clyde walking toward her holding Jimmy around the waist under his arm. Jimmy was kicking his legs and waving his arms and yelling in frustration. Clyde held him away from his own body so the arms and legs wouldn't hurt him and was obviously enjoying making Jimmy feel helpless. Clyde had the gun hanging on a stick in his other hand.

The police drove up and as they got out of the car, Annie pointed to Clyde. "He'll tell you all about it, officer. He's our night custodian."

"Here's the kid and the gun. He fired one shot at Mrs. Kallas and two at me. We're all lucky he doesn't know how to aim."

One of the officers took the gun away from Clyde. "Can we go inside and talk?" asked the other officer.

"Sure, come into the office." Annie led the way. Clyde took Jimmy in and deposited him in the corner seat at the table and sat down next to him. The two officers sat opposite them. Annie leaned against the counter.

She pulled Jimmy's index card and gave it to the officer. "This has all the pertinent data on him: name, address, birth date, parents."

"Thanks," he smiled at her. "That's a help. Your name, please," he asked Clyde. Clyde gave him his personal information and then proceeded to tell what happened.

"I was cleaning room three when this kid comes and says he's got to get into room nine right away to get his homework. Well, man, I don't stop what I'm doing to get some kid his homework that he should've thought about before he went home. Especially when the kid acts like I have to do it for him. I told him no, I wouldn't - to go on home.

"I went back to my cleaning and next thing I know I got a gun stuck in my back. Well, mister, I was in the army. I know when I got a gun in my back. For a minute, I couldn't believe this crazy kid would hold a gun on me. Man, I weigh two hundred pounds. He probably weighs about fifty but I guess he figured the gun was his equalizer. Just as I was wondering if it was loaded, he fired a shot at the ceiling and said, 'Just wanna show you I know how to shoot, so you do what I tell you and maybe you won't get hurt.'

"I thought to myself that this kid's been watching too much TV and if that's true, he might think it's all right to shoot somebody 'cause he's seen it so much on the tube. Anyway, I figured I better go along with the program until I could get my chance. I said, 'Okay kid, we'll go to room nine.' We started walking up the ramp when I guess I didn't move fast enough for him 'cause he shot at my foot and almost hit it and I yelled at him."

"That must have been the shot and yell I heard as I was leaving," Annie said.

Clyde nodded at her. He continued, "I walked him up the playground way to room nine. I thought if I could get him out into the open I'd have a better chance to do something. That's where you saw us, Annie. After he shot at you, I tried to explain to him that no homework was important enough to go to jail for. But what finally gave me my chance was an itch."

"An itch?" Annie asked.

"Yeah. The kid got an itch in his crotch. He wiggled and

squirmed trying to get rid of it but he couldn't. He had to scratch it. He was holding the gun on me with two hands. He had to let go with one. When he did, I got him. When he scratched, the gun pointed at the sky for a minute and I knocked him down and got the gun. It was a pleasure sitting on that kid. I'm real proud of the fact I didn't hit him. Let me tell you, I wanted to. Not many men have bested me - I can't see an eight year old kid even trying."

Annie could see now it was over, Clyde started to get angry. "Clyde, you were great in the way you handled the whole thing. I know the principal is going to be really proud of you."

"He deliberately shot at you, Annie. He could've killed you." He turned to Jimmy sitting next to him, grabbed him by his shoulders and shook him. "You little bastard, who the hell do you think you are?" Clyde turned to the officers and pleaded, "Let me take this kid outside and give him the whipping he deserves."

"Can't let you do it, man, but I know what you mean," the officer replied.

"Let me tell you what happened before he even got to Clyde," Annie suggested to the officers, trying to give Clyde a chance to cool off.

"Go ahead, ma'am."

"I feel like such a fool because I didn't even know the gun was real. It looks just like the toy ones. Now that I think of it, I don't think I've ever seen a real hand gun close up." Annie told them what Jimmy had said to her in the office and how she had shoved him out. "What's going to happen to him now?"

"We'll take him home to his parents. To tell you the truth, not much happens to them if they're under the age of ten. We still have to find out where he got the gun. Has he been in trouble before?"

"Not that I know of," Annie answered. "He doesn't get sent to the office."

"We'll check it out and get back to you. Thanks for your

help. Come on, boy, let's see what your parents have to say about this." One of the officers took Jimmy by the arm and they went out to the police car.

"Do I get to ride in a black and white?" Jimmy asked.

"I wonder if he's all there?" Annie said to Clyde. "I didn't notice he had any feelings that he's done anything wrong. He wasn't sorry or ashamed or even worried about what his parents would say. It's as if he didn't realize he did something very wrong. Wow! We better watch him if he comes back here."

"Yeah, I noticed it, too. No guilt - no fear - no trying to blame it on someone else - no crying that he got caught. Just happy he got to ride in a police car. It's strange, Annie. Even an eight year old should have some feelings that he did something wrong."

"Clyde, are you all right? Can I go home or do you want me to do something for you?"

"Hey, gal, I'm okay. I'll call Joe and tell him what happened. He probably won't believe me."

"Well, if you're all right, I'm going. I'll phone Elizabeth from home."

* * * * * * *

It was eight o'clock Monday morning and the office was in its usual turmoil for the hour: children wanting to pay lunch money for the coming week, bus drivers bringing in naughty students with the resultant bus tickets, parents wanting to enroll children, children who came to school sick or got hurt on the way.

Annie was working at the counter helping Loren handle it all when out of the corner of her eye she noticed Elizabeth bringing Mrs. Wallace in from the staffroom through the office into the principal's office. Neither of them said a word to her. Mrs. Wallace didn't look hurt like the time her husband had beaten her, she just looked wan and tearful. Annie kept working with Loren but noticed a few minutes later that the psychologist also went into the principal's office. Then, shortly thereafter, the nurse went in. She was getting more and more puzzled. What was going on? The conversation in there was quiet and subdued. She waited.

When they came out about twenty minutes later, Mrs. Wallace looked even more tearful and even more subdued. After they left, Annie followed the principal back into her office and asked, "What on earth is going on? Everyone looks like death warmed over."

In a very quiet, controlled voice but with her hands trembling, Elizabeth said, "Mrs. Wallace had Mr. Wallace arrested over the week-end. He's in jail now. She discovered he's been sexually abusing all three of the oldest children for at least the past year. The oldest girl told her and then the other two corroborated it."

Annie sat down. "Oh, God, how terrible! His own children - how could he?" She felt as though someone had struck her in the face.

Elizabeth continued as though she wasn't there. "She's terrified but she's determined he'll go to jail for this and she's also determined to get a divorce."

"Good."

"The children will all have to have a physical by a doctor out of the District Attorney's office. If the father doesn't plead guilty, the children will have to testify against him. Mrs. Wallace wonders how this could have been happening right in her own house without her knowing it. She feels responsible and guilty that her children suffered so and she didn't help them. Annie, I explained to her it was to be expected she wouldn't see it happening. A wife often is, and maybe should be, the last person in the world to believe her husband capable of such actions.

"The psychologist and the nurse have both offered to counsel mother and children as needed. She might come to you for some help. You have my permission to do what you feel you can.

"I feel so incredibly sorry for these people," Elizabeth continued. "Did they ever have a chance? And now look at the children - how much will they be damaged by this? And Mrs. Wallace - she was content to be a wife and mother - proud of her husband and family. This will either make or break her. There won't be a man for her to lean on anymore. She made her first steps toward her own independence this last weekend when she moved to enforce what she believed was right instead of dissolving at what must have been a disastrous shock to her. Well, we'll help her all we can and hope for the best."

* * * * * * *

"Teacher," called a first grade boy as he stood at the counter.

"My name is Mrs. Kallas. I am not a teacher," Annie explained. Even the teachers got irritated at being called 'teacher' instead of by their names.

He looked her full in the eyes. Annie felt she was watching him process the information she had given him. Then he discarded it and again said, "Teacher."

She gave up. "Yes, what is it?"

"Teacher, there's pee-pee in a jar."

"What?" she said. "What do you mean?"

He was annoyed at her lack of understanding. "Teacher, there's pee-pee in a jar in the boys' bathroom," he said loudly and emphatically as only a six year old can do.

Annie was mystified. "Come and show me." Pee-pee in a jar? What could that mean? Had someone taken a urine specimen and left it in the bathroom by mistake? She held the front door open for him and asked, "What ramp?"

"Ramp one, teacher." He was a serious little boy. He was as tall as her hipbone and very important and determined as they walked along. She remembered this boy's family because the mother was white, the father African-American. They had three boys in school - each cuter than the next. This one was the youngest. She had never met the father but the mother was a lovely, cooperative woman.

"Which one are you? I can't remember your name," she asked as they walked along.

"My name is Christopher Bruce Scott," he answered. He had obviously been coached as to how to respond to someone asking his name.

"Here's where it is." He led her into the boys' bathroom. He walked up to one of the urinals and showed her the jar sitting in it. It was the type jar mayonnaise comes in. The cover lay on the floor. The jar itself was three quarters full of urine. "There it is, teacher. There's the pee-pee in the jar."

"Yes, Chris, I see it. Chris, do you know why it's here?"

"Sure I know." He looked at her scornfully.

"Well, why is it here?"

"Cause they're playing Pee-Pee in a Jar."

"You mean it's a game?"

"Sure, teacher. Don't you know that game?"

"No, Chris, I don't know that game." But she had a feeling she was going to learn more about it than she wanted to. "Tell me about it."

"You just put the jar in there," pointing to the urinal, "and see if you can get your pee-pee into the jar."

"I see. Do you know who brought the jar in?"

"It was Raymond."

"What room is Raymond in?"

"In my room, room four."

"Okay, Chris. Well, I guess I'm going to have to take the jar into the office and show it to the principal." Annie picked up the lid, screwed it tightly onto the jar, gingerly picked the jar up by the lid and rinsed it off in the sink. "Chris, thank you very much for telling us about this. You can go back to your room now. Your teacher will be wondering where you are."

"Bye, teacher."

Annie walked back to the office carefully holding the jar at arm's length. "Elizabeth is going to love this."

Loren was helping some parents at the counter and stared, open-mouthed, as Annie walked past her into the principal's office - the jar of urine held prominently in front of her. "I have a present for you, Elizabeth."

"Is that what I think it is in your hands?"
"Yes, ma'am."
"So, we're back to Pee-pee in a Jar, are we?"
"Yes, ma'am," Annie said trying to stifle a laugh. "I see you've heard of it before. It's a new one on me."
"It seems to crop out every once in a while. Did you find out who started it?"
"Chris Scott told me about it. He says Raymond started it and brought the jar in."
"That might be true. Raymond is a walker and could bring the jar in. Chris rides the bus and the bus driver wouldn't let him on the bus with a jar."
Annie looked at Elizabeth in amazement. "How on earth can you remember who walks and who rides the bus?"
"I don't know. I guess it comes with the territory. I'll take care of this," she said as she took the jar. "Send Chris and Raymond to me, please."
"Sure." Annie went back to her desk and called room four on the intercom.
"Excuse me, Mrs. Curtis."
"Yes?" she called into the speaker.
"Please send Chris and Raymond to the office."
"Okay."
When the boys arrived, Annie directed them into the principal's office. "Raymond, did you bring the jar in to school for Pee-pee in a Jar?" Elizabeth asked.
"No, not me." Raymond stared at the carpet.
"Do you know who did?"
"No, not me." Raymond stared at the ceiling.
"Do you know how the jar got into the bathroom?"
"No, not me." Raymond stared at the wall.
"Chris, do you know who brought the jar to school?"
"Raymond did."
"No, not me. It wasn't me," cried Raymond.
"Chris, what makes you think Raymond did it?"
"He told me. He took me into the bathroom and showed me the jar. He said that now we could play Pee-pee in a Jar. He said he brought it in so we could play."

"Raymond, what do you want to say to that?"

"Nothin'."

"Well, boys, I want to explain to you that playing Pee-pee in a Jar is a very dangerous and unsanitary game to play. The jar could break and someone could get cut by the glass. Also, there are germs in the urine - the pee-pee - that could make someone sick so we don't want urine to be anywhere but flushed down the urinal or the toilet. I do not expect to find another jar like this on the school grounds again. Do you both understand?"

The boys nodded at her.

"Chris, you did the right thing in reporting this to us. You may both go back to your room now."

After the boys left, Elizabeth walked into the health office bathroom with the jar, flushed the contents down the toilet and discarded the jar. She thoroughly washed her hands. "They never mentioned things like this in administration school," she said.

* * * * * * *

Annie and Ray were sitting in his living room after dinner. "Ray, I have a story about a first grade kid. Want to hear it?"

"Sure. Why not? But come sit here next to me while you tell it."

"No, I can't. I have to be facing you so I can see your reaction."

"Okay, go ahead. I'm listening," he said as he looked at her affectionately.

"Well, the psychologist - you know, Brigitte Vordstrom - got a referral for testing on a first grade boy - his name's Albert -because he wasn't learning anything and wouldn't work. The teacher had already contacted the mother a couple of times whose only comment was that she didn't know how to make him work. As a last resort, the teacher got the mother's approval for testing. "Brigitte took the little fellow to her office one day and started giving him all the tests she routinely does. He thought it was fun and cooperated with her. The first session went quickly and smoothly. At the second session about a week later, she says he pulled his chair up beside her - instead of across from her as they had done the time before. She was pleased he had enough confidence in her to want to be close to her so they settled down happily to complete the testing.

"Suddenly, Brigitte says, she became aware of a light touch on her thigh. She was concentrating on the testing so she didn't really think about it. She continued on with what she was doing but a few minutes later she felt a more insistent touch right in her crotch area. That got her attention. She and the boy had their heads almost touching working together on the papers. She says her hand holding her pencil froze in mid-air. She held absolutely still without saying anything and waited to see what would happen. Sure enough, the hand progressed further down into her crotch area - remember, this is a first grade boy."

"How can I forget?"

She laughed at the look on his face. "Well, Brigitte took the little hand and placed it back on the table top. 'Do you like me, Albert?' she asked.

'Yeah, you're a nice lady,' he told her.

'Is that why you like to touch me?'

'Yeah, I like to touch ladies,' he smiled.

"Brigitte finished the test on which they were working to gain time to think of the best way to get further information on this latest development."

Annie laughed. "Ray, can you imagine a first grade kid making a pass at the psychologist? Brigitte was absolutely stunned."

Ray shook his head in wonderment. "They sure make them precocious these days, don't they?"

"Well, when they finished that test, Brigitte got out another one which I guess is designed to find out how a kid feels about his family. He drew a picture indicating he thinks his mother is really pretty and nice. He drew a picture of himself - get this - with a penis the size of a club.

When Brigitte asked him if his penis was really that big, he said, 'My what? Oh, you mean my dick? Sometimes it acts that big," and laughed happily. She asked him to draw a picture of his father. He drew a stick figure of a man behind bars.

'Is your father in jail?' she asked him.

'That's what my mama says', he answered in a sad voice. But then he brightened. 'But mama gets me a lot of uncles to take us places.'

'Do you like them?' Brigitte asked. 'Are they nice to you?"

'Yeah, they're nice. They're nice to mama, too. They bring her presents.'

'Draw me a picture of an uncle, will you, Albert?'

'Sure, here's one." He worked a few minutes and proudly showed Brigitte. It was a larger version of himself with an even larger club size penis.

'Is the uncle's dick really that big?' asked Brigitte.

'Sometimes, it gets that big,' he laughed. 'When this one uncle is walking around the house with mama and they don't have any clothes on, his dick gets that big. It's fun watching it grow. He rubs it all over mama and it gets bigger and bigger. I like to watch it,' he giggled happily.

"Damn," said Ray.

"That's what I said when Brigitte was telling Elizabeth and me."

'Then what happens, Albert?' asked Brigitte.

'Mrs. Vordstrom, you gotta know what happens then.'

'You tell me, Albert.'

'Well, he's gotta put his dick inside mama and fuck her to make his dick get small again. When it comes out again, it's just as little as it can be. It's lots of fun to watch.'

'What about your dick, Albert? Does it ever get big and then small again?'

'Sure, lots of times.'

'When?'

'When I have to take a piss.'

'Any other time?'

'When I go to bed sometimes I play with it. Then it gets big. But it gets small again by itself. I try to get it into my sister sometimes but it won't ever go. I asked uncle why it won't go into my sister like his goes into mama and he told me it will when I get bigger. I want to hurry up and grow up. I want to be able to do what uncle does.'"

Annie looked at Ray and tried not to laugh.

"That's got to be the weirdest story I've ever heard," Ray said after a minute.

"I know. Isn't it crazy? And what's even crazier is nobody - including me - can figure out whether or not this is child abuse. The child is perfectly happy. He's doing what comes naturally. He adores his mother. He's got plenty of adult males around for company. His major problem right now is he won't do any class work because he's so interested in sex. All of this at the age of six. I guess the question becomes: Is it an unfit home or just an alternative lifestyle? After all, Ray, our ancestors a few thousand - or maybe just hundred - years ago probably thought stuff like this was perfectly natural."

"What did Brigitte do after that?"

"She spent about half an hour on the phone to Child Protection Services trying to convince them someone needed to examine this child's home life. I understand it developed into quite a debate. Brigitte got furious at their lack of response and I guess the supervisors at CPS are all considering it now. They're going to call her back in a couple of days with a decision. I'll tell you as soon as I find out the end to the story."

MARCH

Loren was upset. Annie could tell by the tone of her voice on the phone. "Why, you can't talk to me like that. How dare you?" A moment's silence - then she gasped and slammed the receiver down. Her usual pink and white complexion had changed to a deep unhealthy red while her jaws were clamped shut and her lips grim.

"What on earth was that?" Annie asked.

Loren waited a minute before answering. "That was an obscene telephone call," she answered in a shocked, unbelieving voice.

"Oh, really?" Annie laughed, relieved it wasn't an angry parent. "Well, that's nothing. I'm sure you've had those before. What did the guy say?"

Loren turned around and looked Annie full in the face. In a very firm, defiant tone she said, "I sometimes don't understand you at all. There is absolutely nothing funny about an obscene phone call." She hesitated a moment, picking her words carefully. "It's dangerous and degrading. It's insulting and I bitterly resent anyone calling me and saying things like that to me."

"Yes, of course, Loren, you're perfectly right. I shouldn't laugh about it," Annie agreed in an effort to calm her. She could envision Loren getting so upset she'd decide she had to go home sick over it. "Of course, it's upsetting. You're perfectly right."

Loren looked searchingly in Annie's eyes for a minute, apparently liked what she saw, gave a deep sigh and relaxed.

Annie gave her a few minutes to get herself back to normal. "Loren, I need to know what the person said."

"Do you really want me to say it out loud?"

Annie had a funny feeling in the pit of her stomach - a premonition. "Yes, Loren. I need to know."

Annie could see her gathering up her courage and determination.

"He said, 'I planted a fuckin' bomb in your school. It's going to go off and blast you fuckin' bitches all to hell. I'll get even with you," she blurted out, her face turning red again in the process.

"GODDAM!!!!" Annie threw her pencil on her desk, went over to Loren, grabbed her by the shoulders and looked into her face. "A bomb! He said a bomb! What else did he say? Loren, did he say where? Or when it was going to go off? Loren, for heaven's sake, is this what you call an obscene phone call? Isn't it a bomb threat?" Annie shook her angrily. She felt like slapping her but stopped herself knowing she wasn't going to help things that way. She'd only make her hysterical. She gritted her teeth and made a massive effort to control herself. "Loren, what else did he say?"

Tears were glistening in Loren's eyes. "He said women were fuckin' bitches and he'd get even with all of us." The tears overflowed.

"Damn it, Loren, don't cry. Did he say anything else about the bomb? Where it was or when it was going off? Loren, it's important, you've got to remember."

"No, he didn't say anything else about the bomb. I think I'd remember if he did. He just said such nasty things about women. No one has ever spoken to me like that in my life," she sobbed.

Annie ignored her. The principal was on campus somewhere. Should she take the time to locate her or make the decision herself but she knew she didn't have any time to waste. The damn bomb might go off while she was thinking about it. She went over to the intercom and pushed the buttons for a fire drill. That would get the students out of the buildings and Elizabeth would contact the office to see why an unscheduled fire drill was being held.

"Loren, pull yourself together, for crissake. You've got two children in the health office and one sitting in the principal's office. Take them out to the playground with the rest of the students and stay with them. You're responsible for them. Don't tell anybody about the bomb. If you do, I will personally see to it you get fired! Do you understand me?"

"I understand," she answered sullenly.

As she went out the door with the three children, Elizabeth came in. "What's going on, Annie? Did someone pull the fire drill by accident?"

"No, no accident. Loren had a bomb threat on the phone. No time or place stated but he had planted a bomb in the school and when it went off he would get even with all of us blankety, blank women. That was about all I could get out of her. All she could think about was he was using bad language to her," Annie added in disgust.

"You call the police and tell them we need a bomb squad while I call the custodian and ask him to start looking around to see if he can spot anything unusual on campus. Then I'll go out and inform the teachers. They'll be wondering why they're being held out there so long."

This was one of the things Annie admired about the principal. She took command immediately. She stayed cool and calm as she gave good, clear, concise directions just as if a bomb threat was an everyday occurrence.

Annie sat at her desk and dialed 911. "Is this an emergency?" he asked.

"Yes."

"State the nature of the problem and identify yourself."

"There has been a bomb threat at the Lincoln Elementary School. I'm the school secretary, Mrs. Kallas."

"Your address and cross street."

Annie gave him the information.

"A car will be there within five minutes."

Elizabeth had punched the buttons for the all-call. "Mr. Sullivan, come to the office immediately, please."

Joe was at the door promptly. "What's up? Got a problem?" he said looking from Elizabeth to Annie.

"Joe, we've had a bomb threat," Elizabeth explained. "I want you to make a quick search of the buildings for anything unusual. I'm going out to the teachers to explain to them why they're out there so long and then I'll help you. Okay?"

"Sure. I'll start right here in this building, so you two don't get blown up." He had sense enough not to waste any time asking questions. Hopefully, there would be time for that later. They left and Annie sat at her desk. There was total silence. She rested for a full minute. Was it strange she wasn't afraid? She felt confident it would be a false alarm. She hoped she was right. She pushed the all-call buttons. "Mrs. Leski, call the office, please."

"Yes, Annie?"

"Since the police are on the way, maybe you and Loren should come down here. They'll want to talk to her."

"Yes, you're right. I'll get her and we'll be right down."

They walked into the office a second before the police did. No one could complain about that service.

"I'm the principal, Mrs. Leski, Officers."

"Understand you've had a bomb threat, ma'am. The bomb squad is on the way. You have the students evacuated?" the older of the two officers asked.

"Yes, Officer. The children are out in the playground with their teachers. Everyone has been evacuated except we three. This is the school secretary, Mrs. Kallas, and the clerk, Mrs. Ash. Mrs. Ash actually took the phone call."

"I'm Officer Brown and this is Officer Delaney," the older one said. "Let's all move outside and talk until the bomb squad clears this building." He held the door open and gently prodded them out. They went to the driveway where the police car was parked. "Mrs. Ash, what can you tell us about the voice of the person on the phone? Was it a man or woman?" Officer Brown asked.

"It was a man. He sounded, well, maybe a little bit young," Loren answered.

"Was his voice high or low pitched? Did he have any kind of an accent? Did you get any kind of impression as to whether he was fat or thin? Tall or short? Sometimes a voice will make us think a person is big and heavy or short and thin," he suggested to Loren. Officer Brown had a nice way about him. He was being kind and gentle with Loren. Perhaps he had enough experience to sense if he wasn't kind and gentle, she would fall apart and he would get nothing out of her.

Loren, too, appeared to be comfortable with his manner. "His voice sounded like he was tall and heavy. That's the impression I got. I hope you're not going to ask me to tell you what he said. He said some dreadful things." She looked at him with her beautiful green eyes pleading for his understanding.

"Just take your time, Mrs. Ash. We have to know exactly what he said. You can understand that."

"Here they are, Chuck," Officer Delaney said to Officer Brown as the bomb squad drove up. One of the men left the truck and walked up to them.

"Lawrence here," he said to the other officers.

"Why don't you get started? We're interrogating here," suggested Brown. "We have no information on location."

"Right," said Lawrence. He indicated to his men where each should go. Lawrence went into the office with his equipment. He came out again after a few minutes. "It's clear. You can go in."

They went back into the office and sat at the front table. "Mrs. Ash, please try to tell me exactly what the man said. When you first picked up the phone, what did you say and what did he say?"

"Well, the phone rang and I picked it up and said, 'Lincoln Elementary, Mrs. Ash speaking' like I always do. Then he said --do I really have to use those words?" she giggled nervously.

"Yes, ma'am, you do."

With a sigh, Loren continued. "Well, he said, 'I planted a fuckin' bomb in your school.'" They all noticed the blood rushing to her neck and face again as she blushed in embarrassment.

"Go on, what did you say and what did he say," Officer Brown prodded. Delaney was taking notes.

"I didn't say anything then. I was so surprised. He said, 'It's going to go off and blast you fuckin' bitches all to hell.' Can you imagine anyone calling a school and talking that way? It's disgraceful." Loren was over her shock and was getting angry. "That's when I said, 'You can't talk to me like that. How dare you?'" She seemed pleased she had reprimanded the caller.

"Then what did he say?" asked Officer Brown.

"Let's see," she thought a moment. "Then he said..." she hesitated but then plunged right in. 'All you fuckin' bitches give us guys a hard time whenever you feel like it. I'll screw all of you good. You'll see when that bomb goes off.' That was when I hung up."

"Anything else?" asked the Officer.

"No, that was everything," said Loren.

"Loren, didn't you mention he said, 'I'll get even with you'?" Annie reminded her.

"That's right, I guess I forgot that. Somewhere in there he said 'I'll get even with you'."

"I remember because I thought it was so strange. It kind of implies he knows us," Annie explained.

"Anything else?" Officer Brown looked at Loren who shook her head, at Annie who shook her head, and at the principal who said, "I have nothing to add, Officer. How soon do you think the children will be able to go back inside?"

"I'll check with the squad. If they don't find anything, and I doubt they will, it should be soon. I'll get back to you in a few minutes," he said as he and Officer Delaney went out the door.

"Annie, I'm going out to the playground to tell the teachers how it's progressing. Ring for me if you need me," Elizabeth instructed her.

"Okay." Annie and Loren went back to their desks. "Well, that sure disrupted this day, didn't it?"

"I will never forget this day. This day has been terrible. This was the first time in my life I ever had a policeman talk to me."

"Is that good or bad, Loren?" Annie tried to keep the sarcasm out of her voice. All that naive innocence got on her nerves sometimes.

"Why, it's terrible. Decent people shouldn't ever have any connection with the police."

Annie moaned to herself. She didn't continue the conversation but picked up the work she had dropped what seemed like hours ago. Loren realized Annie wasn't going to talk anymore so she picked up her work again.

About a half hour passed. Officer Brown came in and said, "We're ready to leave. Will you call the principal so I can talk to her."

She walked in a minute later. "Yes, Officer, do you have news for us?"

"It's all clear, ma'am. The bomb squad went into every room on campus and were unable to find any trace of a bomb. I need to make you aware that this is getting to be a growing fad. The people who used to get their kicks by setting off false fire alarms now get their kicks by phoning in bomb scares. The caller is sitting nearby. He's watching this whole procedure and enjoying the commotion he's created.

"I tell you this to alert you and your people that it could happen again. If so, tell your secretaries to try to find out anything they can about the caller. Ask where he put the bomb, when it's going off, and anything to keep him talking. Have them make notes. At some point, he'll say something we can use. We have to check it out every time, of course, but the chances are it'll be a false alarm. The procedures you followed today were very good. Always most important and foremost - evacuate the students and keep them out until we give you the all-clear. You can get them back in again now. It's perfectly safe."

"Thank you, Officer. We appreciate what you've done for us," Elizabeth said as he left.

"Shall I get them in?" Annie asked.

"Go to it," she answered.

Annie rang the outside bell for fifteen seconds which

was the return to the classroom signal. "That ought to wake everyone up and get them going."

* * * * * * *

Annie hurried home from work so she would be ready when Ray came to pick her up at five-thirty. He had rented a cabin for the weekend near Idyllwild in the San Bernardino mountains and Annie was excited as she hadn't spent a weekend there in almost five years. She had once casually mentioned that it was one of her favorite spots and Ray had planned this weekend as a surprise for her birthday.

Annie found herself floating on clouds ever since the eventful night when she and Ray had made their commitment. He had always been a considerate person but now he didn't seem to be able to do enough for her. She smiled to herself at the thought of how obvious it was that Ray was in love. He was bubbling over with joy and Annie wondered why everyone in the school didn't notice it. At times she caught herself grinning like a Cheshire cat and had to replace the grin with a frown as she sat at her desk so as to keep people from guessing what was happening in her life.

She had no sooner gotten the suitcase packed when the doorbell rang signaling Ray's arrival. She hurried to answer the door and was surprised to find Joe standing outside. "Well, hi, Joe. What a surprise! What are you doing here?"

"Wondered if you'd like to go to dinner and the movies? How about it? We haven't had a night out for awhile."

"Gosh, Joe, I can't. I'm sorry but Ray and I are going away for the weekend. Up to Idyllwild. Why don't you ask me again next week, okay? How're things going for you, Joe?" she asked, feeling badly that she had to let him down.

"Okay. Everything's all okay," he said with obviously enforced cheerfulness.

Annie heard a car door slam and saw Ray coming

toward them whistling a happy tune. He stopped short as he noticed Joe standing in the doorway but quickly recovered and offered his hand to shake as he came up to them. "Hi, Joe, how're you doing?"

"Hi, Ray. Fine, fine. How're you?"

"Great! Did Annie tell you we're going up to Idyllwild for the weekend? It's a birthday present for her. She won't tell me how old she is but I'll find out sooner or later," he reached over and hugged her as he laughed.

It was obvious to Joe that Ray and Annie's relationship had changed. It was clear they were very much in love and since he was sure Ray would be good to her, he bent to kiss her cheek and said "I'm happy for you, honey, have a good time." And to Ray he said as he shook his hand again, "Take good care of her. She's a winner."

"Thanks, Joe, I will."

With a mumbled "I'll see you next week" Joe turned and walked down the path.

Ray went inside and allowed Annie a moment to watch Joe walk away and to get her emotions under control. "I hate to hurt him. He's very dear to me."

"I know, my darling, but it can't be helped. He's only allowed one woman at a time and," he added with a hug, "you're only allowed one man at a time and I'm that man... and I'll fight any man who thinks differently," he laughed as he flexed his muscles with make-believe bravado.

"Yes, dear," she answered in mock femininity. "We better get going, hadn't we? Here's my suitcase."

They drove on Highway 60 to Banning where they had a quick dinner and then turned off onto the Idyllwild Panoramic Highway. After driving for an hour, Ray said, "Sorry it's too dark to see anything, darling, but we can leave early enough on Sunday so we can see the views."

"That'll be fine, Ray. It's not important right now. What's important is that we can get up there without running into any late winter snowstorms."

"There wasn't any indication of danger on the weather

report so I think it'll be all right. Besides, we're almost there now. Only about another half hour to go, I think."

Within another hour they were settling into their cabin that had a blazing fire going thanks to the owner of the resort. "It was good that he thought of starting a fire, wasn't it? It sure makes a nice welcome."

"Especially when the building is surrounded by snow. It must be fifteen degrees outside but at least seventy in here. Annie, it's warm enough to make love in front of the fire."

"Well, Ray,...I guess it is."

* * * * * * *

The recess bell rang.

"Petey, c'mon with me - I got something to show you." Jason pulled Petey along toward the playground.

"What have you got?"

"It's a secret. Shhh! Don't let anyone hear you." As they walked along, Jason put his mouth close to Petey's ear and whispered, "I got something that's the teacher's."

Petey felt a thrill of fear run through him. "What is it?" he whispered.

"I'll show you when we get to the trees." They walked past their friends and other students who were playing ball or jumping rope to the clump of pepper trees near the front fence. Jason led Petey to the largest tree. He parted the hanging branches and led Petey inside. "No one can see us in here. Look at what I found." He proudly pulled out a sheet of shiny, dark purple paper.

"What's that? You made me miss recess for a piece of paper?"

"It's not just a piece of paper, you dummy. It's special purple paper. It's the teacher's special paper. It's like paint - look." He ran it along his arm and showed Petey the purple line which was left on his arm.

"Wow! How does it do that?"

"I dunno, but ain't it great?"

"What are you gonna do with it?" Petey asked.

"How about painting each other up?"

"What do you mean?"

"Well, I can put the purple paint on you and then you can put it on me."

"I dunno about that. Will it come off again?"

"Sure, it will. C'mon, Petey, it'd be fun to be all purple."

"Okay. Go ahead. But I do you next."

"Sure."

They sat on the dirt under the tree and Jason tore off small pieces of the purple paper and smeared the ink on Petey's face. He giggled. "It makes you look like you're from outer space or Star Trek or someplace."

"I wish we had a mirror so I could see what it looks like."

"Hold still," Jason said. He tore more and more small pieces of the paper and spread the ink on Petey's neck, arms, and hands, until all of Petey's skin not covered by clothing was covered with purple. When he finished, he stood back and surveyed his handiwork proudly. "Hey, Petey, this looks baaad!" He jumped up and down with excitement. "You look like a purple man from another planet."

The bell rang.

"There goes the bell. We gotta go back."

"I can't go back in with the purple on me. The teacher will know we took her paper." Suddenly the whole escapade didn't seem like such a good idea to Petey. "How am I gonna get back, Jason?" he asked in bewilderment.

"Why don't you wait until everyone goes in and then go to the bathroom and wash it off? You'll only be a little bit late --I'll tell the teacher you're in the bathroom."

"I never got a chance to paint you. That's not fair, Jason."

"There ain't no paper left anyway, Petey," said Jason pointing to the torn up pieces laying under the tree. "We'll do me some other day. I gotta go now. I'll get a demerit if I'm late. Sure wish you could see in the mirror. You look baaad!" Grinning happily, Jason ran off.

Petey watched him leave. He could see through the hanging branches that the students had lined up and the teachers were leading them back to their rooms. Petey stayed hidden under the tree until everyone went inside. He felt all alone. Jason said he looked like he was from outer space and he felt like a boy from another planet with no place he could go. It was a scary, sad feeling. It was so quiet. No one was outside except him. His eyes got teary and his nose started dripping. He wiped his eyes with his purple hands and wrinkled up his nose. "He shouldn't have left me all alone. I'll get even with him," he said aloud.

When he couldn't wait any more, he crept out from under the tree, ran past ramp one classrooms and into the boys' bathroom. He hurriedly turned on the water and scrubbed one arm and hand with the other. "It's not coming off... how can it not be coming off?" He tried the other arm with the other hand. "It's not coming off," he said aloud. He tore off a piece of paper toweling and scrubbed harder and harder until his arm started stinging. "It's not going to come off. Jason lied. I'm going to be purple forever." His eyes filled up with tears and his nose started dripping again. He let them overflow. He wanted to call for his mother but fought back the need knowing it would make his shame even greater. "I gotta get out of here before somebody sees me. My teacher would help me even if Jason did take her paper but I don't want the other kids in the room to see me. I gotta go to the office. They'll put me on detention for five years but maybe they can get the purple off."

It was ten-thirty and so quiet in the office it broke Annie's trend of thought. She raised her head and listened. Not a sound. Elizabeth was in her office working on the school budget. Loren was at her desk listing the checks parents had paid in advance for their kid's lunches on the bank deposit slip. Annie was composing a letter for Elizabeth reserving spaces at a conference. Recess was over and all the students and teachers were back in the rooms. There weren't any students in the health office being sick and the phones weren't ringing. It was incredible. She didn't remember it's ever being so quiet in here before. She shook her head in wonderment and went back to her letter.

No door opened - no one came in but suddenly she heard, "Jason did it. He made me hold still while he did it! I didn't want to but he made me!" This pitiful announcement was made by a plaintive voice trying not to cry.

Annie looked up in astonishment. Where on earth had it come from? There was no one there a minute ago. She got up and looked on the other side of the counter. A little boy was sitting under the table. "Come on out of there. How long have you been there? Jason made you do what?" she asked.

Elizabeth heard her bewilderment and came out of her office. The boy came out from under the table and they all gasped at what they saw.

His face was a deep, strong, even, purple color. He wore a short sleeved shirt and the skin on his arms and hands was also a deep purple. They were all looking at a seven year old American boy with thick blond hair, blue eyes, and purple skin. The three of them stared as they tried to absorb this contradiction. The same thought occurred to all of them at the same moment. There was only one purple color like that one - it had to be from a ditto master. They started laughing. They looked at each other as they understood and laughed some more. Their laughter confused the boy who started crying. "Jason made me do it. I didn't want to," he sobbed.

Elizabeth turned away from him for a moment to compose herself and put on her principal's demeanor. Then she went to the counter where he stood. "What's your name?" she asked.

"Petey."

"Petey, you and Jason got one of your teacher's old ditto masters, didn't you?"

"What's that?" he whimpered.

"Mrs. Kallas, hand me one, will you?"

"I don't know if I even have one of those things in here. We haven't used ditto masters in ages. Why on earth did his teacher even have one? Okay, here we go." Annie said as she took one out of her desk.

"One like this, Petey." The principal showed it to him. "See the front side of the master is white paper and it has a purple paper in back of it with a lot of purple ink on it. These are what teachers used to use to run off math and other homework papers. Now, isn't it true you and Jason got one of your teacher's and decided to paint you with it?"

"I guess so. Jason did it. He found it and wanted to paint me."

"But you let him paint you, didn't you?"

"Yes, ma'am."

"So, it's as much your fault as Jason's fault, isn't it? I'm going to get you some special soap which will take the purple off and I want you to go into the health office and use the hot water and wash it all off. Then come into the office and let me see if you did a good job of it."

"Yes, ma'am," said a subdued and grateful Petey. He was glad to hear there was a soap that could take the purple off and he wouldn't have to be this way forever. He had been worried at the thought of his mother having to have a purple son forever and ever. He didn't want her to be unhappy and he thought that would make her real unhappy.

When Petey went into the health office with the soap, Loren told Elizabeth the teacher had called reporting Petey missing. He had never returned from recess.

"Did you explain to her what he had done?"

"Yes," answered Loren. "She said she had thrown the ditto master away in the wastepaper basket because it was so old. She didn't notice that it was gone."

"You know, it gave me a shock. For a minute there, I thought we had a Martian on our hands." Elizabeth started laughing again. "Send him into my office when he's cleaned up."

Annie went into the health office to see how Petey was doing. She pulled up the step-stool for him to stand on and took over the cleaning. He was making a mess of it. It took almost the whole bottle of soap but finally all the purple was gone. When she dried him off, she covered him with lotion to keep his skin from reacting to the harsh scrubbing it had received. "Okay, Petey, you're back to your regular color again. You have to see the principal now."

"What's she gonna do?"

"I don't know. You'll have to see." Annie led him into Elizabeth's office.

"All right, Petey, you look much better now. Can you tell me what you did wrong?"

"Jason stole the teacher's paper. And I let him paint me. Am I gonna be on detention for five years?"

Elizabeth put her hand to her mouth to cover her smile. "No, Petey, I have a feeling you've learned your lesson. But your teacher may punish you. That's up to her. You go on back now. I'll call her and tell her you're on your way."

"Bye, Mrs. Leski. Thanks for the soap that got the purple off."

* * * * * * *

"Hey, Annie, what's going on between Joe and Louise?"

"I don't know what you mean." Annie looked steadily at Denise Garcia, the aide in room six. Damn, did they have rumors flying again?

"Oh, come on, don't play innocent with me. You must have heard that Joe and Louise are a twosome."

Denise had met Annie outside as she was walking to the cafeteria and Denise was on her way to the staffroom. No one else was around to hear the conversation. "Well, Denise, if it's true, Joe's single. He can do what he wants."

"Maybe, but should he be doing it on campus? And besides Louise isn't single. People are starting to talk."

Annie nodded in acknowledgement and walked toward the cafeteria. She thought Joe had this problem solved. He had assured her he'd cool it on campus. She wasn't going to talk to him again. He was a big boy and if he wanted to live dangerously, he had to be willing to accept the consequences.

* * * * * * *

"Lincoln, Annie speaking," she said as she answered the inter-office phone line.

"Annie, this is Sue in Transportation."

"Hi, Sue. What can I do for you?"

"Roger, the driver of bus forty-nine, says he reported to your office this morning there was a wire sagging over the street. It was getting pretty low and he thought it needed to be reported."

"Oh? This is the first I've heard of it. What kind of a wire?"

"It's an electric or telephone wire that goes from a pole on your side of the street to the houses on the other side. Anyway, Roger says when he did his noon kindergarten run, he noticed the wire is now down. It's hanging loose off the pole onto the sidewalk on your side of the street. He's wondering if anyone's called Edison."

"Sue, I don't know anything about any of this. I'll check on it. Thanks for letting me know."

"Elizabeth, I'm going outside to check something. Loren's at lunch. Will you catch the phone a minute?" she called into the principal's office.

"Yes, go ahead,"

Annie walked along the sidewalk in front of the school looking for the downed wire. There it was. It was hanging from the pole right outside the playground. It was right where a lot of the children who walked home would go right past it. Geez! Suppose it was a live electric wire? She ran back into the office.

Loren was in the staffroom eating her lunch. Annie went in and whispered in her ear so no one at the table would hear, "Did you call Edison about the wire the bus driver told you was down?"

"No," she answered.

"Why not?"

"I didn't know where to call."

"What?" Some of the staff heard her and were starting to be interested in this conversation between them. Annie calmed herself a moment and whispered, "You just call Edison. What do you mean you didn't know where to call?"

"Annie, there was only one Edison in the phone book. I called the number and it was a private house."

"GEEZ, Loren, that wire is down right outside the playground and right where the kids walking home go past it. If someone gets electrocuted, it's going to be your stupid fault! Why didn't you ask me if you didn't know where to call? Did you think it would go away by itself?" Loren didn't answer and Annie stormed back into the office. She grabbed the phone book, found at least twelve different listings for Southern California Edison, called the "Emergency" listing and gave them the information. They assured her they would send a truck out immediately.

Elizabeth was alone in her office. Annie went in and closed the door behind her. Elizabeth was surprised at the closed door and said, "What's up, Annie?"

"I want Loren fired, Elizabeth. Anyone that stupid shouldn't work in a school."

"Calm yourself. What's going on? Tell me about it."

"I got a phone call from Transportation wanting to know if the wire outside the school was fixed. It seems Roger, the bus driver, came in this morning and told Loren there was a wire hanging very low over the street from this side to a house on the other side. He suggested she call Edison. When he did his noon kindergarten run, he noticed the wire was now broken and hanging down to the sidewalk on this side of the street. He had Sue in Transportation call me to see if we had called Edison. That was the first I knew of it. I asked Loren if she had called Edison and she says she couldn't find Edison in the phone book so she ignored the whole thing. I can't believe it -

she just ignored it. Elizabeth, Edison has twelve different offices and numbers listed in the phone book - I counted them. It's incredible she couldn't find them!" Annie stood up and started pacing the small office.

"Is Edison coming out now?" Elizabeth asked.

"Yes, they're on their way. I told them they had to have it fixed by the time school's out because of the walkers. It's twelve-thirty now. They assured me they would take care of it."

"When Loren comes back from lunch, send her in. I'll talk to her. Annie, you know I can't fire her. She's past her probation and is a permanent employee. She'd have to do a whole lot worse than this to get fired. However, if you feel strongly about it, you can start keeping notes and building a case. We might, at some point in the future, have enough to do something about it."

"I think I'll do just that!" Annie said as she stalked back to her desk.

Loren came back from lunch a few minutes later. "Elizabeth wants to see you in her office," Annie said.

"Oh, what about?"

"She'll tell you."

When she came out she was considerably subdued. "Annie, where did you find Edison in the phone book?"

Annie stared at her a moment wondering where her brains were. She gritted her teeth and went to the bookcase and got the phone book. She flipped the pages until she came to Southern California Edison. She took a red felt pen and circled the almost two inches of Edison numbers listed there. She then gave the book to her. "Here."

Loren took the book, studied it a moment, and then in a surprised voice said, "Oh, it's listed under Southern California Edison."

"Yes, that's true, that's where it is, right where it should be, under Southern California Edison Co."

"But, Annie, you don't understand. I looked under "E" for Edison, not "S" for Southern. That's why I couldn't find it. Everyone always calls it Edison, so that's where I looked." She was pleased with herself for having solved the mystery.

Annie stared at her for at least a full minute wondering if she could get away with strangling her. "Who pays the bills in your house?"

"I do."

"Every month you make out a check to pay your electric bill. Who do you make the check out to?" Annie asked, trying to keep her voice at an acceptable level.

"To Edison. OOOOOOOOH, I see. I guess I do make it out to Southern California Edison Co."

Annie pulled out a psychological report on a student and quickly started typing. Maybe, if she got involved in the report, she'd be able to put Loren out of her mind before she flipped.

* * * * * * *

Annie took her cup and dried soup into the staffroom where six teachers and four aides were eating lunch. All were talking at once. She got her sack lunch out of the refrigerator, made her cup of soup, and found a seat at the table. The teachers were grouped together at one end of the table involved in an intense conversation. They seemed to be upset.

"I'm ready. This has been going on too long. I'm ready to strike. This situation is ridiculous," said Barbara Selby.

"I agree," added Jeanne Curtis. "They've been negotiating for a year and a half and gotten nowhere. We've been without a contract for eight months. They're playing games with us."

"And I'm tired of not making any money," added Janet Reeves. "I've got my master's degree and I make ten thousand less a year than my husband who never finished college. It's crazy."

Annie shuddered to hear them talk like this. The teachers were babes-in-the-woods when it came to things like strikes. Most of them had never worked in private industry and had no idea of the emotional upset that went along with striking. Some teachers, especially the older ones, believed it was degrading for teachers to go out on strike. The younger ones felt it was degrading to make so little money and have no contract to work under. If it came to calling a strike, it would be teacher against teacher. Annie didn't even want to think about it.

She ate her lunch and decided to walk around the campus for her remaining ten minutes and get away from the strike talk. It was a beautiful day. The temperature was about seventy-five with a light wind keeping the smog away. She passed Joe as she walked. "What mischief are you up to?" she asked him.

"I've got Danny here cleaning up the stuff he wrote on the wall. I'm making sure he does as good a job cleaning it as he did messing it up," he said loudly enough for Danny to hear.

Annie beckoned to him to walk a few steps away so Danny couldn't hear what she said. "Joe, the teachers are in there talking strike. You think they'll go out?"

"Maybe they need to. They've been working without a contract for months. Something needs to break this deadlock. We're next, you know. We're not getting anywhere in our contract talks either."

"That's true. But our contract isn't up yet, so we have a little more time. It scares me to death. The teachers don't know how to handle a strike. They're not auto workers or steel workers or truckers. They're people - children oriented. It's going to tear them apart to go on strike."

"You're right, Annie. It'll be a mess, all right. It'll be the first strike this school district ever had, and I don't think anyone will know what to do with it. But you know, if they do it, then we probably won't have to. Got to think about ourselves first."

"I guess so. I want to walk around a little. See you later, Joe."

She walked out to the playground. First lunch - the younger children - was out.

"Hi, Mrs. Kallas," called Freddie who stopped playing ball to come over to her. He knew she thought he was cute and enjoyed her admiration.

"Hi, Freddie," she answered. "Good to see you again."

"Hello, Mrs. Kallas," said Melissa, an eight year old redhead who could sing and was the star of the talent show every year.

"Hello, Melissa," she smiled. And so it was all along her walk.

Sometimes, they got the feeling in the office that there were only naughty children in the world, since those were the ones who were sent to them to be reprimanded. Out here, Annie saw students who never were sent to the office. She enjoyed her quick walk around the campus and was sorry she had to go back in to work.

* * * * * * *

"Annie, I have to tell you something you're not going to like very much," Ray said as they sat on his couch with his arm around her and her head on his shoulder.

"Have you decided you've had enough of me?" she answered, happy she felt secure enough in his love to know it couldn't be true.

"That's never going to happen and you know it, you vixen," he laughed as he lifted her face so he could kiss her. "No, it's nothing like that. But I know you won't like hearing what Pat, my aide, told me today. She's heard a couple of people wondering about you and me. I guess somebody saw you walking into my house and it was all that was needed to start the gossip going."

"Oh, shit!" She stood up and glared at him.

He laughed at her expression. "Oh, c'mon, Annie, it's not the end of the world," he said as he pulled her down on the couch again.

She sat facing him as she said, "It's awful. They're already gossiping about Joe and Louise and I hate it!

They're gossiping and judging them and I don't want them gossiping and judging us."

"I don't know what we can do about it. I told you I won't hide and if anyone asks me, I'll be proud to tell them I love you. There's no way we're going to be able to keep this a secret, darling, so I don't see why there's any point in getting into a sweat about it. Let's just be happy that we've found each other and let everybody know about it. How about it? Want to go public?"

"No, I don't. My private life should be private and that's where I want it to be." But then as she looked into his dear, kind face she relented a little and added, "Well, maybe later on. But what are we going to tell people? That we're having an affair? You know, it gets embarrassing. And, of course, people in schools aren't supposed to do that kind of thing."

"Well, we'll wait a little while and maybe then we'll have something else to tell them," he said as he pulled her into his arms.

APRIL

"Good morning, Officer. What can we do for you today?" Annie asked.

Members of the Police Department came to the school fairly often for one reason or another. There was one regularly scheduled officer who came out to give lectures to the pupils about bike safety and the dangers of drugs, and also let them examine his patrol car while he was on campus. He ran the siren and the radio for them and they loved it. The idea, of course, was to get the students to see the policeman as a friend.

"I need to see the Montgomery children: Joann, Robert, and James," he read the names from a sheet of paper.

Uh-oh, this was no social call. "Yes, of course. Loren, please call the children from their rooms. I'll find the principal. She's on campus somewhere. I'll have to all-call her." She had no sooner hung up when the intercom rang back. She picked it up again. "Office."

"Do you need me?"

"An officer is here to see the Montgomery children."

"I'll be right there."

When Annie first started working in a school, she was dismayed to discover the police had the right to speak to children at school without being required to get the parent's permission beforehand. It was explained to her then that the principal sat in on a police interrogation in lieu of the parent as the child's advocate. Annie's instructions were that the police were never to interview a child without the principal or her designee being present.

Elizabeth came in and invited the officer into her office to wait for the children. They arrived, one by one, from their respective rooms.

"Send them in one at a time, Annie," Elizabeth instructed.

"Joann, go into the principal's office, please."

"Did I do something wrong, Mrs. Kallas?" she asked.

"No, honey, I don't think so. They just want to talk to you. Go on in." Annie held the door open for her.

"What's going on?" whispered Loren.

"I haven't a clue. I hope they haven't done something dreadful. They're such cute kids. Neglected, but cute."

"I'd like to take Joann home with me for a couple of weeks. Did you notice her hair? It looks like it hasn't been combed in a week. It's all matted and she's so skinny and dirty. It makes me want to take her home and bathe her, and fix her hair so it's pretty, put pretty clothes on her and fatten her up."

"I know what you mean. Have you noticed her shoes are always two sizes too big for her? Maybe that's why the police are here. Maybe they're investigating the home situation."

The phone rang, ending the conversation.

* * * * * * *

Rosa Torres, aide in room four, stood at the counter. "Hi, Rosa, what are you standing there for? Come on in - you work here - it's legal," Annie said trying to be funny.

"Come to me, please. I want to talk to you."

With dread in her heart, Annie walked up to the counter. "What is it, Rosa?"

"Do you remember Robert Abados? The little boy with leukemia?"

"Yes, of course," sensing instantly what it was Rosa had to tell her.

"He died this weekend. The brain tumor killed him. The poor little thing."

"Oh, that's awful," Annie moaned, reaching out for her hand. "How is the poor mother doing?"

"She's doing all right. She's known for a long time he would die. I guess in a way she feels it's for the best. At least he's not suffering anymore."

"Does she have a family here to help her?" Annie struggled to blink back tears.

"Yes, all of her family is here so she's not alone. I have

to get back. I thought you would want to know." She pulled her hand from Annie's.

"Thank you, Rosa."

* * * * * * *

The Montgomery children had gone back to class. The officer had stayed to talk to Elizabeth and was now leaving. "Thanks for your cooperation," he said to her. "We'll keep you posted."

After he had gone, Annie went into Elizabeth's office to see if she could satisfy her curiosity. "Can you tell me what's going on?"

"Well, it's very simple, really," Elizabeth answered with a tinge of disgust in her voice. "They suspect the father is making his children steal bikes and then he resells them."

"For heaven's sake!"

"Right," she agreed.

"Did the kids admit anything?"

"No, not this time. But I guess the police are pretty sure."

* * * * * * *

"Ray," Annie said, "do you remember the story I told you about Albert?"

"No. Give me a hint."

"Albert was the first grader who let his hands wander over the psychologist. Remember?"

"Oh, sure. How could I forget that one? Have you got an end to the story?"

"Yup. The psychologist, Brigitte, told me today she had finally convinced Child Protection Services to look into Albert's home situation. They went out to see Albert's mother a couple of days ago. Brigitte says they found a clean, neat home with a cooperative mother as head of the house. The father is in jail for two years. They found Albert and his four year old sister to be well fed, clean and decently dressed, and loved. They discussed Albert's overly active interest in sex. The mother felt proud he was so advanced and 'grown-up'. They must have spent an hour trying to convince her that Albert's being 'grown-up' in a sexual direction was retarding him from growing-up in an academic direction. I guess they finally convinced her by using the theory of: 'to every thing there is a season and a time to every purpose under the heaven.' They managed to make her understand this was not Albert's season for sex - that would come all in good time. Now was the time for him to learn and be a little boy with little boys' - not big boys' - games. The mother understood after awhile and agreed to make every effort to get sex out of Albert's life.

"And so, my darling, all's well that ends well at Lincoln Elementary and the curtain goes down on another drama."

"Well, good luck to Albert. Keep me posted. I'd be interested to know if he has any relapses."

* * * * * * *

The boy sitting at the front table, who had been sent out of his classroom to the office for misbehavior, suddenly began banging on the front window. Loren was assigned to take care of things like that but she acted as if she didn't notice anything. "Loren, what's he doing?" Annie asked.

"I don't know," she answered.

"Would you please find out why he's acting so strangely?" Annie prodded.

Loren stood up and watched the boy without leaving her desk area. "I think he's trying to kill a wasp." She sat down again and resumed her work.

"Loren," Annie said as she tried to keep her temper. "Do you really think we should let a fourth grade boy kill a wasp here in the office while we sit and watch? Suppose he gets stung?"

"He's not in the fourth grade, he's in the fifth."

"What in hell has that got to do with anything?" Annie whispered. She grabbed the flyswatter and went up to the boy and said, "I'll take over now, Bobby. You go stand over there out of the way while I try to get him." Ann swatted at the wasp and missed. He got mad and dive-bombed her. She ducked and he flew the length of the office and back to the window.

Loren screeched and covered her head with her arms. "Oh, Annie, don't chase him. He might sting me."

"He might sting you? I'm the one who's trying to kill him. It's more likely he would try to sting me, isn't it? What do you suggest I do with him?"

"Just let him sit on the window. He's not bothering anyone there."

Annie ignored her and continued stalking the wasp. Bobby cheered her on from the sidelines. "He's over there - now he's over there," he directed as the wasp flew hysterically around and finally settled back on the front window. Annie quickly beat him to death with the flyswatter. "Good way to go!" praised Bobby while she carried the body away in a tissue and flushed it down the toilet in the health office.

Loren gave a sigh of relief.

* * * * * * *

"Anita, can I talk to you a minute?" Annie asked the school nurse.

"Sure, Annie, sit down. What's on your mind?"

"I want to ask you about the Wallace case."

"Okay, go ahead." She sat down at her desk and made herself comfortable.

"Mrs. Wallace told me the other day how happy she was because she was going to visit her husband in jail. I must have looked amazed when she told me because she then explained that the counselor from Social Services is trying to get them back together so they can all be one big happy family again when he gets out of jail. Can you explain to me what these counselors think they're doing by putting this man back into the home after he's sexually abused his children? I would never do that," Annie said.

Anita smiled at her. "Yes, I know what you mean. I tend to feel the same way. Well, first of all, they're not putting him back. It will be Mrs. Wallace's decision. The thrust of the counseling for father, mother, and the children is that father committed some undesirable acts, perhaps because they were committed on him when he was a child. The counselors try to get everyone to understand why it happened. Recovery for everyone seems to be faster if father returns, hopefully cured by counseling, to the family."

"There's a lot wrong with that theory, Anita. Supposing he's not cured? Does everyone in the family live in fear until they find out? Should they be inflicting this fear on the children again? Is the wife expected to have sex with the man who had sex with her six and seven year old children? And you know, sometimes I think we go too far with this counseling and forgiveness. This man has committed one of the most horrible acts of betrayal on those who loved him most and then we turn around and because he's had counseling, say in effect, "Oh, it's okay you did that - we understand. Bull!"

"I certainly understand how you feel, Annie. But the counselors probably have a more positive and hopeful attitude than you do. Their theory is that saving the family group is what's most important. They feel everyone involved has suffered tremendously and breaking up the family permanently would only create more suffering. It will be up to Mrs. Wallace to decide what's better for herself and her children, being without him or being with him. There's no question about it, Annie, she's between a rock and a hard place."

"It's a crock and you know it, Anita, but I guess we'll all just have to wait and see what happens."

* * * * * * *

It was early Monday morning as Annie noticed Joe sweeping the parking lot as she drove in and parked her car. "Hi, Joe," she called and was surprised when he didn't turn around to greet her but called a mumbled, "Hi, Annie."

She thought it so strange that she walked over to him and said, "Joe?" When he still didn't turn around, she was convinced something was wrong and deliberately turned to stand in front of him to look at him. She gasped as she looked at his blackened eyes and cut and bruised cheek and lips. "Joe, you look awful! Whatever happened to your face?" She walked up closer to him and added, "Why, Joe, you've been in a fight."

"Leave me alone, Annie. It's nothing," he said angrily as he continued sweeping. "I fell down some stairs, that's all."

She stared at him wondering what she could do to repair the damage to his handsome face. "Is that the cover story you're going to tell today? Well, the others may believe it but I don't. It's obvious to me you were in a fistfight and from the looks of it you lost."

"I didn't lose. You should see the other guy."

"Who was the other guy, Joe?" but even as she asked, Annie knew the answer.

"You know who it was, Annie. You always know everything, don't you?"

"Why are you mad at me, Joe?" She stopped a moment wondering how best to say it and decided there wasn't any best way. "It was Louise's husband, wasn't it? That's why you're mad at me. Because I warned you you might get hurt. Oh, Joe, my darling Joe." She put her arms around him, being careful not to touch his face, and said, "I wish there was some way I could make it all better for you. Whoops, here comes the principal. I have to go. Come over my house after work. I'll give you dinner and we can talk. Okay?"

"Okay," he muttered.

* * * * * * *

"Loren, I'm going for a coffee break."
"Okay."

It was three o'clock. The students had just left. Annie was alone in the staffroom and found it beautifully quiet.

The quiet was shattered by an angry Susan Woodward as she came in the door. "I can't do it. I know I can't do it. Why don't you quit pestering me? I know I can't do it."

Annie wondered what it was about. The teachers almost always got along and seldom snapped at each other.

"You can do it, Susan, if you make up your mind to it," said Jeanne Curtis.

Susan, Jeanne, and Karen Ramsey had come in together. They were all young marrieds in their late twenties and were friends even away from school. This was Susan's second year of teaching, Jeanne and Karen's third year.

"Susan, you know we don't feel good about this either, but it has to be done. We have to show the administration and the school board that we have some power, too. We have to stick together and show them they can't just continue to ignore us," Karen said.

"I don't care whether they ignore us or not," answered Susan. "I just want to be left alone in my classroom."

"You just want to be left alone, do you?" said Janet. "You don't care if you're underpaid for your work? You don't care if you're not budgeted hardly any money to buy paper and pencils? You don't care if you can have forty students in your room for half the year?"

"We never have forty students in our room," answered Susan.

"Maybe not, but you've had thirty-five at times. The state law only says how high your average can be. That gives the administration plenty of room to manipulate numbers," answered Janet.

Other teachers had come in and were listening to this conversation. Norma Glas, Fred Martinez, Mary Ann Duncan, and Ray Ogilvie were sitting or standing around the original three. Annie knew Ray was worried about the conflict a strike would cause among the staff.

"I'm with Susan," said Mary Ann Duncan. "This is my first year. I have enough problems without even thinking about going out on strike. I only want to be left alone to teach in my classroom."

There was a murmur of disapproval at the statement.

"May I say something?" It was Ray Ogilvie speaking in his calm, quiet voice.

"Go ahead, Ray," said Fred.

"We've been negotiating for eighteen months. We've met and talked and compromised and are unable to come to an agreement. We've been working without a contract for eight months. I have power, so do you - and you, (he pointed around the group) if we have the courage to use it. We have the weapon to demonstrate to the school board that we are displeased with them. If we act together, as a group, we will have all the power we need to get the things we need to work as respected professional teachers."

Ray never raised his voice but his heart was in every word he said. When he stopped talking, they all sat there looking at him a minute. Then everyone started talking at once. Annie looked at the clock, realized she had overstayed her break time, and quickly returned to her desk.

* * * * * * *

When Annie got home that evening, she found Joe waiting at her front steps looking sad and depressed. She knew he wouldn't be there so early if he weren't desperate for some consolation. "Come on in, Joe, and you can relax with a beer and put your feet up."

He followed her inside without a word but as soon as she closed the outside door, he reached for her and with his arms around her could no longer control his sobs. Annie was stricken at the depth of his crying and held him close feeling his tears seep through the thin material of her blouse. "It'll be all right, Joe, it'll be all right," she said as she stroked his back. She was stunned as she felt a bandage wrapped around his chest and back and blurted out, "Why, you've got cracked ribs too, don't you?" After a few minutes, he quieted and groped his way to the couch. "Good, Joe, lay down and rest. You're worn out. You shouldn't have gone to work today. It was too much. I'll fix you a cup of tea with some whiskey in it and that'll help you to relax. After awhile when you feel better, we can eat something light."

As Joe slept, Annie telephoned Ray and explained the situation to him. "After he wakes up, we'll eat and then I'll have to see, Ray. If he's too depressed or hurt, I'll have him stay here for the night. I can't let him go home alone if he still needs me. I hope you can understand."

"Yes, of course, darling. I admire you for taking care of a friend. Is there anything you want me to do?"

"No. Thanks, I don't think so. I think he just needs to rest and be taken care of so he doesn't feel all alone. I haven't found out yet what Louise's reaction to the fight was. I don't think Joe would be so depressed if she had sided with him but I'm not sure. I still have to find out."

"You do what you have to do, Annie. I love you and trust you implicitly. Call me if you need me to do anything."

It was two hours later before Joe woke up and called, "Annie?"

"Yes, Joe, I'm right here. You feeling any better?"

"Pretty groggy. What'd you put in that tea?"

She laughed, "A good shot of whiskey. It did the trick. Put you right to sleep for two hours. You ready to eat now?"

"Have to go to the bathroom. Let's see if I can get up." Annie helped him to his feet amid his moans and groans. "Oh, boy, these ribs are giving me hell. Gotta keep moving or they stiffen up on me."

As they sat at the kitchen table over minestrone soup and sourdough bread, Joe told her the story. "Last night I went into the bar where I always go, you know the one we went to, and as I sat at the bar and looked in the mirror behind it, I could see the reflection of Louise and her husband and another couple sitting at a table in my line of vision.

"I wanted to see how Louise would act with her husband and her friends. I wondered if she was the same with them as she was with me. I noticed as it got later and later, they all started having too much to drink and started arguing and getting mean to each other. The other woman got mad at Louise and in order to hurt her started telling the husband all about Louise's affair and then said, 'and there's the guy sitting right over there' and pointed to me.

"The husband had too much to drink, too, and started slapping Louise around. I couldn't stand it so I went over to the table and told him to lay off. Well, they didn't like the interference, so both guys started taking me apart until the owner stopped the fight and threw them out.

"But I got in a couple of good hits on the husband and the worst part of the whole thing was Louise couldn't do enough for him when he was down and then started screaming at me because I had hurt her beloved husband. I couldn't believe my ears. After all these months of telling me what a rotten husband he was, it turns out she loves the guy. That's the part that gets to me, Annie."

Annie couldn't think of anything to say so just patted his hand and nodded her head.

"I was something for her to play with. She didn't care anything about me. Not really. She wanted to have an affair and I fell for it. Like a blooming jackass. I acted like I was seventeen years old. I can't believe it. I pulled the same stunt on many a woman but now it's been pulled on me. I guess it serves me right." He looked at Annie and grinned as much as he could with his split lips. "You'd tell me that, wouldn't you? It serves me right. Now I know what it feels like and it serves me right."

"No comment," she smiled.

"I'm going home now. You've babied me, fed me, and listened to my confessions, and now it's time for me to go home and start growing up and being a man again."

"Are you sure you'll be all right, Joe? You're welcome to stay here tonight. I've already told Ray you might."

"No, kid. I wouldn't hurt you and Ray in any kind of way. No, I'm okay. I got a little rest and got the story off my chest and now I feel fine." He got up from the table and started walking toward the door. He turned and held out his arms to her. As she walked into them, he held her and said, "Thanks, my little Annie. You're the best."

* * * * * * *

The office bulletin board, put up through the courtesy of Barbara Selby's first grade class, was covered with painted, cut-out flowers some of which were clearly daisies; some of the others defied classification. One of these had light blue tentacles emanating from the purple center and at the end of these tentacles were bright yellow, round petals with another petal colored pink in the shape of a triangle jutting out from the end of the round ones. It was a flower never seen on this earth but showed that some first grader had a vivid imagination along with an aptitude for creating interesting bulletin boards. There was, of course, also a fluffy white bunny rabbit (made from cotton balls) sitting amidst this field of flowers.

It was spring recess time. Their world was populated with bunnies, spring flowers, and Easter eggs.

It had been a long time since Christmas vacation. Important learning had taken place in these past three months. Students who might be retained in June had been identified and parents notified. The gifted student and the learning handicapped had been identified and set on their proper courses. Almost all of them, both teachers and students, were happy and felt proud that they had accomplished so much this year.

For the teacher, of course, there was always the nagging thought that if he or she had handled Johnny in a different way, would there have been a better result? Or if Mary hadn't moved just when they were getting somewhere, the teacher could have performed wonders with her.

However, that was the teachers' life and they accepted it with a sad smile.

But they were all getting tired and looked forward to spring vacation with its change of pace.

* * * * * * *

"Hi, Les, what have you got for us this morning?" Annie said as she walked up to the counter to greet him.

"I've got a fourth bus ticket on Fred Rampart. That puts him off the bus for the rest of the year. I'm sorry, but there was no way around it. He was pushing and shoving with no provocation," Les, the school bus driver, explained.

"Oh, wow! His mom's going to have a fit. It's the first week of April, so that means there are almost two and a half months of school left during which he won't be able to ride the school bus and mom will have to drive him to school unless she wises up and makes him walk. That would teach him something. Okay, Les, give it here."

Les tore off one copy and handed her the remaining two copies of the ticket. "Thanks, Annie. You know, we don't give the tickets - especially a fourth - unless we really have to." He seemed eager for her understanding.

"I don't doubt it for a minute. Les, it's okay! I'm sure he deserved it otherwise you wouldn't have given it to him." She patted Les' hand. He squeezed hers in return.

"Thanks. I have to go or I'll be late on my next run." He waved good-by as he went out the door.

When there was a fourth ticket, there had to be a meeting between the supervisor of transportation, the parent, the principal, and the student. Annie made arrangements for the meeting with Fred's parents to be held on Friday, the last day before spring vacation. That would give Mrs. Rampart a week to figure out how Fred would get to school.

"Elizabeth, Mrs. Rampart is here," Annie said.

"Is Vic here?"

"He's coming in the door now."

"All right, have them all come in," Elizabeth said.

"Please come in, Mrs. Rampart," Annie said. "I'd like to introduce you to Vic Cummings, the supervisor of the Transportation Department."

"I'm glad to meet you, Mrs. Rampart," Vic said while Mrs. Rampart stared icily at him. He motioned to her to precede him into the principal's office. Fred solemnly followed his mother.

"Mrs. Rampart, thank you for coming to this meeting," Elizabeth said after they were all seated. "As you know, Fred has received his fourth bus ticket and as a result is no longer allowed to ride the school bus this school year. I--"

"Yes, I know," interrupted Mrs. Rampart. "What I don't know is how you people expect him to get to school every day. I certainly can't drive him. Both his father and I have to be at work by eight o'clock - unless you want me to dump him at the school at seven-fifteen every morning and then I have no way to get him home until after five at night."

"That would not be acceptable, Mrs. Rampart. There is no supervision for pupils until eight o'clock in the morning nor any after three o'clock in the afternoon," said Elizabeth.

"What am I supposed to do then? He just won't be able to go to school for the rest of the year."

"That would make Fred truant, Mrs. Rampart," said Elizabeth, "and I'm sure you don't want that on his record. Isn't there a neighbor or friend who could drive him?"

"No, of course not," Mrs. Rampart answered. "Everyone I know works and has his own problems." She turned to Vic. "You didn't have to give him that ticket, you know. Fred says he didn't do anything. Fred says other kids push and shove and never get a ticket. He was doing good after the last ticket. That bus driver just doesn't like him" she added.

"Mrs. Rampart, the drivers never give tickets unless they personally see the incident happen," said Vic in a practiced voice trained to deal with irate parents. "These drivers have sixty students on a bus. They don't have time to like or dislike any particular student. They're busy driving safely and they only notice those children who misbehave because it takes their attention away from their driving and thus causes a safety hazard. Have you considered that Fred could walk to and from school?"

Mrs. Rampart stared at Vic, looking like a surprised owl as her lower jaw dropped open in amazement. "Why, it's over a mile!"

"Yes, Mrs. Rampart. It's exactly one and three tenths of a mile. Fred is nine years old. The exercise would be good for him every day." Vic offered the information to her pleasantly with a small smile at the corners of his mouth.

"That's outrageous! How could you even suggest such a thing?" She raised her voice. "Why, that would be almost three miles he would have to walk every day. We don't require our children to do things like that. Never mind, his father and I will figure something out." She stood up so suddenly Vic was caught unprepared and had to scurry to get out of her way so she could get to the door of Elizabeth's office. Without another word she took Fred by the hand and pulled him past Annie's desk, past the counter, and out the front door.

"Wow! What a whirlwind! What did you two say to her?" Annie asked.

"Suggested the boy walk. It must be a dirty word in that family," Vic grinned. "You know, it's amazing how often parents suddenly are able to find a solution to the transportation problem as soon as I suggest the child could walk. It's incredible that walking is not considered a viable alternative in southern California. Do you realize that people in the rest of the world consider walking a respectable means of transportation?"

They all laughed but they knew it was true. Since there wasn't a good system of public transportation where they were located, everyone had his own car. That, combined with the fast pace at which they lived, precluded anyone having the time to walk anywhere and made someone walking an unusual sight.

Vic said his good-byes and they settled down to finish up all the loose ends on this last day before spring vacation.

A lot of the classes were having parties that afternoon so Annie and Loren were busy with cakes and cupcakes and drinks brought in by parents. By two o'clock the smell of sweet icing was permeating the office making them slightly nauseous.

"How can children eat that stuff? Yuck!" Annie said to Loren.

She giggled. "You probably loved it when you were that age."

"I suppose so. It's probably what caused all the fillings I have in my teeth. Loren, did you know the teachers like to have parties only on Fridays because the sugar makes the children so hyper?"

"No, really?"

"Yes. They say they can tell for two or three days after a party that the kids have been eating too much sugar."

"I never heard that before. So, they have the party on Friday and then the children can drive the parents crazy over the weekend."

Their conversation was cut short by the entrance of a tall, good-looking young man. "Hello. Can I help you?" asked Loren.

He flipped open his I.D. showing a badge. "I'm Detective Cutty. May I see the principal, please?"

"One moment, please." Loren went to Elizabeth's office and told her a detective was here to see her.

"Show him in, Loren."

He closed the door behind him.

Ten minutes later Elizabeth opened it again. "Thanks very much for letting us know. It's always interesting to find out the end to a story," she said to him as he left.

After he went out the door, Annie asked. "The end to what story? Are you going to share it?"

Elizabeth laughed. "Sure, you both lived through it, too. Do you remember Mr. and Mrs. Lee who were so irate because we had reported them to Child Protective Services? The ones who locked the door when they came in my office?"

"Yes, of course. The one who threatened you."

"Yes, that's right. He threatened to get even. And do you also remember what the bomb threat caller said? He said he was getting even."

"It was Mr. Lee."

"Yes, it was Mr. Lee."

"I never had anyone talk to me like that in my entire life," said Loren.

"How did the police find out?" Annie asked.

"A neighbor reported to them that he was bragging about being able to make the school do what he wanted them to. He lives right across the street and enjoyed watching all the commotion after his phone call. HE made the kids go out to the playground, HE made the police and bomb squad come, HE made the principal worry. He felt powerful and was getting even."

"Well, I'll be darned! What happens to him now?" Annie asked.

"It's a misdemeanor. I don't know what his punishment will be. The detective didn't say."

"Isn't that something? I never figured they'd catch the caller."

"No, neither did I," agreed Elizabeth, "but I guess the fates work in mysterious ways."

"I knew he would be punished for saying such terrible things to me," Loren added.

They felt that was a fitting close to the last day of school before spring recess. Everyone heaved a hearty sigh of relief when it came time to go home and have a week off.

* * * * * * *

Ann and Ray had made plans to visit Ensenada in Mexico for a few days during spring vacation. They left immediately after work in hopes of beating the traffic but found themselves caught in a traffic jam going into San Diego. "Let's just eat dinner in the nearest restaurant and wait until everyone's off the road. I can't stand this moving two inches every ten minutes," a cranky Annie suggested.

"If we wait until everyone's off the road, we'll grow old and die right in that restaurant," said Ray. "But it's a good idea. I'm hungry anyway."

It was eight o'clock when they left the restaurant feeling soothed and mellow and ready to face the remaining traffic which was always heavy on a Friday night going into Tijuana. The Mexican border guards waved the tourists through the gates and were happy they were bringing their American dollars and hoped they would spend them freely.

When Ray pulled into the parking lot of their motel near the beach in Ensenada, it was almost eleven o'clock. "What do you say we unload and then take a midnight walk on the beach?"

"This is what I call heavenly. Look at that moon and the smell of the water. Ohhh, I love it."

"And I love you, my Annie. Have I mentioned that lately?"

"Not nearly often enough." She reached up and kissed him lightly.

They walked along with Ray's arm around her shoulders and hers around his waist. "You know, Ray, it's almost like being on the moon."

"On the moon? How do you mean?"

"Well, we're so isolated. We're on this narrow strip of beach with the Pacific Ocean on one side and a cliff on the other and we seem to be the only sign of life anywhere in sight. It's kind of weird and if you weren't here, I'd be scared to death."

"If I weren't here, you'd have no business being here either."

"Yes, you're right. I certainly wouldn't be here alone at night."

They continued walking and talking, stopping intermittently to kiss. The further they walked the more passionate their kisses became until Ray said, "Darling, what do you say? You about ready to go up to the room? I don't know how much more teasing I can take. Or," he added, grinning at her, "would you like to try making love on the sand?"

She laughed, "I've heard it can be extremely painful if the sand gets into the wrong places. No, I think the warmth and comfort of the room is about my speed." She reached up and gave him a long, lingering kiss. "Does that prompt you to turn around and walk as fast as we can to the motel?"

"I'd run if it wasn't so hard to do on the sand."

They turned around and were walking in the direction of the motel when she suddenly stopped short. "Oh, for heaven's sake! It can't be."

"What is it, Annie?"

Ray looked at her as she stared in front of them, shook her head as though to clear it, and then said, "I can't believe it. Ray, am I seeing things or is that really Norma Glas coming toward us?"

"It's hard to tell in this light. It looks like her, doesn't it? Who's that with her?"

"I'd know that walk anywhere. Damnit, here we are three hundred miles from home and someone from the school comes walking along on exactly this same beach at exactly this same time. It's incredible! But that's Norma for you. If there's a way to get into mischief, she'll do it. I don't know the guy. He looks like a Mexican. She did say she wanted to brush up on her Spanish. Ray, I don't want her to see us. She'll go back to school and won't see any reason to keep her mouth shut about seeing us here together. C'mon, let's walk over by the cliff. Maybe they won't notice us there." Annie pulled him into the shadow cast by the cliff overhang.

"Annie, is this really necessary? I told you I won't hide. We're not doing anything wrong or illegal. It's humiliating to hide. And it indicates that we feel there's something shameful in what we're doing. I'm very uncomfortable with this."

"Ray, please. I don't want everyone in the school gossiping about us. Just picture for a minute what it would be like to have all the staff members discussing our being in a motel together in Mexico." She shuddered. "It would be awful."

"We're going to have to do something about this. I don't like it at all."

"Shhh. Be quiet for a minute until they pass us," she whispered.

Norma and the man were deep in a conversation in Spanish as they passed when suddenly she called, "What are you hiding in the shadows for, Annie? Afraid I'll see you and Ray cuddling up together?" She laughed and continued walking.

Annie sputtered in fury. "That little snip! Just wait until she asks me for another favor. I'll teach her to have some respect."

"This is ridiculous. I won't be put into such a position, Annie. I have never hidden from anyone or anything in my life and I am not prepared to do it now. Let's get up to the room and discuss this."

When they got to the room all thoughts of making love had evaporated since they were increasingly upset by the problem that seemed to loom larger and larger before them.

"Ray, you've got to understand that I'm not ashamed of us being together or anything. It's just that I like my personal business to be private. I'm a very private person. I'm very uncomfortable with everyone knowing everything about me. The very thought of people talking about me drives me crazy."

"Well, we're in somewhat of a quandary then, aren't we? How do we resolve your need for privacy with my need for honesty and dignity?"

"I don't know, Ray. I want honesty and dignity, too, but I don't actually see how being discreet and private offsets that. They're not opposites. I guess it's a matter of degree. We don't have to go out of our way to flaunt our relationship in front of people. It's nobody's business what we do until we shove it in their faces and make it their business." Annie stopped, "Why, that's exactly what I said to Joe. Oh, that's terrible. I can't stand being in the same category as Joe and Louise."

"Wait a minute, Annie. We could never be in the same category as Joe and Louise because first of all, we're both single and secondly, we're not only fooling around. But that doesn't take into account incidents like tonight. We weren't flaunting anything in anybody's face but, by accident or coincidence, our relationship became known. It seems to me that we have a choice in a case like that of either acknowledging our love or making an attempt to hide it. It's not a choice to me. I don't want to hide it, Annie."

"Are we getting into semantics here? What's the difference between 'hiding it' and 'being discreet'? Are you willing to be discreet?"

"I'm willing to be discreet in the sense of not going out of my way to show the world that I love you. For instance, we don't have to go to a restaurant where we know most of the staff eats every Friday night. However, if we go to a little, out of the way restaurant in another town and still meet someone from staff, I won't hide in the restroom so that I won't be seen with you. That's the difference as I see it. I don't see how we can have a relationship in a place where we're known and expect never to be seen together. I think, Annie, perhaps you need to revise your expectation of privacy. After all, if Norma does go back and talks, the staff will find it interesting for a few days and then forget all about it. It's not a catastrophe, you know. They would all be happy for us and wish us well."

She looked at his handsome face so full of concern and feeling the love for him well up within her said, "All right, Ray, you're right. I guess I've been unrealistic. We'll be discreet but not hide from now on. Okay?"

"Okay. Thanks, darling." And with that he pulled her into his arms.

* * * * * * *

Annie was nervous the first day back to school. She wondered if Norma would start the gossip going but hadn't heard or seen anything all day and when she met Norma in the staffroom after school, she only said, "Hi, Annie, have a good vacation?"

"Very nice, Norma, and you?"

"It was great. I went to Ensenada for a few days and had a good time there."

"Oh, did you? I went to Ensenada, too."

"Surprising I didn't meet you there."

And that was that. Neither Annie nor Norma ever mentioned the subject again and Annie's liking and respect for her increased a hundredfold as she discovered Norma could keep her mouth shut when necessary.

MAY

Annie woke up startled at four o'clock on Wednesday morning feeling like she'd had a nightmare. She lay there wondering why she felt so frightened and depressed. Then she remembered. The teachers had voted for a strike and it was to start today.

"Gad, what a disaster," she moaned as she tossed and turned unable to go back to sleep. She hated to go to work and have to face all the animosity and resentment the teachers were going to feel toward the substitutes and the teachers who didn't go out on strike. "Oh, damn, why did this have to come along to ruin everything?"

The local newspapers had been full of the school district's five by seven inch want ads advertising for substitute teachers and indicating a willingness to pay double what they usually paid. The teachers dubbed it "combat pay." The teachers had ads in the paper, too, telling their side of the story and each side also had billboards along the streets with their respective slogans on them. Annie wondered if all the extra money being spent on advertising the strike wouldn't have paid for a raise for everyone.

The arguments among the teachers themselves started a couple of weeks ago as the strike vote became imminent. Some teachers flatly said they would never go on strike regardless of the provocation because they considered it unprofessional. The other teachers said it was unprofessional not to be paid a decent salary and they were cowards because they weren't willing to fight for what was rightfully theirs.

When she got to work she found the teachers picketing on the sidewalk in front of the school and the parking lot. In order to park, she had to wait for them to break their line. She felt like a traitor. She hated to go through their picket line but the Classified employees (clerical workers, custodians, bus drivers, etc.) had been advised that if they honored the teachers' picket line, they would be fired because their contract was still in effect. The teachers understood and didn't expect them to stay off the job.

"Hi, Annie, give the kids our love. Tell them we didn't want to have to do this," Norma Glas called to her.

"Annie, hold down the fort for us. We'll be back soon," called Fred Martinez.

"I will. I'll do what I can," she called back to them while fighting back tears. She felt as if she was going into her home while her children were locked out trying to get in and couldn't.

"This is terrible, terrible," she said to Elizabeth who had arrived early.

"Yes, it certainly is," she nodded in agreement. She patted Annie's shoulder. "Annie, get the keys, the campus maps, and the instruction sheets for the substitutes ready."

"Yes, I have them ready. They're right here. Do you think there'll be trouble when the substitutes and the regular teachers who aren't striking arrive?"

"It's a possibility. My instructions are to call the police if there's any sign of trouble. The police have been alerted. They're going to try to cruise past each school a few times a day especially in the morning and at three o'clock when the substitutes leave."

Loren came in wiping tears from her eyes. "This is awful. Why did they have to go out on strike anyway? Everything was so nice around here until this happened."

The substitutes started arriving. For the next half hour Annie was busy giving out keys, instructions, and answering questions. She had a hard time being gracious to these people who were willing to benefit from the hardships of others for the high rate they were being paid and hoped they would have to earn every cent.

The buses came in with the students. The teachers called to "their" children. "We'll be back in a couple of days - you behave."

Elizabeth stood outside directing the children to go to the playground quickly. She wanted them safely out of the way in the event of any trouble during the time when the substitute teachers were arriving.

When the eight-thirty bell rang, Annie heaved a sigh of relief. Everyone was indoors now. She looked out of the window and saw the picket line breaking up and guessed they wouldn't be back until about three o'clock.

Ida Pierce, Louise Wong, Deborah Bradford, Diana Neblett, and Margaret Dorner were the five teachers who hadn't gone out on strike. They were subdued and stayed in their rooms as much as possible.

* * * * * * *

Lunch time was dismal. The only people who were talking were the substitutes who talked among themselves. Annie heard one of them say, "They want to pay me all this money to come in here for seven hours of work that's fine with me. I can use this kind of money anytime."

Annie knew the regular teachers could use the money, too, if they could get it.

As the afternoon drew to a close, it was as if they could feel the pressure building. Annie wondered if she imagined it. She looked out of the window and, sure enough, the picket line was re-forming. It was two-forty.

The buses were in at two fifty-five promptly. The drivers probably had instructions to get into the schools and out again in a hurry.

"Annie, get on the all-call and tell the teachers to immediately release all children who walk home. Let's try to get them off campus fast. I'll be outside at the crosswalk."

Annie could feel her nerves jangling and hoped she could keep her cool through all this. It was three o'clock and the dismissal bell rang. The picket line had formed. About ten of Lincoln's teachers were on it and some teachers from another school were there.

The substitutes and the five regular teachers who were working were all out hurrying the children onto the buses. The principal was checking the bathrooms to make sure there were no stragglers around and then walked down to the bike rack to hurry the bike riders along.

The campus was cleared by three-ten. The substitutes turned in their keys and left in groups of three or four. They were obviously worried about going out and getting in their cars while the picketers were there because they would have to break the picket line to drive out of the parking lot.

Elizabeth and Annie watched out of the window. As soon as the substitutes started coming out, the regular teachers on the line started jeering and booing and shouting "scab." They wouldn't break the line for the substitutes' cars. Annie was scared just watching and knew the substitutes in their cars must be frightened. They couldn't get out of the parking lot unless they ran over a teacher. They were trapped inside their cars while the teachers were getting nastier in their language.

Halleluiah! A police car drove up. The policeman shifted into first gear and drove by just fast enough to keep the car from stalling. He must have seen at a quick glance what was happening.

The teachers broke their line and permitted the substitutes to leave. Elizabeth and Annie looked at each other and Annie growled, "Shooooot. How many more days do we have to go through this crud?"

"I don't know." Elizabeth sat down at her desk. "It's a bad, bad situation. Neither the children nor the teachers should be subjected to this type of thing. Their relationship is a delicate, special one that shouldn't have anything intrude upon it - certainly not a strike. A strike is a cruel, amputating situation. The teacher is not in the classroom - not because the teacher is sick which the student can absorb but because he is rebelling against the conditions under which he is in the classroom. How many pupils are feeling somewhere deep inside themselves that maybe it's their fault their teacher won't come back to the room? The pupils can't absorb this absence. It's not in the natural order of things. It's almost like a parent refusing to come home. The child would probably first wonder if it was his fault before he blamed his parent.

"And the teacher - it's hell for the teacher," Elizabeth went on. "He's torn between survival for himself and his own family and the survival of his relationship with each of the children in his room. 'Will the children think he's deserted them?' he asks himself. He hates it, because down deep he's asking himself the same thing. Has he deserted them?

"Get a good night's sleep tonight, Annie. Tomorrow will be more dangerous."

"What do you mean?"

"Well, today was kind of a novelty for the teachers. It's probably the first time any of them has ever been on strike. By tomorrow the novelty will have worn off and the full impact of being on strike should hit them. Things may get a little rougher when the substitutes leave."

"Not in the morning when the subs come in?"

"No, they'll wait until all the children are gone. Those high school teachers who were on the line were also instigators. It's easier to make trouble when it's not your own school - when it's not your students - not your co-workers."

"Oh, cripes!" I think I'll take a vacation for the next week."

"Not on your life," Elizabeth laughed but she knew Annie didn't mean it.

* * * * * * *

The next morning there was a replay of the morning before. The teachers called "hello" to Annie and picketed quietly.

The district phone rang. "Lincoln, Annie speaking."

"Hi, this is Charlene in accounting. How're you all doing in that neck of the woods?"

"We're struggling. How's it going at the district office?"

"It's a total madhouse here. We're all on unlimited overtime if you can believe it. I think everyone in the whole state is watching this strike. The phones are going crazy. I don't have time to talk," she continued. "I have to call all the schools. The superintendent wants attendance reports from everyone. He wants to know the percent of absenteeism today."

"It's high. A lot of the parents are keeping their children home."

"He wants actual figures, Annie. The percent of absenteeism by grade level and then a total for the school - by two o'clock is what he wants."

Annie groaned. "Oh, wow! He doesn't want much, does he?"

"Do the best you can. See you later." She hung up.

Loren had come in while she was on the phone. "Good morning, Annie. Isn't it a beautiful day?"

"Yup, sure is. It's a nice day to walk a picket line."

Loren studied her a moment trying to see in her face what she meant. She shrugged and gave up. She went up to a boy standing at the counter.

"There's a dead bird in the drinking fountain on the playground," he informed her.

"Oh," she said. "What'll we do, Annie?"

"What would you do if I wasn't here, Loren?" She ought to be able to solve a little thing like that by herself.

"I guess I better call Joe. He'll get it." She was pleased with herself for thinking of it. She rang the all-call. "Mr. Sullivan, please call the office. Mr. Sullivan."

Joe came in a minute later laughing aloud.

"What's so funny, Joe? Tell me a joke - I need it," Annie said.

"I just walked past a couple of boys - not more than seven years old. One was trying to explain to the other how to use a condom and what it was for. I wish I could've taken a picture of the look on the face of the kid who was listening. He obviously hadn't heard of sex before and was completely astonished." Joe laughed. "It was funny to see his confusion. What do you charming ladies need?"

Loren told him about the dead bird.

"Sure, I'll get it. No problem," he said as he went out the door.

"I'll be back in a minute, Loren." Annie followed Joe out of the door. "Joe," she called.

He turned around. "Hi, I didn't know you were behind me."

"Joe, what do you think about the strike? Do you think there'll be violence today?"

"Wouldn't surprise me if there was. Yesterday was different being the first day. But from now on it's serious business. It's no fun being out there in the cold and watching someone walk past you to take your job. And it's different for teachers. It's not just a job and their own lives involved like with a steel worker but they're all emotionally involved with the kids in their classroom. Some stranger who doesn't really care about them is taking over their kids, too. It's a mess, all right, and it'll get dirty if it doesn't end soon."

Tears burned hot in Annie's eyes. "It's so awful, Joe. They deserve better."

"Yeah, but I hope they don't get so emotionally involved they screw it up."

"What do you mean?"

"Well, Annie, you gotta remember strikes are something new for teachers. Coal miners, auto workers, and people like that have strikes as part of their lives. They understand them. They grew up seeing their fathers go out on strike. It's always been a part of the overall picture to them. Because they're more experienced, they can cope with it better. So, turn it around. Because teachers have no experience at this, chances are they won't be able to handle it well. Right now they have a lot of sympathy in the community but if they overreact, they'll lose it. We'll have to wait and see, Annie." He patted her arm and walked away.

She went back in and gave out substitute keys. Two

of the subs were replacing two who refused to return from yesterday, she guessed. She gave them the instructions, duty roster, and the rest of the information they needed. Most of the subs were in the staffroom talking until the bell rang. Annie went in and said in her loudest voice. "May I have your attention, please?" She waited a minute for everyone to stop talking. "The superintendent wants an attendance report today so please take attendance first thing and send the sheet down to me with a student. Okay?"

They murmured their acknowledgement.

Annie normally did an attendance report only on Fridays but she'd be willing to bet five dollars she'd have to do it every day until the strike was over. What a pain! She went back to her desk just as Elizabeth walked in.

"I was beginning to wonder where you were," Annie said to her while she followed her into her office.

"I've been in an administration meeting since six o'clock. You have to send an attendance report to accounting every day until this is over."

Annie laughed.

"What's funny?" Elizabeth asked with raised eyebrows and a stern face.

"I just bet myself five dollars that I'd have to send an attendance report to accounting every day."

"Oh," Elizabeth said. She obviously was in no mood for jokes. She had put her purse away and was emptying her leather folder onto the desk. She sat down heavily. Annie sat on the chair facing her and noticed how drawn and tense she looked.

"We now have five contingency plans worked up. Everything should be covered. The teachers' association is moving their pickets to different sites from their home schools," Elizabeth explained.

"What for? What's the point of that?"

"We assume the reasoning behind it is that people are too emotionally involved at their own school. The association doesn't want teachers to see their own students and perhaps weaken in their resolve. We will probably have high school teachers picketing this school and our teachers might picket the high school or junior high."

"What's the word on how long this garbage is going to last? Did anyone know anything?"

"Not much," Elizabeth answered. "They're negotiating again tonight, I guess. It might be a long time, Annie."

"It can't be. We wouldn't survive it. This is too much of a strain on everybody."

"Yes, well, I hope you're right," she replied. She stood up and said, "I'm going out to the playground to see what's going on." She walked briskly out the front door. Elizabeth was upset - no doubt about it.

She was no sooner out of the door when a little girl, about eight years old, was coming in and threw up right in the doorway. Luckily, most of it went on the outside of the frame. "Geez," Annie groaned. She helped her into the health office where Loren was bandaging a scraped knee.

"Got another one for you here. She just vomited in the doorway. Clean her up and call her mother, will you?" she instructed Loren. She reached in the cabinet under the sink in the health office and got a bag of the sawdust type stuff which absorbs and deodorizes vomit. She held the front door open and liberally sprinkled the whole bag of the stuff all over the doorway inside and out. She called Joe on the all-call. He rang her back on the intercom.

"Got a problem?" he asked in a cheerful voice.

"Sure do. A little girl threw up right in the office doorway. I put the sawdust on it."

"I'll be there in a few minutes. I'm right in the middle of something."

"Okay, Joe, as soon as you can."

The bell rang for classes to start.

Elizabeth came back to the office with two boys walking in front of her. "Into my office," she ordered them in a no-nonsense tone of voice. She picked up the intercom phone on Annie's desk and rang room sixteen. "This is the principal," she said into the phone. "Craig Brooks is in my office at the present time." She hung up and punched the buttons for room thirteen. "This is the principal. Jeremiah Cooke is in my office at the present time." She hung up the phone, went into her office, and closed the door behind her.

Annie and Loren looked at each other with questioning glances. "Fighting, I suppose," Annie guessed.

About ten minutes later Elizabeth came out, went to the intercom and called four more boys to the office. She sent the first two to sit at the front table.

Joe came in and vacuumed up the sawdust and the mess it had covered. In Annie's opinion, that sawdust concoction ranked second only to the flush toilet on a scale of the important inventions of mankind. She didn't know how schools functioned before it was available. It seemed like little kids were always vomiting.

* * * * * * *

Attendance sheets were starting to be delivered by students from each classroom. A kindergarten boy and girl came in holding hands. The teachers always sent the kindergarten kids to the office by two's in hopes they would keep each other from getting lost. The girl clutched the attendance sheet in her free hand while the boy tried to get the heavy front door open with his free hand. He got the door open a couple of inches, then using his feet and then his butt, tried to push it open wider all the time keeping hold of the girl's hand. Luckily, Joe was still by the door and helped them when he noticed how the little boy was struggling. They had obviously been told not to let go of each other's hand and they didn't.

"Here's the sheet for the secretary and we didn't lose it on the way," said the girl.

They weren't tall enough to see over the counter so Annie walked over to them, took the sheet, and said, "You did a good job, both of you. I'm very proud of you."

They both giggled in acknowledgement and turned to go. Joe held the door open for them and they went out still clasping hands.

Elizabeth's four boys arrived and she ushered them into her office.

Annie started working on the attendance report. It looked like they had about a forty percent absenteeism rate. That would be a blow to the business office. These would be mostly unexcused absences because of the strike and the state didn't pay schools for unexcused absences. The only absences that qualified as excused were: illness, doctor or dentist appointments, or death in the family. If this kept up, the strike would cost the district a lot of money.

Elizabeth came out of her office. "Mrs. Kallas, I need four detention slips. These four boys are going to have detention for the next two days. Those two at the front table are on suspension until Monday. Their mothers are coming to get them."

"What did they do?" Annie whispered to her.

"They brought firecrackers to school that sound like gunshots when they're set off. Firecrackers at school are always against the rules and we certainly don't need anything that sounds like gunfire around here right now." She went back into her office. A few minutes later the four boys came out with detention slips in hand. "Go back to your classrooms now. Give the slip to the detention teacher this afternoon. Craig and Jeremiah," she called to the two at the front table, "you two go up to your rooms and get your coats and books and get ready to go home. Come back here and wait for your mothers to arrive."

She fixed herself a cup of coffee, went back in her office, and sat down at her desk. Annie followed and sat down facing her. "I've never seen you so tense, Elizabeth. Anything I can do to help?"

"They expect trouble this afternoon after the students leave. They'll have teachers from other schools here picketing - not our own teachers. They expect an effort to be made to intimidate the substitutes. I guess I'm feeling a little resentful that the teachers are inflicting all these additional problems on me."

Annie started to answer, "Why blame the teachers? The administration is at least equally to blame." Remembering that Elizabeth was a member of the administration and was being subjected to all of their propaganda, Annie guessed it probably would be expedient for her to keep her mouth shut! Instead she said, "You tell me if there is anything I can do." Elizabeth nodded and Annie went back to her desk.

The attendance reports were almost all in from the rooms so she sat down in earnest to work on them. The superintendent wanted percent of absences by grade and school so, since they had two or three classes in each grade, she made up a chart and figured it by class, then combined it into a percent by grade. It was a lot of work and she worked on it uninterrupted for the next hour.

About eleven o'clock they had a call from the teacher in room eleven. Deborah Bradfield was one of the teachers who had not gone out on strike because she considered it unprofessional. "Office, Annie speaking."

"Annie, can you send Joe down here? I just had a boy stick a piece of metal into a wall outlet and sparks flew all over. I--"

"Is the boy okay?"

"Yes, he's all right. I guess he got a little shock which taught him a big lesson about electricity. Anyway, I never noticed until now that the wall plate was broken. Can you have Joe come down and fix it?"

"Sure, right away," Annie answered. She punched the all-call buttons. "Mr. Sullivan, call the office, please. Mr. Sullivan."

When Joe rang back she told him about the sparks flying in room eleven. "Damn, what'll they think up next? I'll go right down and check it out."

"Thanks, Joe." As she did at least five times a week, she gave a little prayer of thanks for Joe. She didn't know how the school would manage without him.

Then it was lunch time and after that the clock, in its inexorable way, moved closer and closer toward three o'clock. Annie looked out of the window at two-thirty and saw a group of strangers re-forming the picket line. She guessed these were teachers from other schools in the district. This staff didn't know them and they didn't know this staff. It was a good maneuver on the association's part. Probably all teachers would hesitate to create a ruckus on their own campus but they had no emotional ties to a different campus. If Elizabeth's source was right, they were planning trouble to scare the substitutes off. Annie didn't believe they would do anything really bad but got more and more nervous anyway.

At two forty-five Elizabeth got on the all-call system. "Please release all walkers immediately. All walkers are to be released immediately. I'll be at the crosswalk," she called to Annie as she hurried out.

The buses got there at two-fifty-five. Ann wondered why they couldn't be that punctual when there wasn't a strike. When the bell rang at three o'clock, the students were loaded onto the buses and left promptly at five after three. Again, she wondered why they couldn't do it when there wasn't a strike. In normal times, they sometimes took until three-twenty to get organized and loaded.

The crucial hour had arrived. The substitutes were congregating in the staffroom and left in groups of three's and four's. As soon as they left the shelter of the buildings into the parking lot, the cries of "scab, scum, scab, scum" hit their ears. Tomatoes and eggs started flying and hit one of the young women substitutes who ran wildly to her car, jumped in, and made sure all the windows were up and the doors locked.

Elizabeth, Loren, and Annie watched out of the principal's window at what seemed like an unbelievable movie screening in front of them. They stood there horrified and fascinated. The teachers kept walking, kept picketing, kept chanting "scab, scum, scab" and kept throwing eggs, tomatoes, and other soft vegetable peelings at the substitutes as they ran to their cars.

The first young woman substitute, Annie remembered her name was Cybil, was in such a hurry to get away that she found her car first in line to break through the picket line. "Oh, geez," Annie said aloud, "look at the predicament she's in now."

They refused to break the line for her and effectively trapped all the substitutes in the parking lot. The cars were lined up trying to get out. They sat there for a few minutes while Cybil took the brunt of the verbal and vegetable abuse. Annie started to feel sorry for her. She was just a kid, maybe twenty-three years old, and was way out of her depth in this situation. Her windshield was full of squashed tomatoes and Annie could see she was crying.

After a few minutes of the stalemate, the teachers started leading their picket line toward Cybil's car. She saw them coming toward her and panicked. She must have tromped the accelerator because she made her car stall and then hysterically started it up again and drove headlong out of the parking lot regardless of the fact that picketers were in front of her.

Loren let out a shriek. Teachers, picket signs, and vegetables all went flying as they scrambled to get out of the way of Cybil's car. Once she had broken through, the rest of the substitutes left. Annie held her breath to see if anyone had been hurt, but they all picked themselves up and stood around talking for a few minutes so she guessed they were all right.

"Geez!" Annie turned to Elizabeth. "This is too much."

"I agree." Elizabeth went to her desk and put in a call to the district office. It took three attempts to get through because all the extensions were busy. When she finished talking, she told them, "The same type of thing is going on all over the district. The police are at six different schools.

It's worse at the high schools. I guess they have a near riot going on at one of them. That's why the police aren't here. From the sounds of it, we got off pretty easy."

"If that's easy, I don't want to find out what hard is. Are we going to have this kind of stupidity every day? How long can we live like this?" Annie asked. Joe was right. If they kept this up, the teachers would lose the sympathy of those who had been wishing them well.

"I don't know, Annie," Elizabeth replied, "maybe I'll find out something tonight. They've called us to another meeting."

"I'm going to get some coffee. You want some? Oh, by the way, you'll want to know our absentee rate is forty-three percent. I called it in to accounting."

"Oh, my, that is high. It means we're losing a lot of money. I think probably the teachers got to the parents and convinced a lot of them to keep their children home. The loss of all that money puts additional pressure on the administration. No, no, I don't want any coffee. I'm coffeed out."

Annie went into the staffroom to fill her cup and found the five non-striking teachers in there talking and working.

"Is it all over out there, Annie?" Ida Pierce asked her.

"Yes, it looks like they're wrapping it up for today, anyway."

"Was it bad?" asked Diana Neblett.

"It was bad. You were smart to wait in here. You don't need to get involved in that mess."

"We have to work with those people again, Annie," said Louise Wong in a miserable tone of voice.

"Our staff wasn't out there this afternoon. The people who were there were from other schools and they wouldn't know who were substitutes and who were regular teachers. I think they just assumed everyone they saw was a sub. You know," Annie continued, "I think our faculty understands how you all feel. They might not like it but they do understand it. It's the substitutes they're really mad at."

"They might understand, but things will never be the

same as they once were," said Ida. "The staff will always be divided between those who did and those who didn't go on strike."

"I'm sure that'll be true for awhile but it'll fade as new problems arise. Anyway, let's not worry about the future while we have a very real present to worry about. How're you going to get home?"

"We'll wait until they all leave. We have plenty of work to do while we're waiting," answered Diana. "You know, I feel like I'm in a castle that's being besieged. I have to wait for the siege to be lifted before I can get out."

Annie appreciated her attempt to lift everyone's spirits. "Maybe your Prince Charming will come and rescue you," she added in the same vein.

"The only one around is the night custodian and he's not suitable. I must have someone who loves rats as I do," she joked. She was referring to Clyde's hatred of the white rats in the classrooms.

They all laughed and Annie went back into the office. When she left an hour later, everything was quiet. She was the last one to leave. She stood in the parking lot and thought of how close they had come to a real tragedy. Cybil could have killed someone when she drove out so recklessly. There were pieces of vegetables scattered over the parking lot. She stared at one spot where a half dried squashed tomato lay and thought how at first glance it looked like a small pool of blood. It was like their home had been violated. Many of the staff spent more time here than they did at home and loved it equally. She was glad it wasn't their own teachers who had done this.

* * * * * * *

When she went in the next morning, the teachers on the picket line were quietly walking up and down the sidewalk. She didn't know anyone on it. "Morning, Elizabeth. Anything new?"

"Morning, Annie. They expect a shortage of substitutes

as a result of yesterday's violence. And...the district cut short yesterday's negotiating session because of the violence and no one seems to know when the next session will be."

"Oh, that's just great. How are they going to get anywhere if they don't even meet? And how are we going to cover the classrooms if there aren't enough subs? Shiiiiiittt!"

"Right," Elizabeth agreed. Under normal conditions the principal would have remonstrated at her bad language. They were never supposed to use cuss words on campus for fear a student would hear. "If we don't get enough subs, we'll have to put Dorner in a classroom. Beyond that, I don't even want to think about it. We would have to start doubling up classrooms, I guess. The aides can be a big help to us. They've been invaluable already in keeping some continuity in the classrooms. Most of them could run a classroom for the three hours a day they're here under some supervision from a teacher. Let me know as soon as you find out how many subs we're missing."

"Okay." Annie sat at her desk and figured up how many subs were needed to cover the rooms. They had eighteen classroom teachers. Five didn't go on strike, so they needed thirteen subs. They could put Dorner into a classroom so that meant they could manage with twelve subs.

The substitutes started arriving a few minutes later. No sign of Cybil. Annie figured she wouldn't be back. The substitutes signed in and she gave out keys and instructions. During a lull in their arrivals, she went to the window to see what was happening outside. The picket line was politely breaking to let cars into the parking lot. They were walking proudly but quietly.

"Anything happening out there?" asked Loren.

"No, it's quiet, thank heaven." By eight o'clock eleven subs had signed in. "Elizabeth, we've got eleven. What now? I don't know if any more are coming or not. Hey, wait a minute! Look who's here. It's Linda Chamberlain. Are you coming to work?" Annie asked her as she gave her a quick hug.

"Yes, I'm back. I have no appreciation for what happened yesterday so I decided to come back to work." She turned to Elizabeth. "That is, if it's okay with you. I can't strike any longer."

"Yes, of course it is," Elizabeth answered. "We wish you would all come back. There is a substitute in your room, however. I'll call him and tell him to come up here and we'll reassign him. Annie, what's the count now? What are we short?"

"We have eleven subs, plus Linda now makes twelve and we need thirteen"

"I'll ask Maggie Dorner to take a class. Which are the rooms without teachers?"

"I have no one in room sixteen and no one in room nine."

"Let's put the male sub in room sixteen. Those sixth graders might do better with a man. I'll tell Maggie to go in room nine. Does that make us square then?"

"Yes, that's it."

The bell rang a few minutes later and they settled down to a quiet morning. It was Friday and it seemed like everyone was tired. It had been a hard, nerve-wracking week.

* * * * * * *

Annie got a lot of work done before lunch and was feeling satisfied with herself. There had been only a couple of students in the health office and Loren took care of them. They hadn't even had anyone in the office because of naughtiness. Even the children must be tired. "Any reason I shouldn't go to lunch, Loren?" Annie asked her.

"No, go ahead."

She gathered up her things for lunch and went into the staffroom. Ida Pierce and three substitutes were in there. She sat next to Ida and started eating her sandwich. "How're you doing, Ida?" she asked.

"Okay, I guess. It's all kind of dreary under the circumstances."

"Yes, I know." They sat quietly side by side - they understood each other and didn't need to talk.

The substitutes were at the other end of the table. They were comparing notes. "This is certainly one rough school. I was telling my mother last night the way these kids talk and she couldn't believe nine year olds could talk that way," volunteered one young woman.

"I know what you mean. I told my husband last night about some of the things the kids do to each other like stealing each other's pencils and lunch money. He wanted to know if they were all African-American kids. I told him, no, only about one third were."

This substitute's name was Mary. She had done a lot of substitute work for the school in the past but this was a side of her Annie had never seen before.

Mary continued, "But I really don't think being African-American has much to do with that kind of bad behavior, do you?" Without giving anyone a chance to answer, she continued, "I think it's more a matter of personality than of blackness. I think there's all kinds of good, honest, black people. I had a black teacher in college one time. He was a good teacher and very nice. So, I'm sure it's the personality of the person which makes them steal and fight."

"The biggest thing wrong with these kids is their lack of respect," said a young man sub named Rick. "I'm having a hard time controlling them. You tell them to stop talking and they keep right on talking. You tell them to sit down and they keep right on walking around. If they came from decent families, they wouldn't do that. Their parents would have taught them some respect for the teacher." The other two substitutes nodded in agreement.

"It's a bad neighborhood, all right," said the young woman. "You're right, decent people wouldn't live around here."

"There are a great many decent families living in this neighborhood," Annie said, trying to control her temper. "Many of them might be poor but that doesn't mean they're not decent. How well would you function if you were trying to support six people on about two thousand dollars a month?"

"Why don't they go out and work and not sit home on welfare? They'd get more money if they weren't so eager to make the taxpayer support them," Rick said.

"You're a damn jackass, do you know that?" Annie said, standing up and throwing caution to the winds. "A family of six gets poverty level money on welfare. If you don't think people would rather be out working and making more than that, you're crazy. Most of them would give their right arm to have had the education and opportunities which so obviously have been wasted on you."

Rick was as furious as she was. He walked up to her and said in a tight, controlled voice, "I'm going to file a complaint against you. You're not going to talk to me like that and get away with it."

"Go ahead and complain. You deserved every bit of it. What right have you to come into our territory and criticize our people? You don't know a thing about them." She packed up her lunch things and went banging back into the office.

"What's eating you?" asked Loren.

"Where's Elizabeth?"

"Out on the playground."

"Go on to lunch, Loren. I'll take over here. Anybody in the health office?"

"No. I knew you'd be in a terrible mood so I told them all to hurry up and get better before you came back," Loren said.

Annie had to laugh. "Go on, get out of here."
Rick came into the office about five minutes later. "Where's the principal?" he asked.

"I was told she's out on the playground. You might find her there."

It was lunch recess time so she was busy for the next half hour bandaging scraped knees and elbows, blisters on palms of hands from the bars on the playground, dirt in the eyes, upset stomachs, and trying to find lost soccer balls.

Loren came back from lunch just as Elizabeth came back from the playground.

"Can I see you in my office, please, Annie?"

She went in and Elizabeth closed the door behind them. "Rick Baldwin wants to file an official complaint against you and wants it put into your personnel file," she said in a worried voice.

"Let him do it. I have a legal right to attach my explanation to his statement and it'll be on record what a fool he is. Elizabeth, don't worry about it. I can take care of myself. You have enough to worry about right now."

"Did you really call him a 'damn jackass'?"

"Yes, I did. And I was right, too."

"Your tactfulness sometimes leaves a little to be desired, Annie."

"I know."

* * * * * * *

Things were quiet for about an hour when suddenly there was a loud commotion at the front door. Rick Baldwin held the door open while he ushered his entire class into the office.

"What on earth are you doing?"

"You can have them. You think they're so great - you can have them. I give up. They don't want to learn. They don't even want to be civilized human beings. They only want to make a lot of noise, disobey, and be disrespectful. You take them - I'm leaving," he repeated.

Elizabeth had come out of her office to see what was going on. "Just a minute, Mr. Baldwin. Come into my office, please."

Annie looked at the approximately twenty sixth graders squeezed into the front reception area which was built for about ten people at most. "Don't any of you say one word." They stood there quietly shifting from one foot to another waiting to hear their fate.

Elizabeth opened her door a few minutes later. Rick

Baldwin walked from her office, shouldered through the students, out the front door, and out to the parking lot.

"Do you mean to tell me he actually left? He dumped the class here in the office and left?"

"That's it, Annie. That's what he did, all right." She shook her head. "We only have an hour left. I'll have to take over the class. Boys and girls, I want you to line up by two's and follow me to your room," Elizabeth instructed them.

Annie watched out of the window. Elizabeth never looked back but the students did what she had told them. They were in an almost perfect line, by two's, behind her. "That lady is something else! I guess there are teachers and then there are teachers," Annie said to Loren.

* * * * * * *

The rest of the day passed quietly and quickly which are the two main requirements for a Friday afternoon. If they could get through the going home time with no problems, they would be more than grateful.

Elizabeth came back into the office at two forty-five. "Think there'll be any trouble from the picket line today, Elizabeth?"

"No, I don't think so. They got a bad press yesterday and I guess about fifty teachers throughout the district went back to work today as a protest against the violence. I think they'll be a little more restrained today."

She was right. They got the students off and then the subs out with nary a harsh word spoken. Elizabeth left about three-thirty and Loren and Ann sneaked out at three forty-five instead of four o'clock. "Have a good weekend, Loren. We may have a worse week next week."

"You're a cheerful one, aren't you? I'll bet you it'll be all over by Monday."

"I doubt it. They're not even negotiating anymore."

"Oh? How do they expect to solve it?"

"I don't know. See you Monday."

* * * * * * *

The phone rang as Annie was getting ready for bed Sunday night. "Hello."

"Annie, this is Elizabeth."

Her heart flipped in fear. "What's wrong?"

"Nothing. I just wanted to tell you the strike has been settled."

"Oh, I can't believe it! How did it happen? They weren't even speaking."

"Yes, I know. It's a small miracle. I guess they started a marathon negotiating session yesterday afternoon at about four o'clock and continued until they came to an agreement. It ended about seven o'clock this evening. The teachers will still have to vote on it but it's just a formality. They'll be back at work tomorrow."

"Halleluiah! Gad, that's great. Maybe we can get back to normal now. Thanks for calling me, Elizabeth."

Annie phoned Ray whose line was busy but a few minutes later he called her, "Darling, the strike's over. I can't believe it, it's so great."

"Oh, I know. I feel wonderful. Elizabeth just called me to tell me the news. Do you know what the settlement was?"

"The word is that we got four percent instead of the six we asked for but that's okay. We got something and now it's over which is the important thing. I wish you were here. It seems like we should be together at such a happy time. How about it?"

"How about tomorrow night, Ray? I'm already in my pajamas and ready for bed and tomorrow's going to be a big day so we really should get a good night's sleep, don't you think?"

* * * * * * *

Annie found herself awake again at four o'clock. She lay in bed and worried about how everyone would behave that day. Would there be friction between the strikers and the principal or between the strikers and non-strikers? How should she act? She was so glad it was over she wanted to hug everybody and welcome them back but maybe she had better follow Elizabeth's lead. She'd have it all figured out, Annie was sure. She couldn't get back to sleep so as a result was at work a half hour early. Elizabeth was already there.

"Anything new?" Annie asked.

"The returning teachers have to sign in this morning. I've prepared a sheet for the purpose. We'll keep the staffroom door locked forcing them to come in through the office. I'll tell them to sign in as they arrive. Please try to be alert, Annie, and help me get everyone's signature this morning."

"Sure," Annie answered. Wow, it seemed the teachers were going to get a frosty greeting from their principal as they came in. She wondered if it was the right way to handle the situation. She didn't very often question Elizabeth's decisions because she was almost always right but she wondered about this one. It didn't seem that showing resentment or coolness would be the way to bring the staff back together. She looked at Elizabeth to see if she dared make a suggestion. Her mouth was grim and tight. She was tense. No, Annie didn't think Elizabeth would be receptive to what she wanted to say. Well, it was her ball game. She had to coach it the way she saw fit.

Ray was the first one in. He looked pale and tired and obviously worried about the reception he was going to get. Elizabeth stood behind the counter facing the front door with her sign-in sheet on the counter in front of her. Ray had gone to the staffroom door, found it locked, and in bewilderment and probably trepidation had tried the office door. As he opened it, the first thing he saw was the principal standing grimly behind the counter facing him. Elizabeth was making a big mistake, but Annie didn't know what to do to stop it.

"Hello, Ray," Elizabeth said. "The superintendent is requiring all teachers to sign in this morning." She indicated the sheet. "You still have your key?"

"Yes, I have it," he answered. He looked stricken, embarrassed and resentful. He signed in and then came around the counter toward the staffroom door. Annie had been standing at her desk watching him. She walked up to him holding out her hands, and said, "Welcome back, Ray." He held her hands for a moment with tears in his eyes and went into the staffroom.

Carolyn Tyler was next in. Elizabeth greeted her the same way. Carolyn's face turned crimson in anger and she stormed into the staffroom after signing in. She didn't even look at Annie, so Annie didn't get a chance to try to soften the blow. If Elizabeth kept this up with all the strikers, this staff would never recover from the strike and its aftermath. What could she do? Half-formed ideas raced through her mind.

Janice Sexton walked in at the same time as Loren did. Janice held the door while Loren juggled an enormous flat cake in her hands. She was happy and giggling and exuberant and immediately broke the tension. "I'm so glad it's all over and everybody's back. Now things can get back to normal," she giggled.

Here was the answer to her prayer. Annie hurriedly helped Loren take the cake into the staffroom. The cake was about eighteen by twenty-four inches. It was decorated with yellow and pink and blue flowers and she had written "Welcome Home" on the top of it. It was perfect! Why in hell hadn't she thought about doing something like that?

Loren walked up to Ray and Carolyn Tyler and gave each of them a big hug, saying to each in her bubbling way, "I'm so glad you're back. Get everyone to take a piece of cake for good luck before they go to class. Okay?"

"Sure will," answered Ray, looking like ten years had fallen from him.

Loren bubbled her way back into the office while Annie followed behind her. "Loren, when did you have time to make the cake?"

"Most of the night. I started it after you phoned me at ten-thirty and I guess I got done about one-thirty. I just thought it would be nice."

"It's wonderful! It's an absolutely marvelous idea."

Loren was so happy and exuberant she was totally unaware of any tension on Elizabeth's part. Loren ran up to everyone as they opened the door, swept them into a hug and cried, "I'm so glad you're back." If Elizabeth thought she was punishing the teachers with her icy greeting, she was mistaken. By the time Loren got finished with them, they didn't even notice Elizabeth's coolness.

After five of the returning teachers had come in, Elizabeth was having second thoughts. She couldn't help but notice that everyone was jubilant at being together again. Loren hugged them at the door, Elizabeth greeted them frigidly at the counter, and then Annie hugged them again on their way past her desk. Everyone was laughing and crying together amidst happy greetings. Everyone except Elizabeth. It became more and more noticeable.

She suddenly turned to Annie and said, "Will you please ask the teachers to sign in. I'm going outside."

After she went out, Annie sneaked up to the window to see what she was doing. She blinked back tears as she watched Elizabeth hug each teacher as he/she walked up to the school.

Barbara Selby and Jeanne Curtis came in to the office together. "Well, that was a pleasant surprise," said Barbara. "I was a little afraid of the greeting we'd get this morning. But you sure can't beat getting a hug from the principal, can you? I was afraid she'd be angry at us."

"You get hugs from us, too," said Loren as she hugged each of them. "We're so glad you're back. It was terrible without you."

"Loren made a Welcome Back cake for you. Better go get a piece before it's all gone," Annie added as she gave each a hug.

The school hadn't seen that much hugging during one hour since it was built. The non-striking teachers picked up on the atmosphere and gave their share of hugs and "welcome backs." Everyone felt so good that the strike was over and they had the opportunity to get back to normal there was no room for resentment. Not right now, anyway. It might come later but by then all these good feelings would also be remembered.

It seemed as if at least fifty little children came into the office and asked, "Is my teacher back today? Is my teacher back?"

"Yes, your teacher is back. All the teachers are back today. Isn't it great?" Annie answered.

"Hooray," they cheered.

When the bell rang for class, Annie sat down at her desk and said, "Thank heavens, that's behind us and we can get back to normal." She looked over at Loren and studied her. Loren often irritated her with her constant giggle, her naiveté, her slowness and lack of initiative. But today, it seemed that very naiveté was what saved this school and its staff. She was totally oblivious to any undercurrents of tension or resentment. She did what was right and natural to her and in its very simplicity it was perfect. Sometimes Loren even actually deserved a raise.

* * * * * * *

When Ray opened the door, Annie went into his waiting arms. As he held her close, he nuzzled under the hair behind her ear and kissed her on her warm neck, "I love you."

"I love you, too. Ooh, that tickles. Ray, you better stop."

He kissed her on her mouth but then abruptly said, "Yes, you're right, I'd better stop. We're going to have a great dinner and talk about the strike and then I have something very serious I want to talk to you about."

As they ate, Annie asked how he thought the staff as a group was doing.

"You mean are they going to get along? I don't know. It'll take a long time for the strikers to forget that the non-strikers didn't go out. They can forgive them their decision not to strike because they understand about professionalism but they can't forget that they didn't honor our picket line. They can't forget it was our pain and suffering that got them a new contract from which the non-strikers will benefit as much as we will. It'll take a while. I think probably for the next few years this school district's teacher personnel will be divided between those who went out and those who didn't. It's too bad but I think that's what will happen. We're only human - all we can do is muddle through as best we can."

Annie shook her head in dismay. "It's terrible. It was the cohesiveness of the staff that made them so great. It really hurts me to have this divisiveness take over."

"I want you to think about something else now."

"Oh, what?"

"We've been seeing each other regularly for almost a year. You've become such a part of my life that I can't imagine a life without you so, before some other man comes along and grabs you away from me, I want you to become my wife."

Annie was dumbstruck. She stared at Ray while a thousand thoughts raced through her mind. She knew she loved him but she'd never even thought about marriage. She'd given up on marriage ten years ago. Why couldn't they just continue on as they were? It suited her fine. She felt she had the best of both worlds - the privacy of being single when she needed apartness and the companionship of being married when she needed togetherness.

"Annie?" he prodded.

"I don't know, Ray. I'm afraid of marriage. I don't know how good I'd be as a wife again. Marriage is so confining and stifling. Why can't we go on the way we are? What's wrong with this?"

"There's no commitment. That's what's wrong with it. I want us to make a public commitment to one another to love and cherish each other forever. I want us to have it so we can work and build on it. Then we can get closer and more intimate year after year and get old together. We have nothing now. Sure, we love each other but we're like teenagers. We see each other on dates and make love upon occasion but we both know either of us could break it off tomorrow without a penalty. No, darling, I've got to have more than that. I want my love to have some security so I can make it grow and put out buds and flower and shower us with its petals as they fall.

"You and I have only a beginning now. It's time to take the next step and make it official and public so our love for each other can grow and mature. How about it, Annie? Do you love me enough to want a life like that with me?"

"Ray, I wasn't kidding when I said I don't know how good a wife I could be. I've been single and selfish for a long time. Let me think about it for a few days. I promise I'll give you my answer the next time we see each other. Will that be okay?"

"It'll have to be. I don't know that any man has ever figured out how to get a woman to say 'yes' on demand. Sure, on Friday then?"

"Okay, on Friday."

As Annie drove home she felt a rush of varying emotions from dismay at the seriousness of the decision she was now faced with to elation that Ray loved her enough to want to marry her. Her thoughts swung from fear at the thought of being married again to pride that Ray had chosen her over the younger, prettier women he met daily including all the single women on the staff. But marriage? She didn't know if she was ready for it but she knew if she didn't agree to marry Ray, he wouldn't see her any more since it was obvious he wanted to be married and he would want to spend his time looking for someone who would agree to be his wife.

As she lay in bed, she moaned in disgust at the uncontrollable way thoughts were racing around in her head. She knew she wouldn't be able to get to sleep until she had made her decision and she knew it might take hours. She finally decided to make a mental list of pros and cons. Cons first: she didn't know if she was ready to be married with all the patience, hard work, and adjustments it entailed. Being married meant that from that day forward she would have to take another person into consideration. All the time. Every minute. She'd been single for ten years - when she was home, she didn't have to think about anyone except herself. It was nice. Selfish but nice. If she wanted a peanut butter and bologna sandwich for dinner, she could do it and not have to answer to anybody else. Did she want to give up her selfishness and freedom?

On the other hand, if she wanted a peanut butter and bologna sandwich for dinner if she was married to Ray, she was sure he would make it for her even though he might think she was crazy. And freedom? What did she do with her freedom now? It wasn't as though she went to wild parties. Mostly freedom meant she could stay in her pajamas all day on Saturdays if she wanted to.

Okay, get to the pros. The biggest one, of course, was that she would never be lonely again. She would have someone she loved and who loved her to go places with, to go away on week-ends with, to cuddle up to in bed at night with, and to whom she would be the most important person in the world. Would it be so hard to give up her desire to stay in her pajamas all day Saturdays in order to be Ray's wife? She'd have more interesting things to do with him than stay in her pajamas. Or maybe he'd stay with her in his pajamas. How about that? They wouldn't answer the phone or the doorbell. They'd just make believe they weren't home.

What would her life be like if he wouldn't see her any more? She'd gotten used to seeing him at least once during the week and almost always on week-ends. He usually had some interesting thing he'd thought up to do. She was never bored with him and he was always kind and considerate. Suppose it was taken away? She'd have a hard time adjusting to life without him. It would be harder than adjusting to life with him.

As more and more pros were added to the imaginary sheet in the air above her bed, she knew what her answer would be. She'd be crazy not to accept him. As she had told him at the beginning of school, he was a very eligible man and a very fine, honorable, sweet, loving person. Why was she even hesitating? What possible advantages of singlehood could outweigh the joy of being Ray's wife?

She couldn't wait another minute and turned the bedside light on and called his number. He picked it up on the first ring and she could envision him in bed wondering what this late phone call could be. "Yes, yes, yes, yes," she said in a deliberately sexy tone of voice.

He laughed and said, "Are you sure?"

"I can't understand why I didn't say yes right away. Of course, I'll marry you, Ray. I'm honored you want me and I'll try very hard to adjust well and be a good wife to you."

He laughed again and said, "You'll adjust well enough. Darling, we'll work it out - whatever it is - don't worry about it. That's part of the fun of being married - to be building something greater than each of us. I love you, Annie, and it will be wonderful to have you here with me every night and every day, too. You can't know what a relief it is to have it settled. I didn't know if I could wait until Friday to find out your answer."

"Just one thing, darling. Can we wait until the end of school before we announce it? Then we don't have to go through weeks and weeks of having people talk about it. We can tell them the last day or two of school and then maybe we can get married during the summer and we won't have to be around when people are talking about us. Can you live with that idea?"

"I'd like to go out on my porch this minute and yell as loud as I can 'Annie agreed to marry me' but I won't in deference to your desire for privacy. I guess I can wait until the end of school but it'll be hard. I'm so happy I want to share it with everyone."

"Good. Well, now it's all decided maybe we should try to get some sleep. I love you, Ray."

"I love you, Annie. Night."

JUNE

COUNTDOWN: Fifteen and a half more days. That was the message written on the chalkboard in the staffroom. It was the beginning of the end of the school year.

There were a sprinkling of days with temperatures over ninety degrees which immediately triggered a rash of misbehavior by the students. "Annie, please type this memo to the teachers with suggestions to help them with discipline now that it's getting warmer," Elizabeth said.

"What's the weather got to do with it?"

"You didn't know that when the weather gets warmer, the children start to act up?"

"No, I never heard that one before."

"Well, when the weather gets colder, it seems to dampen their exuberant spirits. The heat revives it which can create a lot of mischief and when it rains, it makes the children nervous and irritable. I don't know if anyone has ever done a study on weather affecting schoolchildren's behavior, but that's the way it seems to work out in practice. We need to get the memo out today, if possible, to help keep the lid on things."

"I'll do it right away, Elizabeth." Annie was doing a lot of word processing these days. So many things were scheduled for the last three weeks of school that a calendar had to be made up to remind teachers of: the last day the children could bring back library books, when to send letters home to parents to see if their children would be back at Lincoln in September, when report cards were due to the principal for review, the date of the party for staff members who were leaving, when the cum folders on each student had to be completed and returned to the office, and on and on and on.

This was the time of year, too, when many of the teachers took their one allotted field trip. They were allowed to choose where they wanted to take their students from a list of places published by the business department. Each school had an allowed amount of bus mileage they could use for field trips. It was the principal's responsibility to see the mileage was distributed fairly among the staff.

The teachers of the youngest students liked to stay close to home. One of their favorite spots was a small farm just outside of town where the owners - an elderly couple - enjoyed having the schoolchildren come visit. There, the children could see farm animals close enough to touch them and eat their lunches on picnic tables the owners had set up for that purpose. They could pet the lambs, piglets, and ducklings, and watch the colt run around behind his mother.

Jeanne Curtis and Patricia Campos had decided to combine their mileage and take their first graders to the local farm. The bus had been ordered, permission slips had been sent home to parents, parent volunteers had been recruited, sack lunches had been ordered from the cafeteria, and today was finally the big day.

The school buses finished their morning rounds and one sixty-passenger bus returned at nine o'clock to take them on their trip. Two of the Spanish speaking children in Mrs. Campos' room hadn't returned their permission slips so she needed to phone the students' homes to get verbal permission. One of the students had no phone at home and after a tearful conference with Elizabeth, Patricia had to leave him at school. The principal was adamant - no parental permission, no field trip. She was luckier with the other student. The mother admitted on the phone she had forgotten to return the slip and so the student could go.

They were finally all on the bus and ready to leave at nine-fifteen. Annie waved good-bye to them with a sigh of relief that all the commotion was over.

* * * * * * *

They pulled up in the big open space in front of the barn twenty minutes later. The farmer's wife was waiting for them. She walked up to the teachers and said, "We glad to have you here. I'm Mrs. Weissenhausen."

"Hello, Mrs. Weissenhausen. I spoke to you on the phone. I'm Jeanne Curtis and this is Mrs. Campos. It's so nice of you to let us come to visit."

"We like to see the children. Since our own boys are grown up, we like to hear the children run and play. So, now, let them get off the bus and we go up there to the picnic tables and they can run around and stretch their legs and look at the animals," she said with a heavy German accent. "There is nothing will hurt them but they cannot take a baby from a mother. We go with them to see the babies and tell them about it. You have baby soon, too, yes?"

"Oh, yes," Jeanne laughed as she patted her very obvious bulge. "I'm due in about three weeks."

"And they don't make you quit your job?"

"No, they don't do that anymore. We're allowed to work as long as we feel well and the doctor says it's all right."

"Let's get these children off the bus, Jeanne, before they explode in there," Patricia prodded.

"Yes, of course. Come on, everybody. This side of the bus first, row by row, in an orderly manner. I'll stay here, Patricia, and unload them. Since you're faster than I am these days, will you take them to the picnic tables and start organizing things?"

"Sure. Let's go. Everybody follow me. In a nice line. That's it."

The farmer had set up six picnic tables under big eucalyptus trees in the middle of a meadow. Off to the right was a fenced field with a few horses and colts in it. As soon as the children saw the horses, they broke their orderly line and ran to the fence to see the horses close up. Patricia called to them, "Don't be too loud. We don't want to scare them and of course you never, ever, go through or over a fence. Remember, we talked about it in class?"

"We remember, Mrs. Campos," they called.

Jeanne followed along with Mrs. Weissenhauser at

the end of the line of children. Mrs. Weissenhausen was explaining, "We have new baby pigs, a calf, and puppies. Our 'Lassie' dog had five puppies about two weeks ago. We take the children to see them in a little while when they calm down a little from their long bus ride. Okay?"

"That would be fine, Mrs. Weissenhausen. They'll love it."

The two teachers and the four parent volunteers sat at the tables and watched the children run around looking at the horses and the pens of goats and pigs which were also nearby. The children squealed with delight as a family of ducks walked by in a line, seemingly unimpressed by so many noisy children so close to them.

Mrs. Weissenhausen returned in an hour and asked, "Are you ready to go in the barn and see the animals? Inside the barn, you must be a little quiet, okay? We don't want to scare the mothers."

The teachers got them lined up and they solemnly walked behind Mrs. Weissenhausen and visited a cow with a three day old calf, a pig with a litter of six squirming around all over her, and the collie named Gretchen with her five puppies who didn't have their eyes open yet. Patricia was explaining about all these babies - how old they were, how they were nursing, when they would be able to see - both in English and Spanish to her bilingual group. The children were fascinated. They went from the calf on his wobbly legs, to the squirming piglets, to the blind puppies and back again and were quiet and orderly the whole time.

But finally stomachs started growling and sensing a restlessness stirring, the teachers and parents guided them back to the picnic tables. The children eagerly attacked the contents of their sack lunches and afterward played their games or watched the horses some more.

"But soon it was time to leave and get back to school. The parents and teachers rounded them up and seated them on the bus. Jeanne routinely counted them: fifty-seven, fifty-eight, fifty-nine. Fifty-nine? I must have counted wrong. Patricia, would you count too, and see what you come up with?"

They stood at the front of the bus and counted silently. "I get fifty-nine, Jeanne."

"And I get fifty-nine. Oh-oh, we started out with sixty. Who've we lost?"

"We'll have to call roll. I'll go first." Patricia called off the names on her class roll. Each child answered, "here" as his/her name was called. When she got to Heriberto Torres there was no answer. "Heriberto, are you on this bus?" There was no answer. "Well, that's it then. He's gone off some place. We'll have to go find him."

"Mrs. Brown, can you and Mrs. Garcia and Mrs. Hollis keep the children in order here while we go searching?"

"Sure, we can. We'll have a sing-a-long or something."

Patricia and Jeanne walked back to the picnic area and called, "Heriberto, Heriberto!" He didn't respond so they walked rapidly through the barn looking in all the stalls calling his name. There was still no response. Jeanne sat down heavily on a bench at the door to the barn. "I'm starting to get worried, Patricia. Where on earth could he be?"

"I don't know," she said, shaking her head. "Maybe we should get Mrs. Weissenhausen. She might have some ideas. Why don't you rest there while I go find her? You look kind of pale."

"Thanks. I am a little tired."

Patricia returned five minutes later with Mrs. Weissenhausen. They both looked worried. "Where can the boy be? You called and called and he not answered?"

"No, he didn't answer. Mrs. Weissenhausen, you don't have any old wells or holes around here he could fall into, do you?"

"No, no, nothing like that here. We very careful. Nothing here can hurt children."

"Well, where could he be? We've looked all over and called and called."

"Why don't we look again? I take the milking house. Mrs. Campos, you take the chicken house. And you, Mrs.

Curtis, you take the horse stalls. We meet back here again. The boy's name is...?"

"Heriberto."

"Heriberto? What a strange name," said Mrs. Weissenhausen.

Ten minutes later they met again and Jeanne sank gratefully to the bench. No one had seen or heard anything.

"Jeanne, are you all right? You're really pale."

"I don't know. I feel funny. But never mind me. Where can he be?" She suddenly started sobbing. "Where can he be? Have we lost a child? Patricia, have we lost a child?"

Patricia put her arms around her and comforted her, "No, no, we haven't lost a child. He's temporarily misplaced, that's all. We'll find him. You just stay here and rest. Mrs. Weissenhausen and I will search some more and be back in a little while."

Patricia and the farmer's wife walked slowly through the barn looking right and left. "Look, look, Mrs. Campos, look there."

"Where? I don't see anything."

"With Gretchen. The boy - he there. He sleeps with Gretchen and her babies."

Patricia looked closer into the dimly lit stall and finally saw Heriberto on the straw sound asleep curled up against Gretchen's back. It looked like Gretchen was sleeping too, with her puppies nursing fitfully in their sleep. "What a picture! I wish I had a camera," she said as she smiled in relief. "Thank you for seeing him, Mrs. Weissenhausen. I was getting really worried. Wow, what a scare. It's frightening to think we might have lost a child."

"Yes. yes, but he's safe. I go in and get him." She opened the door to the pen and talked softly to the dog as she gently shook Heriberto awake.

Patricia called to him in Spanish and he woke up. He asked his teacher sleepily what he was doing there and she told him he had scared them half to death and to come on out, they needed to get the bus going. Rubbing his eyes with his fists, he followed Mrs. Weissenhausen out of the stall. Mrs. Campos hugged him fiercely, all the while scolding him in Spanish for making her worry.

They hurried out of the barn to share the good news. "Jeanne, we've got him! We found him! He was in the stall sleeping with Gretchen. He..." Patricia stopped talking as she realized something was wrong. "What is it, Jeanne? Are you all right?" She leaned over and looked into Jeanne's face. "Oh, my goodness! The baby... Has the baby started, Jeanne?"

"I don't know. I guess so. I'm all right. Is he okay? Heriberto, is he all right?" she asked between gasps for breath as the pain receded.

"He's fine. Just fine," she patted Jeanne's hand. "Now, what about you? Are you having pains?"

"Just two. About ten minutes apart. Let's get back to school, Patricia. I just want to get back to school."

"Okay, let's get to the bus. We'll be at school before you know it." With Mrs. Weissenhausen's help, they got Jeanne and Heriberto onto the bus. Patricia asked the bus driver to come off the bus and she explained to her about Jeanne.

The driver said, "I'll have you back at school in twenty minutes. If she's only had two pains and this is her first baby, she's not going to have the baby all that fast. It'll be okay. I'll give you a smooth ride back. Come on, let's get going."

Patricia turned and shook Mrs. Weissenhausen's hand. "Thanks so much for everything you've done. We had a marvelous time."

"Come back again soon. Auf wiedersehen. Auf wiedersehen," she waved as the bus pulled away.

* * * * * * *

"Annie, Annie, come out to the bus - I need you. Come on, hurry! Jeanne's having her baby!" An excited Patricia Campos called in as she slammed the front door open.

"Geez!" Annie jumped up from her desk and followed Patricia out to the bus. "What's going on? What happened?"

"She's had four pains now. They're ten minutes apart. Help me get her into the office, okay?"

"Sure." They both got back onto the bus which was empty except for Jeanne and the bus driver. The children had been sent back to their classrooms with the parent volunteers. "Your little gal there just couldn't wait until school was out, could she?" teased Annie as she leaned over Jeanne, held her hand, and peered into her face. "What's happening?"

"The pains are ten minutes apart and I've had four pains." She looked up at Annie with a mixture of fear and exhilaration on her face.

"That's fine, Jeanne. You've got lots of time. Do you want me to call your doctor?"

"No, I want my husband. We're going through this together, so he needs to be here. Will you call him, Annie?"

"Sure, honey. You come on now and lay down on the cot in the health office and get a little rest." Jeanne slowly and carefully stepped down the steep steps on the bus with Patricia and Annie helping. "Patricia, you better go to your classroom and see what's going on there. I'll take care of Jeanne."

After she settled Jeanne on the cot, she said, "If you're all right, I'll go call your husband."

"I'm fine. Oh-oh, I think another one is starting now. Oh, Annie!" she gasped as she reached for her hand. She gave quick, short pants as she had been instructed to do.

Annie tried not to let the pain of Jeanne's pressure on her hand show but as soon as Jeanne's pain let up she gently released her hand and furtively rubbed it behind her back. "That lady is strong," she said to herself.

"I'm going to call your husband now, Jeanne. You rest there. Call me if you need me." She went to her desk and after looking in the personnel records, placed a call to Jeanne's husband on his cell phone. He was an outside salesman for an office machine company. When there was no answer, Annie phoned the company office and was informed by his secretary that Tim Curtis was out of the office but she expected him to call in soon. She would give him the message that his wife was in labor at the school. She sat down next to Jeanne and told her what the secretary had said.

"That's okay, Annie. I think he calls in every hour or so. Maybe the battery on his cell ran down or something. He talks on it all the time."

"I think I should call your doctor and alert him, Jeanne, don't you?"

"I guess so. His number is in my bag. Will you hand it to me, please? Here it is. It's Dr. Gordon - and here's the number. Thanks, Annie. Tell him I've had five pains now. The last one was seven minutes apart."

"Okay, I will. Do you want some water or anything?"

"No, I'm fine. But even if I did, I could get up and get it. You don't need to spoil me."

"It's my pleasure to spoil you right now." Annie leaned over and kissed her hair.

The nurse in Dr. Gordon's office gave Annie instructions that Jeanne should go to the hospital when the pains were three minutes apart. She would alert the hospital to prepare for Jeanne's arrival.

* * * * * * *

The bell rang for the end of the school day. Annie was kept busy helping Loren handle students, teachers, and parents until the buses pulled out, parents left, and teachers settled down to work on the next day's lesson plans. Word had spread throughout the school that Jeanne was in labor in the health office.

Patricia Campos was the first one in to see her after the students left. She sat on the end of a cot while Jeanne nervously paced back and forth in the small office. "Annie, would you call my husband's office again for me? He should have called in by now."

"Sure." She learned that Tim Curtis had not yet phoned his office for messages. She convinced his secretary it was getting urgent and the secretary agreed to call around to see if she could locate him. Annie told Jeanne and then asked, "How about your mother or sister, or someone?

Isn't there someone who could stay with you at home until it's time to go to the hospital?"

"Yes. Call my mother, will you? Her number is on my emergency card." Annie called the number but there wasn't any answer. "Nobody expected me to be so early, that's the problem. Well, I'll wait a little while longer. Patricia, you don't have to sit with me. I'll be all right."

"No. I'll stay. I was there at the beginning of the labor and I want to see it through. I want this baby to be part mine when it's born."

"That's really nice of you, Patricia. Maybe I can do the same for you someday."

"Not on your life! I've got my two and it's enough for me," she said so vehemently they all laughed.

As other teachers came in to see Jeanne and hold her hand during the pains, Annie went back to her desk to finish up her day's work. She was starting to get worried about their inability to contact Jeanne's family. It was almost four o'clock and still no word from Tim Curtis. She called Jeanne's mother's house again but still no answer. Jeanne's pains were every five minutes now and the time was rapidly approaching when she would need family - not friends - to be with her.

Loren left at four o'clock and the teachers gradually started leaving to attend to their own commitments at home. Annie, Patricia, and Jeanne were there alone. At four forty-five Annie called Tim Curtis' office again and received the same answer. He had not called in but messages had been left everywhere he was expected to stop that afternoon. Their office would close at five o'clock.

Patricia went back to her classroom to lock it up. Annie was about to try phoning Jeanne's mother again when she heard a startled cry, "Oh, Annie, look what I've done!"

She ran into the health office and asked, "What, Jeanne, what? What have you done?"

Looking tearful and embarrassed, Jeanne answered, "I've wet my pants. I've wet my pants! I can't believe it. I'm all wet, Annie, and I didn't even feel like I had to go to the bathroom. I'm so embarrassed. What am I going to do, Annie? I'm all wet."

She looked like she was going to cry so Annie gave her a hug and said, "You haven't wet your pants, Jeanne. Your water broke, that's all. You're going to have to get to the hospital. Here are some paper towels to clean up as best you can and dry yourself off. I'll try your mother again and then we'd better make some plans."

Annie went back to her desk and called Jeanne's mother again. She gave a sigh of relief when the phone was answered. She explained the situation to the mother, Mrs. Adams, who promised to be there within ten minutes. She then called the doctor's office. The nurse advised her to have Jeanne meet the doctor at the hospital as soon as possible. Annie called Patricia on the intercom and advised her of what had happened and asked her to come back to the office. She then went in and helped Jeanne become more comfortable.

"How close are they now, Jeanne?"

"Still about five minutes, maybe a little faster. I'm starting to get tired, Annie."

"Sure you are. But you'll be more comfortable in the hospital when you're in that adjustable bed they have. You'll be able to rest a little in between pains when you're there."

"I want Tim. Where is he?"

"I dunno, but the messages are bound to catch up with him soon or else he'll just naturally come home. It's getting late now. It's after five o'clock, so you should be able to reach him at home pretty soon." The phone rang. "Maybe that's him now," she said as she picked up the phone. "Lincoln - Mrs. Kallas speaking."

"Mrs. Kallas, do you have my wife there? This is Tim Curtis."

"We sure do. Am I glad to hear from you! We almost have your child, too. She needs to get to the hospital pretty quick now."

"I'll be right over - I'm about fifteen minutes away. Wait for me. Don't let anything happen. I'll be right there." He slammed down the phone in his excitement.

"He's on his way, Jeanne."

"Oh, that's good. I need him."

"Sure you do. Maybe this is your mom now." Someone was coming in the front door. Patricia Campos and Mrs. Adams came in the door together.

"Hello, mother. I'm glad to see you. I was beginning to wonder if I'd have to go to the hospital alone."

"Hi, baby. How are doing?" Mrs. Adams asked as she went to Jeanne and gave her a gentle hug and kiss.

"I'm starting to sweat, mother. All the old wives' tales were right, weren't they? It's no picnic giving birth, is it?" She grimaced and panted as another pain started up. Her mother gave her her hands to hold onto and never gave a sign that Jeanne was hurting her. They both relaxed together when the pain was over.

"Has anybody ever heard that school secretaries can get sympathetic labor pains - you know, like husbands get sometimes?"

They all laughed. "Honest," Annie continued, hoping to lighten the atmosphere. "I'm starting to feel them come and go along with Jeanne."

"Well, maybe it's true. Probably husbands feel them out of love for their wives. And certainly, Annie, no one could ever doubt you feel love for the teachers on this staff," Jeanne said with a catch in her voice. "I'm well aware you should have gone home hours ago and that you wouldn't think of leaving me until you're sure I'm in safe hands. I love you for it."

Annie felt hot tears spring to her eyes. She kissed Jeanne and turned away so no one would see her moist eyes.

A banging of the front door indicated the arrival of a distraught young husband. "You in here, Jeanne?"

"Here, Tim. In the health office."

"Oh, honey, are you all right?" he asked, burying his face in her neck and gently hugging her. "Have we got time to get to the hospital?"

Jeanne laughed. "We better have. I know all of you

don't want to deliver it here. But, let's get going. I don't want to have to go ninety miles an hour to get there."

"I'll go with you, Tim. Jeanne can sit in the back with me while you drive. Dad and I can come back here later and pick up Jeanne's and my cars," Mrs. Adams said.

"Sounds good, mom."

"Will one of you call me as soon as something happens?" Patricia asked. "I've written my name and number on this paper. I would appreciate it."

"Yes, of course, I will. I'll call either tonight or early in the morning before you go to work," Mrs. Adams said.

"And, Annie, as soon as I hear, I'll call you," Patricia said.

Jeanne walked slowly and stiffly to the car with her husband's arm around her waist. Tim got his wife and mother-in-law settled in the back seat and then got into the driver's seat. "Wish us luck," he called.

"Good luck, Jeanne, good luck."

"Thanks for your help, you two. You've been good friends." Jeanne and her mother waved as they drove away.

"Well, Patricia, that's as close as I ever want to come to helping a baby get born. How about you?"

"I know what you mean, Annie, but it's an interesting process."

"I'm sure it is. However, I'm perfectly happy leaving it to the professionals. Well, let's lock up and get out of here. I'll be expecting your call."

The call arrived at ten-thirty that evening. The baby girl had been born at eight-fifteen, about two hours after they left the school, and was named Patricia Ann after her mother's two good friends.

* * * * * * *

Annie and Ray stood together in the staffroom before the morning bell rang while Ray made their announcement. "Could I have your attention, please?" He waited as they gradually stopped talking. "Annie and I have something we want to share with you - our good friends. We are going to be married on July 24th and would like all of you to be there with us. We will--" But he was unable to finish as the commotion reached a roar.

"We didn't know--"

"How long has this been going on?"

"Why didn't you tell us?"

"You sneaky guys--"

Amidst congratulations and hugs, Annie could hear snatches of conversation about someone having guessed months ago, someone else never had any idea, someone else had been suspicious, and someone else had always thought they'd make a wonderful couple. As the questions about where they were going to live, would they both keep their jobs, where were they going to honeymoon, and on and on, the bell rang much to Annie's relief. She and Ray smiled at each other and then everyone went to work.

She went into the office and told Loren who screeched in delight and told Elizabeth the news when she came in from the playground.

"Annie, I had two people come out to the playground to share that information with me. You and Ray have dropped a bombshell here. But it's wonderful. I'm very happy for you both." She laughed, "I hope you can deal with being the topic of conversation all over this campus for the next day or two."

"I hate it. That's why we left it for the last days of school to announce. Hopefully, the talk will be cut short because everyone is so busy."

* * * * * * *

No graduation ceremony was held since the school only went to the sixth grade but there was an awards assembly. It was held the day before the last day of school.

The office stocked a supply of certificates for Perfect Attendance This Quarter, Perfect Attendance for the Whole Year, Good Academics, Good Citizenship, Most Improved Student, and a blank one which allowed teachers to write anything they wanted on it. Most teachers made an effort to see each child received some kind of award.

"I've got one boy though, Annie, who just doesn't deserve any award. He hasn't done one bit of work, he's always in trouble - fighting or picking on the other students, and sassy to me. What award could I possibly give him?" asked Mary Ann Duncan, as she counted out the exact number of each award she needed.

"He hasn't improved at all?"

"No, nothing, and I've tried everything."

"How's his attendance?"

"He's absent a lot."

"He's not good at anything? There's nothing he likes to do and is good at?"

"Nothing. He doesn't want to do anything. Oh, Annie, I know," her face lit up. "He's a good cook. When we made the yeast bread that time, he was the leader of the group. He seemed to understand about yeast and showed the other children how to punch down and roll out. Oh, Annie, thanks so much. You're a genius."

Annie laughed in surprise. "What did I do? You thought of it."

"I never would have thought of it if you hadn't said what you did." Mary Ann happily walked off with the certificates in hand.

Awards assemblies started in the multi-purpose room shortly after the bell rang at eight-thirty. The classes assembled by grade level - all the first graders at eight forty-five - all the second graders at nine-fifteen and so on. The principal called each child up and read off what the certificate was for. Applause was only allowed at the end of each class. Elizabeth had to stop for recess and lunches so almost her whole day was spent giving out awards. It was probably deathly boring for her, but it was an important event for both the teachers and students and was the climax of the school year for them.

One could feel the frenzy in the air. Teachers and students alike were hyperactive. The students because the end of school and freedom was only a day away; the teachers because they had so much to do and only one day left to do it.

They wouldn't be able to leave for the year until they had finished report cards for the students to take home tomorrow, completed the test and grade information on the cum folders, got all their media equipment into the library (which was tied into the burglar alarm system), stacked all P.E. equipment and textbooks onto shelves in their room, covered the books with paper (to keep the dust off), gave the lists of returning students to Annie so next year's class lists could be made up, and straightened up their rooms before the principal inspected them.

They held a science fair with students bringing homemade exhibits, there was a softball game between staff and sixth graders watched by the whole school, there was an ice cream party for students who didn't have any disciplinary actions to the office all year put on by the PTA, and a funny hat contest with the prize a free meal at McDonald's.

There was also the annual staff luncheon on the next to last day of school. It was a pot-luck and everyone brought something. Delicious chickens, cold cuts, salads, vegetables, dips, and desserts of every description were there. As usual, the staff was voracious and it was all soon demolished.

* * * * * * *

The last day! By nine o'clock Annie had a terrific headache which was unrelieved by aspirin. All was barely controlled chaos. Today was a minimum day. That meant the students left at twelve-thirty instead of three o'clock. The principal had to rearrange the schedule so the students would get lunch and be back to their rooms by twelve-twenty so they could get their things and be ready to leave when the buses were due to arrive.

Annie went in to eat with second lunch. "Gad, everybody looks exhausted," she commented as she looked around the table at the drawn, tired faces of the teachers.

"We are, we are," they answered.

"This last week of school is just too much, Annie. Do

you realize how much we have to do?" an irritated, short-tempered Norma asked.

"Yes, I know."

"And the kids are so up - it's like trying to keep the lid on a volcano about to blow and all this paper work. I can't stand all this paper work!" Norma's voice got shriller and shriller as she vented her aggravations. "We have to figure all the grades for the report cards, figure how many days present and absent for each student and put those figures on each report card and each cum, figure out who's coming back and who isn't, write up all those certificates, and heaven only knows what else. I'm so sick of paperwork, I could scream. Yuck!!!" Norma threw away the remains of her lunch and went storming out of the door.

"Whew!" said Mary Ann Duncan.

"She's right, you know," added Fred. "Teaching would sure be more satisfying if we didn't always get drowned in paper work."

"Sure, but how are you going to get rid of it?" Annie asked.

"We can't. We have to learn to live with it."

* * * * * * *

The buses were in. It was twelve-thirty. The principal said on the loud-speaker, "Teachers, please release all walkers now. All walkers may leave now. Will kindergarten and first graders load the buses, please. Only kindergarten and first grades to the buses now.

"Annie, I'm going out to the buses to keep things moving. Wait a couple of minutes and then let second and third grades out and so on every few minutes. Try to give each group a chance to get on the buses."

The last bus left at twelve forty-five. Many of the teachers stood and waved good-bye to their students with tears in their eyes. They were happy summer was here but they had grown to love their students during the year and were sad they would never be able to recapture those precious special moments of growth and development which made teaching so satisfying to them.

Even if the children returned the next year, things would never be the same again. How to recapture the moment when the frightened little boy from Viet Nam felt secure enough to give his teacher a timid hug? Or the day when Tanisha made the breakthrough and finally connected the looks of a letter with a particular sound? Or the time when homely, neglected Mary Ellen felt enough confidence to offer her help and friendship to a new, scared little girl?

The teachers knew something was forever lost as they waved good-bye to those buses. The only way they could survive the loss was to remind themselves that the next school year would soon be here with its own special moments of growth and achievement.

"Here's my key, Annie. Bye, see you at the wedding."

"Annie, here's my key and give me a hug. Thanks for all the help you've given me this year. I couldn't have done it without you."

"Bye, Annie, I'll try to get to the wedding. Give me a hug good-bye."

Annie hugged and hugged and in between put the keys away in their assigned places in the key box on the wall. In September she would give them all out again. And in September she would get and give all those hugs again as she helped to set the stage for the new school year.

The End

Made in the USA
Monee, IL
25 September 2022

14622713R00152